Die Cold

Graham Smith

[I've] had a wonderful evening but this wasn't it.
Groucho Marx

Author's note

"One or two readers have commented that the Boulder novels are written using UK English, rather than US English, despite them being set in the United States. This was a conscious decision I made when first starting to write about Boulder. To my mind, he is born and bred in the UK, therefore, UK English fits him and his stories best. Any mistakes made with the American language are my mistakes, although I make no apology for the fact that Boulder still thinks of certain things in a British way."

Cheers
Graham

Chapter 1

Singers aren't supposed to scream. Not even thrash metal singers – if they can be classed as singers – make a sound like the one emanating from Debbie Boitoult's mouth. Her scream, magnified around the room by the microphone in front of her, gets everyone's attention.

It doesn't take much to understand why she's screaming. The black-clad men holding submachine guns could well be blamed for her terrified wails, but I think it's the brunette holding the hunting knife to Debbie's throat who scares her the most.

My first thought is to grab my cell and dial 911. As my hand is reaching into my pocket, the lights go out.

The lights come back on within seconds, flooding the blackened dining room with an eerie half-light that seems to echo the fearful shrieks and screams emanating from the customers.

I stop myself, and leave my cell where it is. In today's world, just about everyone has a cell phone on them at all times. For a group of armed people to invade a place like this there will have been a certain amount of planning beforehand. I figure almost two hundred people trying to call 911 would have been very near the top of their list of things to consider.

Therefore, I think it's only fair to credit the terrorists with enough intelligence to have blocked any cell signals and disabled all other communication methods.

The way they are moving tells me a lot. They're organised, and each terrorist seems to know their role. This means they're well trained and working to a pre-arranged plan.

Other than the woman, I've counted five armed men, and I can see other members of staff being herded out from the kitchen areas.

When I look at the faces of the waiting staff, chefs, pot washers and chambermaids as they are driven out of the service areas, I see fear, trepidation, and very little fight. I also see more black-clad figures. My best estimation is there's at least a dozen of them in the dining room. How many have been stationed outside the room or are engaged in searching the other areas of the resort, is an unknown.

The fact none of the customers or staff are have-a-go-heroes is a good thing. The terrorists appear to be professionals and it would also appear that they've all had some level of military training. Should any of the staff or customers try and take them on, it will be suicidal at best.

For the time being, other than a body bag and a mention on the local news, there's little to be gained from heroics.

I have to marvel at the ingenuity of the terrorists; a ski lodge, halfway up a mountain, that's only accessible by cable car or helicopter, is the ideal place to stage whatever they're planning.

The fact they've chosen the most exclusive, most expensive resort in Vermont suggests the reason they're doing this is money related. The resort's clientele is made up of the obscenely wealthy. At twenty big ones per person, per day, RidgeTop Resort excludes the vast majority of the population through price alone.

How I managed to land a job tending bar in such a place is beyond me, but then again, since the events that drove me to leave my home in Casperton, Utah, I've been something of a drifter, and, with no ties, working twelve hour shifts right through the holiday season appealed to me in a way that repulsed others.

My loved ones are left behind for their own safety. In the last year alone, I've witnessed the deaths of five people I cared for, and I blame myself for each of the lives that were taken.

I may not have killed them myself, but four of them died because of actions I'd taken and decisions I'd made.

Rather than endanger any more lives, I left town and drifted until I wound up taking on the role of bartender at RidgeTop Resort. I'm now earning big bucks on New Year's Eve, while all those I care about are getting ready to party.

The resort is an ideal target for terrorists in a lot of ways. It's isolated, near the summit of a mountain, and the snowstorm that's raging outside gives them a perfect cover for whatever their nefarious plans entail.

For the police to respond to the threat they'll have to fight through the blizzards that are covering the valley floor, just to get within a couple of miles of RidgeTop resort. After that, they'll have to find a way to get up the mountain. The cableway will deliver any would-be rescuers into the terrorists' hands, and the snowstorm is sure to prevent a helicopter from ferrying a police assault team to the resort.

One of the terrorists ushers me and my colleague out from behind the bar and directs us over to the knot of staff occupying the left-hand side of the dining room.

On the right, two gunmen are standing guard over the customers, while a steady stream of people are being shepherded into the dining room by more gun-toting hoods.

I figure there will be demands made of the customers' loved ones – for their safe return in what is basically a mass kidnapping.

The terrorists being predominantly western in their appearance gives me hope that this isn't some kind of religious attack, but I could be wrong.

What takes that hope away is being able to see the faces of all the terrorists. That isn't good, because, with so many witnesses also being able to see their faces, they're sure to be identified by the authorities once they leave.

Unless they don't plan to leave any witnesses to give descriptions.

Chapter 2

I take my place with the other staff and, at the insistence of the nearest terrorist, we sit on the floor.

The last vestiges of staff and customers are being brought out from the bedrooms and service areas.

Next to me on the floor is Sharon Bairden. Like me, she's ex-Glasgow and, unlike me, she has military training. Upon leaving the army she had a couple of kids and divorced the major she'd married in haste.

Sharon is a typical Glaswegian woman; she has short hair and a shorter temper, which she uses to disguise a heart of gold. I don't have the heart to tell her that the disguise doesn't fool anyone. Her sharing a Christian name with my sister is just one of the many things that draws me to her. She's a good woman in every sense of the word: straight-talking, honest, and, best of all, she's laden with a garrulousness only a Glaswegian upbringing can foster.

I can see her eyes flicking around the room, taking in the position of every terrorist and assessing their weapons. Her face is stern and gives me the impression that my own opinions about the terrorists are shared by her.

Rather than do nothing, I focus on the nearest guard. He's around forty and has the wedge-shaped body of an Olympic swimmer. What disconcerts me about him more than anything is that he appears to be relaxed as he watches over us. The expression on his face is akin to that of someone sitting on a beach watching the world go by.

Like his fellow terrorists, Swimmer wears a black T-shirt and combat pants. The boots on his feet look to be military grade and there's a pistol in a holster on his right hip. His left hip has a knife handle sprouting from a sheath. It doesn't take much imagination to picture the knife as being razor sharp with a row of serrated teeth on the top edge of its blade.

I cast my eyes along to the next terrorist. He's got the same knife and gun combo as Swimmer. His hair is cropped close in a military buzz cut.

The most disconcerting thing about him is his gaze. Where Swimmer is relaxed and confident, Buzz Cut seems to be strung out. His eyes are darting back and forth all the time and there's a quality about his sneers and snarls that tells me he's just itching for someone to try their luck against him.

His eyes find Sharon and he gives her a thorough looking over. I don't like the way his eyes lock on Sharon's chest and, knowing her as I do, I'm sure if he looked at her like that in a bar, he'd get either a beer shampoo, or a knee buried into his groin.

From the corner of my eye, I see her trying to suppress a shudder. She's too strong a woman to let him see she is disgusted by his lechery, but I can tell how she's feeling.

A gunshot pierces the quiet sobs and turns all our heads. The female terrorist is still on the stage and she has a handful of Debbie Boitoult's hair that she's using to pull the singer's head back, exposing her throat.

I take a look at the knife she has pressed against Debbie's larynx, and it's just like the one I imagined Swimmer having. A proper military knife with a serrated top edge and a blade that's sharp enough to shave with.

The woman presses the knife a little bit harder against Debbie's throat. I can see the skin indenting under its pressure and the beginning of a trickle of blood forming.

'Ladies and gentlemen, if I can have your attention.'

Chapter 3

The woman's voice is clear and crisp with the hint of an accent. To my ear the accent is French, which makes sense given our proximity to the Canadian border.

However, it doesn't mean the terrorist is necessarily French Canadian. Terrorism is a global problem faced by virtually every country on earth, in one fashion or another.

The woman, whom I'm starting to think of as being in charge, is addressing the crowd. She's tall, lithe and clad in the same black clothes as the men. A lot of men would call her pretty and, despite being on a mission, she's styled her hair and put on lipstick. While it would be easy to picture her as a ballerina, I can't christen her that in my mind; it would be too ridiculous to call her that when she has a knife at someone's throat. Instead, I simply think of her as Hannah. The name is innocuous and unthreatening. A friend's two-year-old daughter is the inspiration for the name, and, while it might be trite to use her name for the leader of a group of terrorists, I want to manage my own growing fears that everyone who's not a terrorist will die tonight.

Now that Hannah's speech has got past the 'do as we say or else' part, I pay closer attention.

'My colleagues will come round and ask your names. You are to reply truthfully. Once we have all of you identified, we'll be speaking to each of you on a one-to-one basis. Again, I cannot stress enough how little harm you'll come to if you cooperate. On the other hand, should you fail to do as I, or my colleagues request, we will not hesitate to harm you. I should imagine a lot of you are thinking about the cell phones in your pockets or purses. Don't waste your time. We've been blocking the signal since we got here. You can't call for help, either with your phone or via social media.'

Hannah takes the knife from Debbie's throat and slips it under the thin shoulder strap of her dress. A quick jerk severs the strap and the knife is moved to the other side.

As Hannah is slicing through the other strap, two of her goons take hold of Debbie's arms.

One has a bald head and the other has tattoos that come up to the underside of his jawline like a multi-coloured beard.

Debbie's dress slips down her body, baring her breasts before catching on her hips. Hannah's knife slides inside the folded dress and severs enough material to allow the gown to gather around Debbie's feet.

Debbie struggles and tries to free herself from Bald Man and Tattoo Neck without success. She's now topless and is wearing what I assume are control pants beneath her nylons. Debbie is a good-looking woman, with the kind of figure many women aspire to, but I get no thrill from seeing her exposed like this.

I steal a glance at Buzz Cut and see a lascivious grin on his face as he enjoys the floor show.

Hannah grabs Debbie's right nipple and pulls until her breast is drawn up and away from her body. I can hear Debbie pleading for Hannah to stop, but she doesn't pay any attention.

The blade of the knife is placed under Debbie's breast and her nipple is released. As the breast sags down, a pained whimper escapes Debbie's mouth and a thin line of blood runs down the knife's serrated blade, dripping to the floor.

I expect, like me, everyone else in the room is holding their breath and fearing the worst for Debbie.

Hannah pulls her knife downwards, without cutting any more of Debbie's breast, and stares into the singer's face. Whether she's making her point or feeding on the fear in her victim is irrelevant. She hasn't gone ahead with her implied threat.

The knife rises up and is held in front of Debbie's face.

The singer turns her head to one side and cranes her head back, but Hannah grips her hair again, and before ten seconds have passed she's looking front and centre at the knife.

Hannah twists and turns the knife before Debbie's eyes then slashes it across her chin. Before the blood rushes to fill the wound, I see a flash of bone that shows just how deep the cut is. To my eyes, the cut has made Debbie look as if she has two mouths.

Bald Man and Tattoo Neck release Debbie, who falls to the floor pressing blood-soaked hands to her ruined chin.

When Debbie's agonised screams subside into adrenaline-cushioned sobs, Hannah turns to face the room. 'I always prefer showing to telling. Cooperate and you'll be unharmed. Refuse and you'll die screaming.'

Beside me I hear a hissed intake of breath from Sharon. She doesn't have to speak, there's no need for anyone to give voice to their thoughts as all of us will be thinking the same thing.

Debbie's mutilation has had the desired effect of horrifying everyone into compliance.

It isn't just the brutality of the act, it's the cold manner in which Hannah has gone about it.

The way that she'd humiliated her victim by exposing her to the room was bad enough, but the way she'd cut Debbie had elevated her point to unnecessary levels. Had she just threatened her, we would have been compliant – the point would have been proven. Yet she'd chosen to do what she did, and had done it without hesitation. This tells me that Hannah is by far the most dangerous of the terrorists.

Even now, she stands with droplets of Debbie's blood splattered across her hands and is making no effort to wipe them away.

When one of her minions steps forward with a clipboard, she nods at two others and starts walking down the hallway. She opens the door of what I know to be the manager's office and leads her men inside.

I've only been in there a couple of times, but I know, as well as being a working office, it has a table with six chairs in it for staff meetings.

The guy with the clipboard is confirming names and using a black marker to write the name of every person he speaks to on their left forearm.

His reason for identifying each person is a mystery to me, but I'm sure it will become evident as the night passes.

A look at the staff and customers shows me a sea of nervous faces. A lot of the women are weeping, or cuddling into their partners for support, while the men are grim. I imagine some of the big hitters in the room are wondering if they can barter or buy their way out of danger.

There's a huge glass window behind me; I turn my head and look down the valley towards the cableway station at the bottom. I see no lights other than those leeching out from the resort.

The snow falls thick and determined. Its presence the reason for ours.

Whether or not someone at the bottom cableway station has noticed we've lost power is unknown.

Perhaps they've tried to communicate with us and failed. Maybe they've called the cops, maybe they haven't.

Whatever they've done or not done is irrelevant. Unless someone has a platoon of marines hidden away in their room, we're at the mercy of the terrorists.

Chapter 4

Leslie Trouseau gives the man his name when asked and offers his left arm forward so the guy with the marker pen can do his stuff.

As soon as Leslie had realised they were being over-run by gunmen, he'd loosened his bow tie and unfastened his top button. At sixty years of age, with a history of ulcers and heart problems, he knows it's imperative for him to remain calm. Beside him, his wife, Lily, is bearing the situation with her usual fortitude.

Lily is the rock that grounds him, and without her support he'd never have risen to the heights he has. Throughout his life, Lily has given him many reasons to be grateful to her, and very few to make him love her.

He only found out when he married her that Lily was a cold woman, who believed sex was for procreation alone. Once she'd had the three children she wanted she moved herself to the spare bedroom, from where she issued threats that were designed to prevent him from having affairs. If only she knew: all the times he'd told her he was working late at the office, he'd been at his desk, alone with a bunch of numbers and a glass of iced tea.

He'd stuck by her out of duty, and this ski holiday was his way of keeping her happy over the holidays while he worked. She would take to the slopes and he'd stay in their suite and hunch over his laptop.

After their children, banking was his life.

The problem was, it may also be his death.

As vice principal of foreign investment, on a daily basis he dealt with sums of money that could bankrupt a small country. The smallest transaction he'd done in the last year was eight figures.

If these terrorists are after money, he has access to the kind of funds that would make their wildest dreams come true. To counter this, he keeps his head down and avoids looking their way – lest they decide to pay him special attention.

The attack on the singer was gruesome. The female terrorist who'd disfigured the singer was beyond evil as far as he was concerned. How one woman could debase and torture another in such a fashion was beyond his comprehension.

As the macabre scene had played out, he'd felt Lily's grip on his arm tighten. She'd not cried once when she'd had her left breast removed last year, but he caught her muffled sobs as she'd cowered behind him while the singer was being mutilated.

With his and Lily's arms branded with marker pen, he follows orders from one of the terrorists and takes a seat in the same area the staff are occupying.

A millionaire several times over in his own right, he wonders just what the night will bring. Will he be alive to see the sun rise? If he is, will he be penniless, or will he be the man who'd financed terrorists with other people's money?

He offers up a silent prayer to Saint Matthew the Apostle, the patron saint of money. Leslie's belief in religion is a fleeting thing, wheeled out in times of need and ignored when the sun shines and life is good.

The man with the clipboard repeats a name. His voice shows exasperation as he glances at the fifty or so remaining people who've yet to be identified.

A twist of the man's mouth precedes him moving on to the next name on his list.

Celeste Powell is a name Leslie is familiar with. She has been in his office on more than one occasion and he knows her story. Her blood is bluer than a summer sky and her ancestors had no doubt owned shares in the Mayflower when they'd travelled to America.

She'd had a significant family fortune handed to her at an early age due to her parents' fondness for too much whisky and fast cars. To cap it off, she married the only son of one of the few families that were richer than her own. Her in-laws had poor health and had both died within two years of Celeste saying her marriage vows. Their son had joined them in the family plot when an aneurism had burst inside his head. He was dead before his body had hit the carpet of the apartment where he housed his mistress.

Leslie watches as Celeste stands and walks across to the man with the clipboard. She is trailed by her two children: a boy of around twelve and a sullen girl a year or two older.

Tragedy may have struck Celeste Powell's life with the force of a wrecking ball, but she carries herself with poise, as if her deportment matters at all times, regardless of circumstances or threat.

As she walks over to join the staff and those already identified, she gives Leslie a tiny nod and ushers her daughter into the space behind a table that was upturned in the panic of the terrorists' arrival.

The boy, Leslie can't remember his name – isn't even sure he'd ever known it – wears an expression that is part fear and part fascination. For him, this will be the best kind of adventure to experience – horrifying and thrilling in equal measure. So long as he makes it out alive, and his family all survive, the boy will dine out on tonight's events for the rest of his life.

Leslie hears the man with the clipboard raise his voice again, as another person refuses to step forward when their name is called.

He doesn't see any reason not to comply with such a basic instruction; after all, once there are only a few people left to match with the names on his list, the man with the clipboard will only have to harm one or two people to make the others fall into line.

Chapter 5

The whole room has descended into a hushed silence with the exception of the odd sob coming from one of the women, and the occasional rustle of clothing as a man rubs a soothing hand over his wife or girlfriend's back.

Clipboard has whittled down the remaining unidentified to three couples and a single man. When none of them answer he gives an exasperated sigh and nods at a squat colleague.

Squat takes his cue with indifference as he points his gun at the nearest man and drags his partner away from him.

He removes the knife from his hip and uses it to slice through the woman's halter-neck top. A second later the top is pulled down to expose the woman's breasts.

'I'm Frederick Houston.' The man steps in front of Clipboard, his voice betraying his fear. 'Let her go, you've made your point.'

Clipboard doesn't even look at the man. 'You may think that. I don't. If I were you, I'd concentrate very hard on not being uncooperative again.' He gives a nod to Squat then looks at the distraught man. 'I think she ought to be naked from now on. I trust you have no issue with that? Or perhaps you'd like to be uncooperative?'

Squat takes his knife, points it at the woman's trousers and gives the knife's tip a couple of bounces. 'You heard the man.'

The look the woman gives Houston, as she peels down her trousers and underwear, is one of pure hatred. I can imagine what she's thinking about the man and know none of it will be charitable or forgiving. He's tried to hold out and it's her who has to suffer the consequences.

Granted she got off lightly compared to the singer, but she's still had to endure the humiliation of stripping.

Clipboard's loud threat that anyone who offers the woman a jacket will suffer, makes her lips twist into a snarl as she struggles to cover herself with her hands.

True to form, Buzz Cut waves her over and instructs her to wait near him.

The remaining hostages offer up their names with only the briefest of hesitation.

Beside me, I hear a hissed whisper from Sharon.

'We're gonnae have to do something about this. These bawbags are no' getting away wi' this.'

The Scottish terminology would bring a smile to my lips were it not for the fact that, as much as I might agree with her, there is little an un-armed couple can do against up to a dozen heavily armed terrorists.

I keep my own voice low. 'I agree that something needs to be done, but the question is what? And how?'

I let the reality sink in for a moment. Other than a couple of steak knives I've managed to filch from a table, we don't have any weapons.

If all the men in the room charged the terrorists we'd be able to overpower them and snatch their weapons. The problem with that is the complete lack of communication we're able to have with the other men and the way the terrorists are guarding us.

At all times they keep five yards away from the throng of frightened bodies. The losses we'd incur crossing those five yards would be horrific. At least half of us would die.

I'm not averse to risking my life, but at the same time I have no desire to throw it away in a foolish gesture.

There's also the possibility that our plan would be thwarted before it even got started. Should that happen, it would take Hannah less than a minute to get someone to point a finger at the ringleader.

I've never liked the idea of becoming a martyr. It's bad enough that I've had to remove myself from the lives of my friends and family, without throwing my life away for a bunch of people I hardly know.

There's also the fact that if I'm to make any moves against the terrorists, I'll have to use extreme force. I don't want to do that. Too many people have died, either by my hands or because of decisions I've made. I don't want any more deaths on my conscience. Not even those of terrorists.

Another point to consider is the time. It's still early and we've only been held for a half hour or so. There haven't been any demands as yet and this whole thing may well play out without any loss of life.

If it comes to it and I'm forced to act, I will, but for now I plan to observe, to scheme, and to find a way to stop thinking that the terrorists will kill us all because we've seen their faces.

There's also the question of what the terrorists' goal is. The idea that each of the customers are to be taken for a one-to-one meeting with Hannah both intrigues and worries me.

What happens in that office will dictate whether or not the terrorists achieve their aims, and I'm already convinced Hannah is ruthless enough to do whatever is needed to ensure her hostages do as they're told.

Chapter 6

Sharon Bairden flexes her fingers and leans on the floor with her right hand. Or to be more accurate, she leans on a steak knife. When she lifts her hand off the floor the knife is hidden inside her sleeve for use at a later date.

The brutal attack on the singer disgusted her; she'd wanted to act, to take on the guys, but as Boulder had pointed out, how could she without a decent weapon?

She might manage to get the jump on the nearest guard and get his gun, but the odds are stacked against her and she knows it.

Even if she does make such a move, and it is successful, what then? It will still be one against many, and the only cover available is a sea of seated bodies.

She'd be cut down in seconds. One or two if she turned the gun at the other terrorists; five or six, maybe seven or eight if she dived for cover behind innocent people and used them as a shield.

Her death would, at best, achieve one or two dead terrorists.

If Boulder were to help her she'd have more chance of success, but, in her mind, he seems reluctant.

When she'd chatted to him a couple of weeks ago, she had learned little about his life – except that he liked reading and was filled with a sadness he didn't express but couldn't hide. His laughs were polite, but his smile never got close to touching his eyes and, on the night she'd had a long talk to him, it became clear he was haunted by something that had happened in his past.

As conversations go, it was the gentlest, most sincere she'd ever endured. Part of her was glad she had got to meet the real Jake Boulder, another part told her he was a dangerous man. He was well-mannered at all times, but she'd caught the flashes of anger he displayed when a customer was rude or arrogant. That he'd taken on a job like this, with a temper like his, was unusual if not rare.

Any job where you deal with customers face to face requires an even temper. When they are rich, and are paying through the proverbial nose for what you're serving them, they can be a lot more difficult than someone who is down to their last.

Since starting work at RidgeTop Resort at the beginning of the skiing season, Sharon had been insulted, threatened, or belittled at least twice a week.

When you added in the sexual harassment and groping, from those who thought they could do as they pleased, or make you do whatever they wanted, just because of the size of their bank balances, it was little wonder the resort's owner had to pay thrice the going rate for bar and waiting staff.

At this moment, though, she dismisses all that as just another chapter in her life, the bigger issue being what they can do to fight back at the terrorists and shift the narrative.

A look across at the hotel manager gives her no reassurances; he is quivering, sitting with the security manager. Kirk Fleming may be good at schmoozing customers and keeping staff in line, but he isn't the kind of popular leader she would be prepared to follow.

The fact Fleming had hired his twin brother as security manager said everything. Patrick is a decent enough guy, but he is more like Columbo than James Bond. His remit is making sure the customers are confident their valuables are safe, and the staff have no opportunity to pilfer from the company. In a lot of ways he is little more than a stock-taker with a shiny badge.

Her mind returned to the present as the last few people join their group and the guy with the clipboard goes to the manager's office.

Sharon experiences a mixture of dread and morbid fascination when he returns a minute later with the woman who seems to be in charge.

The woman takes up position in front of the hostages – Sharon isn't under the illusion they are anything else – she is flanked by the guy with the clipboard and a man who looks more like a computer geek than a terrorist.

The woman holds up an arm and waits for the small amount of chatter to subside before she speaks.

Chapter 7

Like everyone else in the room, I'm watching and waiting for Hannah to speak. It's obvious she knows how to read a room, she's aware we're hanging on what she's about to say, and she's milking the situation like it's a prize cow.

'Ladies and gentlemen, you have all been identified and I'm sure you've learned the value of cooperation.' She gives a pointed look at the naked figure of Houston's partner. 'In a moment, you will all be called to come and speak with me privately. I hardly need emphasise the benefits of cooperating to you, but I think it would be remiss of me to assume you're all going to do as you're told.' She pauses and licks her lips in a way that's almost seductive. 'The first person to refuse me or my men, at the time of asking, will be punished severely. The second will die screaming. In fact, they'll be begging for death. This is something you'll all witness because I will execute them in front of you as a reminder to anyone else who may have foolish ideas about heroism.'

The way Hannah is ramming home her point seems off to me. Debbie Boitoult's plight remains at the forefront of our minds, and Houston's girlfriend is still naked. There is no need for Hannah to keep reiterating that we must cooperate.

It's overkill – unless what she's going to ask us to do is so horrific that we are tempted to refuse. So far as I can work out, that can be the only explanation.

Those who've paid to be here are all wealthy or influential people. Most of them are both.

Sharon, who's far more interested in these things than I am, has pointed out a few reality TV stars, an alleged singing sensation, and a former wrestler who has risen up the ranks until he's in sole charge of a franchise that has grown men play-fighting for the amusement of small children.

The only customer I've recognised myself is a former captain of the England football team.

When I first met him, it was all I could do to control my temper and not shorten his over-sized nose for the goals he'd scored against Scotland in the European championship.

The game took place years ago and it was one I'd watched on the Internet a day after it was first broadcast. That didn't stop my sense of outrage at his overly-elaborate celebrations though. As for the former captain, he's now the BBC's go-to-presenter for all major sporting events.

None of that is important though, what really matters is why Hannah is having private meetings with people. My first thought is that she'll be pressing them for the contact details of someone who'll pay a ransom for their safe return. My second, is that it's Hogmanay, and likely payers of ransoms will not be easy to contact. There's also the fact that communications have been cut. Hannah and her cohorts may have a satphone, or some other way of contacting the outside world, but I don't know how their being able to contact others will help them unless the team here is only one part of their organisation.

Another consideration is how they plan to make their escape; whatever happens tonight, there are only three ways to get to and from RidgeTop Resort.

Number one is the cableway, but they won't use that as it would deliver them right into the hands of anyone who might be waiting for them.

Number two is by helicopter. It would work, but only to a certain extent; the current snowstorm, and the reduced visibility it has brought, will make flying incredibly dangerous – if not suicidal. Plus, it's possible their crime will have been detected when they decide to leave. Therefore, there would be a full-scale attempt to track the helicopter to wherever it eventually lands. The tracking would be done by radar, and other technologies, until a police helicopter or two could be put on their tail. Depending on how serious their crimes get, there may even be military involvement. I can't imagine having an Apache Gunship on their six is part of their plans.

The third way to get to and from the resort is perhaps the foolhardiest. A top-class skier may be able to navigate their way down the slopes in darkness, but, like the cable car, they'd head right into the arms of any welcoming committee organised by the police.

None of these seemed like good ideas to me, but, then again, I'm a former doorman, current bartender and occasional whatever-I-need-to-do-to-earn-a-buck guy, not a master criminal. The idea they've got a master plan is a given; what it is, is something for me to wonder about.

I see Clipboard lift one of the A4 envelopes from the pile, which some of the terrorists have been creating on the bar's counter, and approach Hannah.

Hannah looks at the envelope and turns her head so she's looking at the assembled crowd.

'Zack Longhorn. Will you and your wife please come to the front?'

Chapter 8

Nathan Miller looks at the console in front of him and sees nothing except the glare from the light, which tells him there is a power failure at the other end of the cableway. That shouldn't be a problem: if there is no power, the operator at the top can throw a lever to disengage the gearing mechanism and the entire cableway can be controlled from the base station.

It may not be as speedy as having both the top and bottom stations supplying power, but it will still work.

Yet when he tries to set the motor into gear it whines and protests until its powerful motor causes the wheel to turn without achieving anything bar the tightening of the pull cable.

He stops the motor at once, before either the motor burns out or the cable becomes over-stressed.

His next move is to radio his counterpart, Steve, at RidgeTop. There is no point in him looking out of the window as he thumbs the key, but he looks anyway. As has been the case since dawn, thick, wet snow is falling – he knows 'falling' is a misnomer for what the snow is doing.

Rather than drifting to the ground in a more or less vertical path, the ferocious winds that power the snowstorm are driving each flake two feet across for every foot that gravity is pulling it.

He can see nothing because of the blizzard, he hears nothing because nobody answers, and he says nothing because there is nobody to speak to. All by himself, he's covered the same bases as the three wise monkeys.

Steve may well have gone to the can, but Nathan knows Steve is a stickler for protocol, and his counterpart always alerts him whenever he'll be away from his post and when he's got back.

With no response, he pulls his backpack from under the desk and grabs himself a sandwich from the box he brought with him.

Tonight wasn't supposed to be his shift, but he swapped it so he could have Christmas at home with his family.

Boy, had that been a mistake.

His father was as ornery as ever. The day had been spent with the man, whom Nathan had never been able to respect, complaining about the noise Nathan's kids made, about the meal Nathan's wife had spent hours cooking, and then, to cap it all off, he railed on Nathan, blaming him for his mother finding the man from the dime store preferable to her husband.

The day had ended with a lot of harsh words and a standoff that had been one wrong comment away from evolving into a fist fight.

With his sandwich finished, and a smear of mayo decorating the tips of his moustache, Nathan tries to contact Steve for a second time.

Once again there's no answer. Another look out of the window returns the same twenty feet of vision-obscuring blizzard.

Nathan now faces a dilemma: he can dismiss Steve's absence from his post as an inconsequential one – there are no passengers scheduled to travel on the cableway tonight, he and Steve are only in post in case there is an emergency of some kind – or he can listen to the prickle in his gut and call someone else at the resort.

Sure, it may get Steve in a spot of trouble, but, on the other hand, if something is wrong, the sooner he acts the better.

He puts down the radio and picks up the telephone handset. As soon as he dials the number for the resort's reception desk he is met with the same flat monotone he got before he dialled.

Nathan tries dialling a second time and gets the same result.

By now, the prickle in his gut is a full-blown porcupine charging around looking for escape.

Nathan's instinct tells him that something is wrong up there. It's one thing Steve failing to answer his radio, but for the telephones to be out too suggests there is a bigger issue, such as a power cut.

The problem is, he knows there is a generator at RidgeTop that is more than capable of powering the resort.

It may just be a series of coincidences, but it may be something more serious. If the resort has no power, the residents will be in for a long, cold night.

Rather than take any chances, Nathan dials another number and relays his concerns to Olly Attwood, the manager of RidgeTop's sister resort, RidgeWay.

RidgeWay is aimed at the everyday person, rather than the elite, and its resort is based further along the valley. With six times the bed space of RidgeTop, RidgeWay is a much larger complex, its hotel at the bottom of the mountain and nothing more than a cafeteria and small medical centre at the end of its cableway. It is, however, the hub of operations, and as such, the manager there is in overall charge of both resorts.

The man listens to what Nathan has to say and promises to contact Fleming up at RidgeTop to see what's going on.

With his concerns passed up the chain of command, Nathan abdicates himself from any responsibility and rummages in his backpack for something else to eat. His groping hand finds a candy bar and an apple. One of the two will have to be kept for later, so he flips a mental coin and makes sure it comes down on the side that lets him have the candy.

He peels the wrapper from the candy bar and looks out of the window, wondering, as he stares into the blizzard, whether there is something amiss at RidgeTop, or whether he's just hit the panic button for no reason.

Chapter 9

I watch as Zack Longhorn levers himself upright and strides forward. He's a proud Texan, made obvious by his cowboy boots and the metal tips on the collar of his shirt, and his voice is a languid drawl as he addresses Clipboard. Longhorn is either completely unafraid, or too stupid to realise the danger he's in.

The wife he trails behind him suggests he may be stupider than he is brave. She's half his age and, judging from the way she's made up, she's all about style rather than substance. Nothing about her looks real; her nails are fake, as are her eyelashes, and her face has been made up in a way that suggests she'd be unrecognisable if seen without the layer of slap she's applied. The breasts her gown is struggling to contain are way too large for her frame.

All in all, she carries the look of someone who's out to snare a rich man, and if Longhorn has fallen for her charms, there's every possibility he's not as bright as he'd like people to think.

Tattoo Neck is standing beside Clipboard and he pats down Longhorn with a thoroughness that speaks of much practice, or his having been the recipient of a nasty surprise at some point in his nefarious career. Either way, there's no chance that Longhorn has gotten anything larger than a toothpick past him.

When Tattoo Neck turns his attention to Little Miss Made Up she pouts, and looks to Longhorn to stop the terrorist from touching her.

Longhorn fixes her with a commanding look, so she submits to Tattoo Neck's professional pat-down with ill grace and the sullen pout perfected by teenage girls.

She shudders when the backs of Tattoo Neck's hands glide over her hips, but it's when they slide up between her legs that she reacts in a way that risks her life.

Her knee pulses forward towards the crouched terrorist's nose and her hand is pulled back ready to throw what I'm sure she intends to be a devastating slap.

Tattoo Neck is too fast for her and, as he ducks his head away from the knee that is arrowing for his nose, his hand reaches for the knife on his hip.

Longhorn is even quicker. He doesn't just grab the arm that's arcing towards Tattoo Neck, he uses it to reposition Little Miss Made Up so she's behind him.

'That's enough, my dear. The man is only doing his job.'

Tattoo Neck has a scowl on his face, but he lets the matter drop when Longhorn ushers the young woman back to his side and tells her to stand still.

It's an interesting exchange as it denotes the balance of power in the Longhorn household, as well as Tattoo Neck's professionalism. Like a good security guard, he used the backs of his hands to pat down the Longhorn's intimate areas. While the process was invasive, it was carried out with the maximum humanity.

Had Buzz Cut been the one to pat them down, I'm not sure he would have used the backs of his hands, or passed up the chance to grab a handful of Little Miss Made Up's more rounded assets.

Even Tattoo Neck's response to the girl's attempt to strike him had shown his professionalism. Not only had he avoided harm, he'd also reacted by reaching for his knife.

I've more experience than I care to regarding gun and knife fights, and it's taught me, at such close quarters, the knife is better than the gun. Yet Tattoo Neck had shown enough restraint to not use the knife until he'd assessed the changing situation and realised that Longhorn himself was offering no threat and was nullifying the one presented by Little Miss Made Up.

Nor does he press the matter while he finishes his pat-down of Little Miss Made Up. A spot of petty retaliation may have been enacted to establish superiority and quell any further uprisings, but he doesn't go down that road.

This tells me, for this part of their plan, the terrorists are not putting undue pressure on their hostages. The only reason for this, that I can think of, is there must be further coercion to come, and they want their victims to be compliant rather than defiant.

While it may work on a group level to make an example of someone, it will carry a lesser impact to each individual couple if it isn't directed specifically at them.

My guess is that Longhorn is the terrorists' target of this couple, and Little Miss Made Up will be used as leverage to make him comply with their wishes.

As Tattoo Neck leads them to the manager's office where Hannah awaits, I hope for Little Miss Made Up's sake that Longhorn truly loves her. Otherwise, she may find herself at the receiving end of Hannah's brutality.

Chapter 10

The threat to Little Miss Made Up is palpable to me, but it's not the thing giving me the cold sweats. Much as I hate to see anyone suffer, the overly made-up young woman isn't someone I know or care about. Having been in a similar position to Longhorn, as the protector of a loved one, I can only hope for her sake he makes better decisions than I did.

The knowledge that you're responsible for the suffering of someone you love is a burden that never lightens. I'd tried to deal with my guilt in a variety of predictable ways.

First, I ran away. Leaving Casperton and my friends and family behind had been cowardice, disguised as my removing myself for their benefit. I kidded myself that I had to leave so they didn't become victims of my poor choices. That didn't work out well for anyone, and the infrequent contact I have had with my mother and my best friend has engendered little more than homesickness and a deepening of my guilt.

My next attempt to escape my problems was to climb inside a bottle or six. This was an even worse solution than running away. I can be a mean drunk and I got myself into bar fight after bar fight. I won each fight as they happened, but the reality of my actions was that I was looking for someone to kick my ass in a grandiose bout of self-flagellation.

The end result was me picking on the wrong man when I was half done-in with drink and the night's previous battles. The guy I selected as my target was the biggest guy in the bar. Considering the shape I was in, he had every advantage he needed, and I was too drunk to realise he had three buddies with him.

When I came to, it was under the harsh lights of an emergency room.

A few days later, when my bruises had healed, I got a handful of quarters and found a working payphone.

Doctor Edwards had initially refused to take my call. I could understand that: he'd been fond of Taylor too. She was his receptionist after all.

I persisted throughout the day and eventually I persuaded him, via his new receptionist, to give me a telephone consultation.

The half-hour conversation I had with him ate up a pocketful of quarters and left a hole in my chest.

He started out by insisting I ran through the whole sequence of events.

When he heard the unbridled truth, he offered neither consolation nor condemnation. Like the psychologist he was, he asked what I thought about my actions.

Again, I told him the truth: how I was compelled to seek vengeance; how the fury inside me had driven me to kill. Not just in the moment, but in a series of deliberate acts.

I told him that, as much as I blamed my father for his part in Taylor's death, it was myself I held most responsible as it was my decision that had put Taylor in harm's way.

When he asked if I would do things differently a second time around, I snarled, 'Of course I would', and damn near hung up on him. I hadn't though; some part of me knew I would need his help if I am ever to manage my guilt.

His next question skewered me with a mixture of perception and dread.

At that point, I hadn't thought about the future much beyond the next day or week. I drifted from town to town, my Mustang eating up the miles as I tried to leave behind the troubles I carried with me. I took odd jobs in bars, and laboured for builders where I could find them, and I lived in crummy motels and ate in diners. From time to time I'd visit bars and not drink in them.

Once or twice women sent me the kind of signs I'd always followed, but I turned away from them. For the first time I could remember, since arriving in America as a cocksure fifteen-year-old, I had no interest in female company, whether for a few hours or a lifetime. My company was my own and I didn't want to bring anyone else down with my morose feelings.

Since that call, and the emotions it concerned, I've been calling Doctor Edwards once a week. Some of the calls salve my wounds, whereas others feel like I'm applying salt to raw flesh.

On the whole the calls are working, but I know I still have a long way to go before I'm anything like the Jake Boulder I used to be.

As much as I feel guilt for Taylor's death, I loathe myself for becoming a killer. It was hard enough coming to terms with the lives I had taken in self-defence; but to see the man in the mirror and know he is capable, guilty even, of premeditated murder, is taking a lot more getting used to.

In another act of cowardice since leaving Casperton, I've taken to shaving only once a fortnight. That's thirteen days straight that I don't have to look at myself. Thirteen days when I don't gaze into my own eyes, trying to see the spark that used to be there and instead seeing the dullness that has replaced their once piercing quality.

Maybe one day Doctor Edwards will be able to help me find myself, but until that day dawns, there's no way I'm going to put myself in a situation where I have to take another man's life.

It's a nice thought, and one that would be a lot easier to envision were I not held at gunpoint by a bunch of terrorists.

Chapter 11

When Longhorn is led back by one of the terrorists, Sharon can't help but notice the shocked look on his face. His slapper of a wife – Sharon can't think of her in any other way – wears a similar expression, although she is sporting a cut lip and a swollen nose, whereas Longhorn is unmarked.

It is obvious to Sharon what has happened: either Longhorn refused the terrorists' demands and they roughed her up to bend him to their will, or the girl was defiant and again lashed out at one of their captors.

Having seen the way the girl reacted to being patted down, Sharon's money is on the girl acting out, or insulting one of the terrorists. The few dealings she'd had with the slapper showed the girl's lack of intelligence. Just yesterday morning she had complained that the vegan meal she'd ordered didn't taste very meaty.

Sharon had relayed the girl's comment to the chef, who made sure to drizzle every other meal she was served with at least one type of meat stock.

It was a minor revenge, but one that Sharon had enjoyed. Now, as she looks at the slapper, she feels the first twinges of remorse.

What is puzzling her is the way Longhorn and his wife, or whatever she is, were herded to the opposite side of the room. They have a guard to themselves, and she surmises that the terrorists are segregating them so they can ensure Longhorn doesn't forewarn his fellow hostages about what to expect when they are taken into the manager's office.

Another couple have been frisked and as soon as Longhorn reappeared they were led along the corridor at gunpoint.

The next name to be called is Celeste Powell. Sharon doesn't know much about her – except that she has good manners, impeccable breeding, and the kind of figure Sharon has only ever dreamed of having. Celeste's son is a good lad who echoes his mother's manners, while the daughter expends most of her energy enacting a familiar tale of teen rebellion. Despite the girl's efforts to be different, she is treading down a path so well-worn it has achieved the consistency of concrete.

She might think she is being rebellious by being sullen and uncooperative, but she is conforming to type. The fact her mother has to scold her into using better manners, or tell her things twice, is no surprise; the girl is testing boundaries, struggling to cope with the changes to her body as she begins the transition from child to woman.

When Sharon thinks back to her own teenage years, she again throws a silent apology to her parents. She bunked off school, got into fights, shoplifted, and, on her sixteenth birthday, she'd taken the next-door neighbour to bed then walked down to the army recruiting office and signed up without even listening to what the recruiter was telling her.

She'd imagined a world away from her parents and that's what she got. Instead of parental discipline wrapped up with love, she went through the worst fourteen weeks of her life as she endured basic training with nothing more than her ingrained stubbornness to prevent her from quitting.

Sharon's mother had forgiven her after a few weeks, but it hadn't been until her passing out parade that she'd earned her father's approval. Even that had been tempered by a lecture on what her running off had done to her mother.

Impulsive as she is, Sharon knows that going off like that was cruel from her mother's perspective, and she hopes the sullen Miss Powell doesn't go on to cause her mother the same pain she gave hers.

Regardless of what the girl may do in the future, Sharon is more concerned about what she may do today. The terrorists aren't the forgiving type, and if the girl has one iota of sense, she'll do as she is told, when she is told.

If Sharon were in Celeste's place, she would have had a word in the daughter's ear to stress the importance of complying with the terrorists. On the other hand, she knows that her own teen self would have scoffed at the warning. Perhaps such comments would be likely to send the girl down the path of obstinacy.

There is nothing Sharon can do about it, other than cross her fingers and hope that fear overrides the girl's teenage hormones.

A more pressing question for Sharon is what will happen to them once the terrorists have gotten what they want? The lack of masks is bugging her, and her army training is compelling her to fight back in whatever way she can.

Even if she can't fight back, there must be some way she can escape from the terrorists and alert the authorities.

That's where Boulder will come in. When she first met him, his name had been familiar to her but she couldn't remember why. Google had filled in the blanks and she liked that he'd twice thwarted killers: it made him that little bit dangerous. Sure, he was all brooding machismo when not flashing a false smile at customers, but she also found herself attracted to the vulnerability he tried, and failed, to hide.

If she is to find a way to get out of the terrorists' clutches, she can think of no one better to aid her. Patrick Fleming is a non-starter in the hero stakes – Sharon doesn't believe he can contribute anything beyond a bunch of keys and maybe a set of handcuffs.

None of the other staff are made of the right stuff. They are either teens or twenty-somethings. The exception to this is a pastry chef who possesses a military background. The problem with him is that he's into his seventh decade and has a fondness for hard liquor, which has put a shake in his hands and a spiderweb of broken veins on his face. He'd be useful if you put a gun in his hands and asked him to provide covering fire, but there is no way she's confident she can trust him to make a decisive shot if the pressure is on.

When push comes to shove, she knows the only person who can provide her with any kind of backup worth having is Boulder.

Chapter 12

The more I think about it, the less I like the way things are transpiring. The first four groups of people have returned from Fleming's office wearing shocked expressions.

As they join the others who've visited Hannah, their faces transfer from shock to anger.

I'm working on the theory that they are all intelligent people; therefore, I'm sure they'll be trying to work out ways to counteract whatever happened in the office. Whether they've been extorted, ransomed, or coerced into some deal or other is irrelevant. What matters is that it's happened to them and they're angry about it.

Whatever it is, it's clever enough to have them showing an inner fury rather than the impassive faces that denote deep thinking. This tells me their initial thoughts are bouncing back at them without solutions. These are powerful, intelligent people, yet they're all dumbfounded, too distracted by the trauma of what happened in the office to make sense of it.

The point I keep returning to is that the terrorists have shown their faces. Whichever way I examine it, I can't help but sense that all the hostages will be killed before the terrorists leave.

For me the biggest surprise is that the people who've visited the office have returned more or less unharmed.

Part of me had expected them to be dispatched with a bullet to the back of the head once their purpose had been served. The only reason I can think of for this not happening, is that the hostages are still required: either for proof of life – if this is a mass kidnapping – or to complete whatever scheme the terrorists are working to achieve.

The connection between their survival and everyone else's compliance doesn't escape my attention. Their return, albeit in a state of shock and anger, means those yet to be called forward by Clipboard will do as they are told without resistance.

I hear the next couple get called up and watch as a man offers his wife his arm and guides her through the mass of people towards Clipboard.

By now, those being patted down by Tattoo Neck are soft and compliant. By letting them see the others return in one piece, the terrorists have shown the benefits of doing what they say without question.

The woman's face twists as Tattoo Neck's hands slide down her thighs. I'm guessing it's the intimacy of the touch that bothers her. He stops and feels round her upper thighs with the palm of his hands.

When he straightens he's wearing an amused grin and the woman's face is the colour of beetroot. I can't work out what's caused this until I notice she's wearing nylons and surmise they're either stockings or thigh-highs. His extra touches weren't fuelled by lust, but professionalism as he checked to make sure the strange feel to her upper thighs wasn't caused by a gun, strapped to the inside of her leg.

I'm moving my thoughts on to the next issue when I hear a gunshot followed by a loud feminine scream.

Chapter 13

Like every other captive in the room, my eyes spring to the door from where the gunshot had sounded. Other than agonised screaming, nothing happens beyond muffled shouts.

The gunshot shows an escalation. I have no idea what's happening in that office, but I'm sure someone has just paid a steep price for refusing to cooperate with the terrorists.

The next two minutes pass as if hours, but eventually the door opens and a couple are marched out by Swimmer.

The man is trying to help the woman but it's obvious, despite the pain she's in, she wants nothing to do with him.

Her right arm is cradled in her left and there's blood gushing from her elbow. It would appear that's where the bullet struck. As they walk past me, I can see scorch marks on the less bloody inside of her elbow.

Despite myself, I wince.

It's now clear what happened in the office. The man, in a fit of foolish bravado, must have refused to do what Hannah had wanted. Either she or one of her lackeys had put their gun against the inside of the woman's elbow and pulled the trigger.

The action is a variation of the old IRA trait of kneecapping their enemies. That it's happened to the woman's elbow rather than her knee has left her mobile. She's still able to walk and therefore will not require any carrying by the terrorists. Her arm, however, will be as good as ruined.

If she gets to a hospital that has a team of crack surgeons, she may retain the use of her arm, but up here, at the mercy of Hannah and her cohorts, she's odds on to lose the use of her lower arm forever.

Perhaps she could get a new elbow joint fitted, after all, hips and knees get replaced all the time, but before that can even be considered she has to get off this mountain alive.

She'll be entering a state of shock very soon and, when the initial rushes of adrenaline and endorphins pass, she's going to experience pain like she's never dared to imagine.

In a lot of ways, her sobbing and screaming will work in the terrorists' favour. After seeing what's happened to her, and hearing her pained moans, the chances of someone else refusing Hannah are now minimal.

'Jake.'

I turn at Sharon's hiss and look at her. The determination that was there earlier has doubled itself and brought along a hefty amount of righteous fury to keep it company.

'I know. I want to do something as well but it's too dangerous.'

My words surprise me. There is little doubt in my mind that someone has to do something about the terrorists, but I'm still at a loss as to what needs to be done and how to do it.

'I thought you were made of better stuff than that. You're feart, aren't you?'

'I'd be a fool not to be afraid.'

'We cannae let them keep maiming folk. We have to stop them.'

'Agreed.' I fix her with a look. 'Why you asking me?'

'Because you're the only real man here. I cannae dae it ma'sel'.'

Sharon's speech has gone right back to Glasgow from its more universal English, and as much as it takes me back to the old city, I don't have the solution she's looking for.

'Nor can I.' I take a deep breath. 'If you come up with a good plan, I'll help.'

'Good, but what we gonnae dae and how we gonnae dae it?'

'I haven't got a Scooby. You?'

She shakes her head at me, to indicate she hasn't a clue either.

'All I can think is that we have to get away from them and raise the alarm. If we can take one of them down and get his weapons, so much the better.'

What she's saying makes sense to me. I just need time to think about how to get free.

However we do it, we must make sure we both escape the terrorists. If either of us should fall into their clutches after making a bid for freedom, we'll suffer a brutal punishment – if we're not killed outright.

Now I've decided to act, I realise the hypocrisy of my thoughts. Ever since the terrorists announced themselves I've been monitoring them, watching what they're doing, trying to work out what their goal is.

As much as I may be denying it to myself, I'm itching to get involved so I can try to save the hostages' lives. Were the terrorists masked, I'm sure I'd take a different stance, but as they aren't, I'm driven to believe they'll massacre every last one of us before they leave; and I'd rather die fighting than wait around for death.

The one concession I make is that I won't kill any of the terrorists if it can be avoided.

Chapter 14

Leslie Trouseau helps his wife onto a seat and sits on the one opposite her. She wears the same disbelieving look he can feel on his own face.

What happened in the office is a thing he'll never be able to forget. As soon as the woman had threatened Lily, he knew he would do as he was told. It wasn't because he loved her as a person, more he respected her as a woman. As the mother of his children, he couldn't let any harm come to her, regardless of his own feelings towards her.

As he'd expected, she was stoic in the face of the threat. Lily Trouseau is neither a weak nor cowardly woman. She isn't the type to shy away from any confrontation, yet she is wise enough to know when to pick her fights.

She'd gone along with events as they'd unfolded and retained her haughty dignity even with a gun pointed at her. More than that, she'd refrained from telling him to do as the woman told him. She had, quite literally, put her life in his hands, and despite the terror she must have been feeling, she made no effort to press him to do what the terrorists wanted, and left him to decide her fate.

Upon their return to the dining room, she'd maintained her icy composure and only shown her gratitude for his decision with a quick squeeze of his fingers.

As he settles into his seat he feels his heart pounding, and that old, familiar burning in his gut. What he'd been forced to do didn't sit well with him on any level, and, as such, his body was reacting to the ethical dilemma he hadn't been given a choice in.

Much as it galls him to have done what he did, he can see the simple brilliance of the terrorists' plan. When he looks at the other people in the room he can gauge the effect of the scheme, and the only word he can find to describe its final impact is significant.

In all his years of studying the world's news, to predict the potential financial effects of events, he's never heard of anything like this. If the terrorists can get away undetected, it will become the gold standard for audacious crimes.

He scrabbles in his pockets and pulls out a blister pack of pills. He is overdue his heart medication and the way it is pounding doesn't bode well for him. As he feeds the last two pills into his mouth, he curses that he has left the next pack in his suite.

Trouseau sees his wife notice the empty blister pack that he tries to secrete into his pocket, and witnesses the flash of understanding in her eyes as she realises its possible implications.

Had it not been his own heart he was worrying about, he would have enjoyed the irony of one of the hostages fearing for their life in a way the terrorists hadn't anticipated.

Chapter 15

The cop who clambers up the stairs to Nathan's control room looks as if he is carrying his own weight in stress. His face is set in the kind of grimace that inspires gargoyle sculptors, and there's a stoop to his shoulders that speaks of a long-running injury or ailment he's battling to work through.

Nathan waits until the cop has got himself in the room and shut the door before speaking. The cop dusts snow from his coat as Nathan explains that he's been trying to contact Steve for over an hour without response.

'Could it be his radio isn't charged, or that it's broken?'

'It could, but he has a backup.' Nathan tries not to pull a face at the cop. The man is doing his job, but the way he is going over the basics makes him feel like he is being patronised. 'And that wouldn't explain why the phone lines are dead.'

While waiting for the cops to respond, he and Olly Attwood had examined everything they knew about the communications up at RidgeTop. Rather than waste time answering the cop's questions, he decides to lay out everything they'd been through.

'We tried calling the landline, which is a system phone, and it's dead. Next, we tried calling the cell phones of the RidgeTop manager and the other senior members of staff. All went straight to voicemail. When that didn't work, we tried emailing the resort. All we got were bounce-backs, so we tried looking at their PCs remotely. We couldn't connect to any of them.' The cop isn't responding to anything Nathan is saying, but the cableway operator can see the information is being taken in and analysed. 'You're probably thinking some kind of power failure accounts for the lack of communications, and you'd be right. Except we know there's a backup generator. Like all the company's mechanical equipment, it's serviced and tested on a regular basis. Even if there was a power and generator failure, it wouldn't account for the fact we can't contact the manager on his cell. He has a company one that's always in his pocket. If he was dealing with a customer, I'd be able to leave a message for him and he'd call back. We've left ten messages and had no response.'

'What about the customers' cell phones? Have you tried calling them?'

Nathan tosses a look at his boss and gets a nod of confirmation that he can answer the question.

'That was our next move. We tried five and got the same straight to voicemail message on all of them. Yes, they might have left them in their rooms, switched off, but we purposefully chose the younger customers as they'll be more likely to have their phones with them so they can show social media what a great time they are having. Also, we've been monitoring incoming calls and emails along with our own social media feeds. We've heard nothing since seven thirty. Before that, we were tagged on Facebook, Twitter and Instagram.' Nathan shakes his head. 'I don't know what's going on up there, but it's like they went into lockdown. No matter what we've tried, we just can't raise them.'

The cop purses his lips and peers out of the window. Nathan follows his gaze and sees the same whiteout he's been looking at all night.

'What provisions do they have up there? Is there plenty of food and water for the number of people who are at the resort?'

'There's enough of both to last them several days.'

'Then we'll leave it until the storm passes tomorrow morning, unless someone at the resort can find a way to get in touch and lets us know there's a problem we need to act upon.'

Nathan disagrees with the cop's plan of waiting as he is sure there is more to the lack of contact than a power outage or mechanical failure. However, unless he can find a way to persuade him, everything his gut is telling him is going to be ignored until morning.

'Excuse me, officer, but would you look at this?' Nathan holds up his cell phone for the cop to look at. 'See how I've got five bars of signal, and the same for Wi-Fi?'

'Yes. I'm very pleased for you, having such a great signal at work must be a great boost to your productivity.'

Nathan ignores the cop's sarcasm. 'The signal for both resorts is beamed out from here. We know it's working because we've not just checked it's working, we've also rebooted our Wi-Fi booster. RidgeWay is further away from the cell mast, and our Wi-Fi system, than RidgeTop, and it's working fine. Now I'm only a guy who works a cableway, whereas you're a cop, but can you answer me something – why would the Wi-Fi signal be out when it's not connected in any way and it's transmitted from here?'

'I don't know, but I'm sure it's not what you're thinking.'

'How? How can you be sure?' Nathan points out of the window at RidgeTop. 'There's over a hundred very wealthy people up there and they're totally isolated. We have no way of communicating with them when it's been proven that our systems are working. Does that not tell you something is going on up there that shouldn't be?'

The cop lifts a hand to stall Nathan. 'Say you're right, what do you expect me to do? You say the cableway won't work because the gearing at the other end is locked in place, I don't think we'll find a helicopter pilot crazy enough to try and land on a mountaintop in the middle of a snowstorm, and you'd need to be a certifiable lunatic to try hiking up there. If you've got any bright ideas on what I should do, please, let me know what they are. If you've got nothing, don't expect me to magic up a solution. The storm is due to blow over by morning, we can get a helicopter up there as soon as there's visibility. If you manage to contact them, or they contact you, let me know, but until we know there's definitely something wrong up there, we can't do anything. And even then, we can't get up there until this storm has passed.'

Nathan turns away from the cop. He is disappointed with the man's logic, but he can find no way past what he is saying.

As Nathan slumps in his seat, the cop leaves and closes the door behind him.

Nathan doesn't even hear the door latch click home, as his mind has fast-forwarded to a possible way to get to the lodge. He would have shared it with the cop, but the man was too dismissive. Rather than have the cop around, should he be proven wrong, Nathan plans to check things out for himself.

Chapter 16

I scooch my backside back and forth and try to get comfortable. Sitting in one place for any length of time isn't my thing, and I can feel my muscles stiffening and protesting at the lack of exercise.

Across the crowd of people, I see a man crawling his way through the mixture of customers and staff. With nothing to do beyond worry, I watch him with interest.

The man stops his crawl when he reaches the manager. Kirk Fleming looks at him, part fear and part empathy. I can't hear what they are saying, but they become more animated as they talk then Fleming gives a nod.

Whatever the man has asked of Fleming, it's something that scares him. The manager shakes his head at him. A finger is jabbed in his chest and a look of fear encapsulates Fleming's eyes.

Fleming levers himself to his feet and steps between a group of hostages about to approach the nearest terrorist; he is holding his hands above his head and there's a tentativeness to his movements, which is understandable given the circumstances.

The terrorist aims his submachine gun, but I can see he's curious, rather than worried that Fleming is going to attack him.

'I'm sorry to bother you, but one of the ladies needs to use a restroom, and I'm sure there will be others who do too.'

The terrorist stares at Fleming for a moment then tells him to return to his seat.

As he picks his way back through the throng of bodies, Fleming tosses an 'I tried' look to the man who'd approached him. The woman beside the man looks at Fleming with fury. I guess her need is pressing and she doesn't want the humiliation of soiling herself to add to what is already a stressful ordeal.

From the corner of my eye I see the terrorist has relayed the request to Clipboard.

It doesn't take Clipboard long to reach a decision. He steps forward to address the group. 'Ladies and gentlemen. It has been brought to our attention that some of you need to use the facilities. You will be taken in groups of four.' He gives a vicious smile. 'I'm sure I don't need to remind you of the consequences of trying to escape, do I?'

A sea of heads rotate left and right. Nobody except Sharon and me has escape plans on their mind.

This is where our opportunity will arise, though there are a few points to consider: first of all, the terrorists will be alert for any attempt to escape or fight back at them; therefore, neither Sharon nor I must act until there has been a number of uneventful visits to the restroom. When the terrorists become bored escorting compliant prisoners it'll be easier for us to get the jump on one of them.

The second point is that while we may get the jump on a terrorist, he'll be missed within a minute, two at most. This means we'll have very little time to hide ourselves. Plus, if we use lethal force it sets a precedent for the terrorists' retaliation.

After being responsible for so many deaths in the past, there's no way I want to get any more blood on my hands. Doubly so if it means I'm putting my own life in jeopardy. The counter-argument to this is that the terrorists haven't hidden their faces, they haven't even worried about taking our cell phones from us. In their position, I'd have claimed all the cells so nobody could take pictures. They haven't, which reinforces the point they aren't worried about being identified by any of the hostages. Had they been masked, I'd be a lot more reluctant to strike against them.

If we don't use lethal force on the terrorist we jump, we'll either have to incapacitate him or take him with us. I've no problem with knocking someone unconscious, but there's no way I want to deal with a reluctant prisoner while attempting to evade his comrades.

It would be better all round if one of us could get away unnoticed to raise the alarm. I know if I can get in touch with either Alfonse or Chief Watson back in Casperton, they'll take me seriously enough to send the cavalry. however, were I to dial 911 there is every chance my call would be dismissed as a prank.

This begs the most important question of all: even if I can get word to the correct people, what can they do about it?

By its very design, RidgeTop Resort is remote and inaccessible. There's a chance a special forces team may be able to storm the place if given a few days to plan their assault. Even then, they'd only be able to get here via two methods: the cableway and a helicopter. I've already discounted both of these ideas as escape methods for the terrorists and the same reasoning applies to incoming forces.

If this were a Hollywood movie, a team of Navy SEALs, led by a heroic character called Clint Squarejaw, or something equally ridiculous, would launch themselves from a plane and parachute their way through the snowstorm to unerringly land on the helipad. After that, it would be a case of Clint and his buddies out-shooting the bad guys before a final stand-off with Clint and the leader of the terrorists. A big fight would ensue, which Clint would win, despite being at some disadvantage, and then the erstwhile hero would make a couple of wisecracks and seduce the prettiest hostage.

The problems with this are numerous: this isn't Hollywood, it's real life; I'm not Clint Squarejaw, and the terrorists appear to be the real deal. Every one of them will be a better shot than me, and they will all have been trained in hand-to-hand combat, whereas I'm unfamiliar with guns, a questionable shot, and the only fight training I've ever had was an afternoon spent in a back garden being shown the dirty tricks my grandfather had learned while battling on the infamous Clyde shipyards.

If I'm going to act against these terrorists, I'm going to have to outwit, rather than outfight them.

Chapter 17

I'm still working out the details of what can be done when a boy in the crowd catches my eye. He's around fourteen or fifteen and he's sat beside a woman I assume is his mother. Both of them look scared, but I can see an inner strength that's fortifying them against the horrors of the evening.

The boy's jaw is set and there's a whisper of fine hair caressing his top lip. The mother is familiar to me from her habit of stationing herself at the bar so she can observe the whole room.

She's no bar-fly though, she'd have three, maybe four drinks per night. If my memory serves me right her name is Helen Prior, and the boy is called Daniel. I don't know her story, or care too much if I'm honest, but more than once I'd spotted the collection of rings she wears on a thin, white-gold necklace. I clocked two wedding rings, an engagement ring, and what I presumed was an eternity ring.

The presence of the rings tells me she still loves the person who put them on her finger and had worn the one she'd given in return. Whether they're on the necklace because of divorce or bereavement is her business, and I only had a fleeting look at them. Their position said something, but I wasn't listening, and I sure as hell didn't want to get caught gawping at a customer's chest.

Daniel unwinds his mother's arm from his shoulders and shuffles his way over to me.

'Do you think we're going to be okay?'

I don't know why he's asking me this question; to get to me he's passed three other guys, but to be fair to the kid, they're all city types who probably think arguing over a restaurant bill is a manly way to act.

'I'm sure we will be.' I don't like lying to anyone, let alone an impressionable youth, but there's nothing to be gained, other than panic, by telling him what I really think. 'Don't worry, I'm sure it'll all be over soon.'

He looks at me with the kind of wisdom that takes some people a lifetime to accrue. 'When you make your move, watch out for the guy with the tattooed neck. He keeps looking your way.'

It's all I can do not to let my mouth hang open in amazement. In a flash, I wonder if I'm being so obvious with what I've been hoping was covert surveillance, that everyone in the room is aware of what I'm doing and is waiting for me to make my move.

'You sure?'

'Yeah. The others are watching the crowd in general, but he keeps glancing towards you.'

'Thanks for the heads up.' I need to know what else he's spotted. He's observant and has made the right connections. He didn't have to come and warn me, but he did, which shows he's got a good heart. 'What else have you noticed?'

'You've got at least one steak knife stashed and the lady behind you has one as well.'

The fact that he's spotted me and Sharon collecting potential weapons speaks well of his observation skills, and poorly of our attempts at subterfuge.

I'm glad of his warning but it has cast doubt into my mind about the chances of either me or Sharon being able to get away and raise the alarm.

Over Daniel's shoulder I see his mother looking our way. She's worried, and if I've been spotted by Tattoo Neck, she has good reason to worry about her son. If I do try anything and fail, the repercussions may fall on his shoulders as well as mine.

It's a responsibility I neither want nor am comfortable with. If I try something and I'm the one to suffer, it's fair enough. However, if there's a potential for backlash against others, I'll have to do everything I can to make it appear as if I'm a lone wolf.

I'm about to tell him to go back to his mother when a pair of gunshots ring out in quick succession.

Chapter 18

The gunshots were too close together to have been a warning: to me they sounded like an assassin's double tap. As these thoughts are whirling through my head, the office door opens and the limp body of a woman is dragged into the corridor.

The blood all over her chest tells me where the bullets have struck. The woman is lifeless and, from what I can see, if she's not already dead she will be very soon.

A scream erupts from the mouth of a woman being led along the corridor on her way back from the restrooms. She's hustled away from the shot woman by Tattoo Neck and re-joins her companion.

The significance of the woman's death isn't lost on any of the hostages. The mutilation of Debbie Boitoult, and the woman whose elbow was shot out, were indicators of the terrorists' resolve, but the fact they had escalated to homicide indicates a raising of the stakes.

Both of the women who received injuries have been swathed in bandages made from shirts. There will be a risk of infection to each of them, but, in the greater scheme of things, there are more pressing issues than infection.

I watch as Hannah strides down the corridor from the office. Her face is grim, and she's got her knife in her hand.

'Listen up.' Her tone is hard and there's no doubting the fact that she's pissed at the situation. 'If you don't want to suffer from the sudden onset of rigor mortis, you'd better do as we say. I need hardly add that non-compliance will not be tolerated.'

Hannah nods at Clipboard, who calls out a name as she turns on her heel and returns to the office.

There's something amiss about what just happened. It all seems too calculated, rehearsed even. Hannah was too quick to come from the office, too erudite with her quip about rigor mortis.

My first thought is that killing a hostage in this way was always in their plans; therefore, Hannah has had time to script what she'd say. There's no doubt in my mind that she's cruel enough to have planned this, what bugs me is the why?

A punishment has already been meted out; therefore, doing a second is overkill.

The only explanation I can come up with for the homicide, is that the guy must have refused to cooperate, thereby gambling with his wife's safety. It seems like a reasonable assumption until you factor in the knowledge that the terrorists were willing to maim *before* the guy and his wife entered the office.

The demands that Hannah and co are putting on people in there must be horrific for a man to risk his wife's safety. Now that someone has been murdered, there will be less chance of someone else refusing the terrorists' demands.

I cast my gaze across the room and look at the guy whose wife has been shot. Like the others who've entered the office, he's in a state of shock, but he doesn't quite seem shocked enough to me.

He's sitting with his back against a wall. His gaze is at the ceiling and, while I can't see his face too well, his body language doesn't speak of anger, or even shock. His wife has just been killed, he should be trying to rip the terrorists' heads from their shoulders; he ought to be shouting abuse at them, or at the very least, trying to get to his wife in a desperate attempt to save her.

That he's doing none of these things makes alarm bells ring in my head. Yes, he might be a couple of stone overweight, and have the pasty skin of someone who rarely goes outdoors, but he should still have enough anger in his gut to react in a more human way.

I stop my thoughts where they are and look at things from a different angle. Rather than question what the terrorists were asking of the man, I look at reasons why the man wouldn't have moved heaven and earth to save his wife.

The first thing I do is remember them as a couple. When I take away the fact they can afford RidgeTop's inflated prices, I figure he'd punched above his weight in snaring his wife. Set against his pasty bulk, her slim and tanned figure had only accentuated the difference in their appeal. While it is natural to think that such an imbalance would have him acting in a way that was almost subservient, he didn't. The two of them had bickered with each other and the looks they'd exchanged were anything but loving.

Where he had been courteous, she'd been waspish and offhand with me and other staff members. That she's got a good tan, while his skin is ghostly in its whiteness, speaks of her lounging around while he slaves over a desk. It doesn't take a great leap from there to imagine her cheating on him with a fitness coach or a pool cleaner.

This would be a huge reason for the guy to refuse Hannah's demands. When I add in the woman's acerbic nature I can almost hear their arguments: he'd be throwing accusations of infidelity at her, asking her why she cheated on him when all he did was provide for her.

Her responses would be that he was always working and was never at home. Maybe she'd been nasty and criticised his manhood or sexual prowess.

It's possible she had some dirt on him, and he was forced to tolerate her presence in his life, lest she expose whatever he'd done.

It's a terrible thought for me to have, and I hope for humanity's sake I'm wrong, but I figure he's chosen to refuse Hannah's demands so she'd save him the hassle of what would have been a toxic and expensive divorce.

Whatever the reasons, to my mind he hadn't fought hard enough to protect her, and has reacted to her death in all the wrong ways. So far as I'm concerned, he's as guilty as the person who shot her.

Chapter 19

Sharon outlines her plan to me and I listen without commenting. If she has her way, there's every chance she'll instigate a manhunt that will see us both either mutilated or dead.

My own thoughts centre on one of us slipping away, without our absence being noticed, and raising the alarm.

She plans to thrust her knife into Tattoo Neck's throat and bolt, whereas I'm against taking life.

'That's not going to work.' I'm not worried about sparing her feelings. She's ex-military and ex-Glasgow, there's no way she's going to take any offence to a different opinion.

'How?'

She means why, but being Scottish myself, I understand what she's asking.

'They'll be after us in seconds. We'll be hunted down and killed in no time.'

'What do you reckon we should do then?'

I outline my plan to her in a few short sentences. It carries a certain amount of danger for her should my absence be noted. After all, she's the one whose role it is to create a distraction and be the source of confusion.

She falls silent as she works through my plan in her mind. I'm cool with her finding faults, the more that are found and corrected before the plan is put into action, the better our chances of success will be.

'Do you really think you can get away without them noticing?'

I shake my head. 'No, but if I can, we have a chance. If not, I'll just have to take my chances.'

'It's not just you, but.' Sharon appending her sentence with a 'but' takes me back to Glasgow faster than any aeroplane ever could. It's a trait local to Glasgow and one that I'd dropped when I moved to America. It wasn't a conscious decision, I was just a teenager doing whatever was needed to fit in. 'If you fail, we'll all die.'

I look at her without speaking. She huffs out a breath and shrugs her shoulders.

'If you fail, I'll not be able to get another chance.' Sharon nods towards Buzz Cut. 'We've seen their faces, they've made no attempt to disguise who they are. When they leave here, we'll all be dead.'

The look on her face tells me she knows I've worked this out for myself. What it also says is that she trusts me to deliver.

It's the second piece of information that sits heaviest on my shoulders; that I'm being trusted to save the lives of all the staff and customers is both humbling and terrifying.

If Sharon or any of the others knew how much I'm doubting myself, I'm sure they'd feel their trust was misplaced.

Regardless of their confidence and my lack of it, I know, when the moment for action comes, I'll do everything I can to ensure I raise the alarm and get help coming our way.

Chapter 20

Nathan bangs on the door of Roger Knightly's chalet and pulls his hood tighter. The snowstorm is ferocious in its intensity, but it's part and parcel of living and working in a resort that only exists because of skiers and the money they spend to indulge their passion.

When Knightly opens the door, he looks as he always does: unshaven and red-eyed. That he is a high-functioning alcoholic is an open secret, yet he's been allowed to keep his job because, even when he is full of bourbon, he is better at it than any of his contemporaries.

When people pay the kind of money the customers of RidgeTop are asked to, they want the very best of skiing; the slopes have to be perfect, and this is achieved with snow groomers.

Every night a gang of snow groomers, or piste bashers as they are better known, ascend the mountain. Their great wide tracks haul them up impossible gradients as their ploughs level drifts. The tracks destroy clumps of snow and the comb at the back leaves a perfect surface for skiers.

Roger Knightly has been driving the piste bashers on the RidgeTop slopes since the resort opened, and his knowledge of the mountain is legendary. Where other operators rely on modern piste bashers – with their wealth of technological gizmos such as GPS systems that not only pinpoint their location, but also give readings about snow depth – Knightly relies on experience and instinct. The fact his piste basher is more than thirty years old, and considered to be un-driveable by the other operators, is something that appeals to the cent-sensitive company accountants.

When he eventually stops working, they will have to replace not just the man who drives the machine, but the machine itself.

At upwards of $300,000 apiece, Knightly is cut a lot of slack to defer the expense of replacing him for as long as possible. It doesn't hurt that he maintains his piste basher himself and refuses to let anyone else touch it.

'What d'you want?'

Knightly's breath carries enough bourbon fumes to suggest at least a half bottle has been consumed, but Nathan doesn't let it bother him. Drunk or sober, if anyone can get up the mountain tonight, it's Roger Knightly.

In the general course of things, he'd have been out there by now, but there is little point in grooming the slopes when there is continuing heavy snowfall, and a strong wind creating drifts. On nights like this the piste bashers remain in their sheds, ascending the mountain in the early hours. It puts more pressure on their operators, but when the weather is a factor it's the only way.

'There's something going on up at RidgeTop. I can't raise Steve and they're not responding to emails or phone calls.'

A wry twist caresses Knightly's mouth into a grimaced smile. 'So what do you want me to do about it?'

'Take a guess.' Nathan knows Knightly well enough to know that, despite his fondness for bourbon, he is smart enough to read between the lines. 'The question is, are you going to offer me a solution or become another part of the problem?'

'Seriously, what do you want me to do? Drive up there, knock on the door and ask if everything's okay? You've been watching too many movies.'

Nathan ignores Knightly's sarcasm. 'No, I want you to take me up there so I can find out what the hell's going on. Trust me, there's something wrong up there and we've got a lot of very wealthy and influential people as our customers. If I'm right, the bad publicity could close this resort and then where would we be?'

'Gimme five minutes to get my stuff together; and get yourself some warmer clothes – if you're going walkabout up there, it's gonna be a lot colder than it is down here.'

Chapter 21

Sharon stands in line and waits for Tattoo Neck to pull her and Boulder forward. There're two other guys standing with them, along with a woman in her sixties.

It's rude of her, but Sharon makes sure she's in front of the other woman in the queue. For Boulder's plan to work, they must be in the same group as they're led to the restroom.

As luck would have it, Tattoo Neck waves all five people forward at once.

'Use the men's room, and the men's room only.'

Boulder had predicted this would be the case and it's what they were banking on.

Sharon lets Boulder enter the restroom first and turns to face Tattoo Neck.

Her role is to distract him long enough for Boulder to make his escape. She also has to block the other two guys from witnessing anything.

'I can't go in there.' Sharon glares up at Tattoo Neck and shakes her head to emphasise her point.

He shrugs at her. 'It's there or nowhere.'

'You don't understand. I need to go to the ladies'.'

'Why?'

His tone is becoming more aggressive, but that doesn't matter to Sharon, the two of them arguing will eat up time and create a better distraction for Boulder.

Sharon glances up and down the corridor as if she is reluctant to speak. Everything she is doing is designed to use up valuable seconds.

'Because I need to get something from the ladies' that isn't available in the men's room.'

Incomprehension covers the terrorist's face until he makes the connection. Then there is a brief spell as he debates with himself. He gives a sharp nod. 'Go on then.'

As Sharon makes her way to the ladies' restroom, she is aware of the other woman following her. This can only be a good thing as it will help to muddy the waters.

As she waits in a cubicle, to give the illusion she is using the restroom, she offers silent prayers that Boulder has made his escape without detection.

Boulder's idea of her claiming to need sanitary products was a good one; like so many macho guys, Tattoo Neck had shied away from talk of a woman's menstrual cycle and, by doing so, he'd allowed Sharon to create an environment where there was room for confusion and mistakes.

When she exits, she finds that Tattoo Neck has positioned himself at a point in the corridor where he can watch the doors of both restrooms.

To further distract him, she walks across the corridor and stands in front of him. 'Thank you. You didn't have to do that, but the fact you did is greatly appreciated.' As she goes back to her space on the floor of the dining room, Sharon wonders if Tattoo Neck had been able to tell the smile and the thanks she had given him were false.

Chapter 22

When the bartender doesn't return from the men's room, Daniel wonders if he's the only one who's noticed. He's sure the server has, but she'd been talking to him, so he's confident that she's in cahoots with him.

The bartender seemed like a decent guy, unlike Double M, the former wrestler who is now in charge of the World Federation of Wrestling. He is nothing like as cool as he seems on the TV. He'd been rude when Mom had taken him over and introduced him; her explaining how he always cheered for Double M had been so embarrassing, he wished he'd never pointed out the wrestler to her.

His pops had always said you should never meet your heroes, and this afternoon had taught Daniel why.

Daniel casts his eyes towards the clock and sees that a full ten minutes have passed since the people who went to the washroom in the same group as the bartender had returned. The bartender hasn't come back with them, which means he must still be in the toilet.

Except, Daniel doesn't think he is still in there – the way he'd watched the men with guns, and their woman boss, had been different to everyone else.

The bartender hadn't looked at them in fear, he'd been checking them out, observing their movements and, from what Daniel could gauge, looking for a way to stop them doing what they were doing.

In Daniel's mind, the bartender is a spy, or a cop working undercover. Before long, he'd call in the army and they'd all be rescued from the evil men who'd taken over the resort.

He also likes the idea that the bartender used to be a crack soldier, and he will return with a pair of blazing guns and shoot all the terrorists dead. It would be cool to see them get what they deserve.

As much as his mind is creating fantasies, Daniel knows the truth is a different matter. The bartender is just that: a bartender. He isn't a hero, or any kind of undercover agent, he is nothing more than a man who pours drinks.

A commotion causes Daniel to turn his head and look at where Double M is standing. In his wrestling days Michael Malone was known as the All-American Hero, before he'd morphed into the faux bureaucrat at the head of the WFW company.

Standing at six nine, he is a big man who used to use his great strength to throw his opponents around the ring as if they were ragdolls. Daniel can remember watching Double M fighting all the modern greats and beating them.

Double M was a mean wrestler who'd pummel his opponents long past the point necessary to allow him to pin them.

Daniel knows all the wrestlers' moves by heart and he remembers Double M's finishing one: The Leveller. It had incapacitated so many of those who'd stood against him in the ring. When his opponent was reeling from the beating he'd dished out, Double M would launch them against the ring's ropes and, when they were catapulted back at him, he'd lift a size fourteen boot into their chin.

The Leveller was always preceded by a ritualistic beating of the chest and three slaps to the right thigh.

As Daniel watches Double M beat his chest like a gorilla, he fears for Michael Malone as a man far more than he had ever feared for him as a wrestler.

Chapter 23

I crawl along the top of the air conditioning duct, taking care to keep my weight to the sides where the metal has more strength in case the thin metal of the top flexes and makes a noise that gives my position away.

As soon as I had entered the men's room, I clambered up the wall of one of the stalls, popped a ceiling tile, and slid myself into the opening between the false and real ceilings. I'd helped the maintenance guy make a repair to the air conditioning duct a couple of days ago, which had made me aware of the space between the ceilings.

Now all I have to do is follow the boxy metal until I'm in a part of the hotel where I can climb down and raise the alarm. It's just as well I have the duct to follow: I can't see a thing and I daren't use the torch on my cell phone in case a terrorist below sees the light through a chink in the ceiling tiles.

It sounds simple, and in theory it is, but this crawl space has twenty years of accumulated dust and it's all I can do not to sneeze as every movement I make disturbs enough particles to send a whole new cloud billowing up.

The duct is warm to the touch as heated air is pumped throughout the hotel in a bid to combat the temperature outside. Fortunately, the heat in the ducting isn't so great that it burns my hands.

I follow the duct round a corner and bump my head against a supporting wall. My groping fingers tell me that the duct disappears through the wall, but there's not a chance I can squeeze myself through the three-inch gap I can feel above it.

By my calculations, I've passed over the ladies' restroom, and I'm above the corridor that runs from the dining room and bar to the part of the hotel that houses all the suites.

If I was to lift a ceiling tile and hang down before dropping, I'd still have at least six feet to fall. The drop holds no fear whatsoever for me, but the fact I'd almost certainly make a noise upon landing means it's a non-starter. For me to thump down so close to the terrorists would be stupid at best, suicidal at worst.

I consider taking off my shoes to land barefoot but dismiss the idea. If I have to take on a terrorist after dropping down, I'm certain I'll need my kicks to have the maximum effect and there won't be time for tying laces.

The last thing I want to do is get into a fight with a terrorist. Not only are they all heavily armed and trained fighters, the noise is sure to bring the other terrorists running.

I feel again where the duct goes through the wall. While there's no chance of me getting through the gap above it, there may be a space to one side, or some loose bricks I can remove.

My fingers scrabble against the masonry until my hand goes down the right side of the duct. I slide my hand away from the duct I'm lying on. With every inch my hand moves away from the duct, I'm expecting it to collide with rough bricks.

When my fingertips bump against something, my arm is three-quarters extended.

I don't feel anything rough like masonry, instead I feel something smooth, metallic, and warm.

It's another duct.

I reassess my position in the hotel and realise that the one I've crawled along has taken the turn left because it was heading towards the boiler room. If there's another off to my right, it'll probably turn left and take me in the direction of the suites.

That's where I want to be: away from the terrorists, somewhere they won't be looking and, most of all, somewhere that has a telephone connected to the outside world.

I reach across to the other duct. When I have my right hand planted on top of it, I shift my weight across and put my left hand beside my right. My back skims the underside of the floor above me as I bridge the gap and pull across one leg then the other.

Once again, I set off on a slow crawl, pausing every now and then to squeeze the tickle from my nose. After five or so paces, my forearms bang against something.

I use one hand to fumble at the obstacle and surmise it's a cable tray. It's halfway between the duct and the floor above so I have to wriggle my way over it.

The burgundy vest that's part of my uniform snags on a sharp edge and tears, but that's the least of my worries.

I keep going until the duct turns left, and I follow it until I've passed over two more cable trays and a collection of pipes.

The duct takes a turn right and, as I progress along it, I feel smaller sections of ducting protrude from either side and head off to heat the adjoining rooms.

This is all good news, as I figure that the ducting is following the corridor to the point where the corridor turns to provide access to the cable car station. Along either side of the corridor there are storerooms, an office, and the reception desk.

When my head bumps against another wall, I reckon I'm at least fifty feet from the toilets.

It's crunch time; I reach down from the duct and locate the edge of a ceiling tile.

Using my fingertips, I lift it just enough to allow me to see if there's anyone below.

There isn't, and I don't hear anyone shout a warning, so I lift the tile a little higher and crane my head to look along the corridor as best I can.

When I see nothing, I mentally cross my fingers and move the tile to one side.

I now have a twenty-inch square to drop through.

As I adjust my position and get ready to lower my feet through the square, I hear a sound I shouldn't hear.

Fingers drumming against something metallic.

The space below the hole darkens as a terrorist wanders below me and stops in his tracks.

He's got a submachine gun in his hands and the same weapons on his hips as the other terrorists. If the way he's moving his body is anything to go by, he's bored. First, he leans left, then right. His next move is to lean forward, as if touching his toes.

His presence is a nuisance in every possible way. I can't drop down when he's there, but if he takes a few steps and returns, he's bound to see the missing ceiling tile.

I'm left with no choice but to act. I position myself ready to drop and make the best plan I can think of as I'm shifting my weight off the duct and starting to fall.

Chapter 24

I don't have a lot of options for dealing with the terrorist I'm dropping towards, but there's no doubt in my mind that this is a time to hit first and ask questions later.

As I drop, I swing my right hand towards the side of his neck. My hand is flat to deliver a karate style chop rather than a punch.

By design, my left hand slides over his left shoulder and down his chest.

I'm hauling him back as I fall. The impact, of both my blow and my weight, landing on his left shoulder drives him to the floor as my left arm snakes up and under his chin.

Unlike the movies where a hero will fight for minutes with his enemy trying to strangle him, a good chokehold takes only a few seconds to render someone unconscious, as it cuts off the blood flow to the brain rather than oxygen to the lungs.

The terrorist drops his gun as he reaches up to scrabble at my arm. He's too late. The suddenness of my attack has caught him unawares and, by the time he remembers the knife on his hip, his movements have become sluggish and uncoordinated.

Even as I'm grappling with him, I'm looking left and right along the corridor in case he's not alone.

I give him an extra couple of seconds of pressure then poke him in the eye with my right thumb.

It's a sure-fire test of his consciousness.

He passes my test by failing to respond.

I roll him off me and strip him of his obvious weapons. A quick pat down reveals no hidden knives or backup guns.

His pistol goes into the small of my back, and his knife – sheath and all – is added to my belt. I keep the submachine gun in my hand as I fish a set of keys from my pocket and open the door to the room where the drinks are kept.

With the door open, I lay the submachine gun on an empty beer keg and grab the terrorist by the ankles.

I drag him into the beer cellar and lay him face down. He still has a pulse and when I pinch the skin on the back of his neck he doesn't respond.

My next move is to search the room. I find a roll of tape left on a shelf with a bundle of other odds and ends. I go back to the terrorist and bind and gag him.

As an extra precaution against him getting free, I lay him on his side and surround him with beer kegs.

One down, umpteen to go.

The pat down had revealed no wallet or any form of ID. This speaks of professionalism to me, and if I'm honest with myself, I hadn't really expected to find anything. Everything about the terrorists has shown experience and planning.

Whatever their aim is by speaking to each customer, I reckon they're likely to achieve it. Not only are they well-drilled and armed to the teeth, but their plan has worked well for them so far.

The only error they have made was falling for the diversion that Sharon created, which allowed my escape, and I'm not even sure they have missed me.

Their primary focus has to be the customers they've identified. They are the people who're wealthy and powerful. The terrorists not bothering to identify a single staff member speaks volumes to me. My first instinct was a mass kidnapping, but the more I think about it, the more I wonder if there's another angle that I'm missing.

My next move has to be contacting the outside world. How they'll be able to help is beyond me, but knowing they're aware of the situation will give me confidence about surviving the night.

Should I be captured, I can use that confidence to put fear and doubt into the terrorists' minds. It might not save my life, but forcing them to abandon their plan may well save the lives of others.

I lock the beer cellar door and walk along the corridor. Its warm décor and pictures of skiers on the mountain are supposed to offer comfort and excitement to new arrivals. I feel neither warm nor excited. My primary emotion is fear, not just for myself, but for every customer and staff member who is being held hostage.

The reception desk is right in front of me, but the area is open plan and the last thing I want is to get caught calling for help. All the same, I pick up the phone and listen for a dial tone.

Nothing.

I try pressing 9 for an outside line and get some more nothing.

I press 0 with the same results.

It's obvious they've either cut the phone lines or disabled the system.

There being nothing else I can do, I creep my way towards the cableway station. If I can't call for help, I'll have to go and get it myself.

All I have to do is figure out how to get the cable cars running, and then jump in one.

As plans go, it's a simple one. Too simple.

If I were a terrorist and I saw the cableway running, I'd do one of two things.

First: stop the car and leave it hanging – that would leave me safe from the terrorists but exposed to the snowstorm's vicious winds and sub-zero temperatures.

Second, and least preferable: reverse the controls and kill the first person found in a cable car.

Neither option appeals to me, but I have very little choice – there's no way I can hike down the mountain.

Chapter 25

Daniel watches as two hostages carry Double M back from where he'd landed after his wild charge at the terrorists.

The former wrestler hadn't stood a chance; as soon as he'd got within striking distance of the nearest terrorist, it was obvious who'd win.

The terrorist awaited Double M's arrival without reaction. He didn't even lift his gun. As the famous size fourteen foot arced its way towards his head, the terrorist ducked to one side and crashed the stock of his gun into Double M's groin.

With his aggressor doubled over in pain, the terrorist removed his knife from its sheath and stabbed it into each of Double M's thighs.

Like the woman whose chin had been cut, and the one was shot in the elbow, Double M's wounds are now bandaged up with shirts.

As Daniel watched the shirts being applied, the former wrestler's face was slick with sweat as he fought against the pain.

What Daniel finds strange, is the expression on Double M's face, and the way his eyes keep flicking among the crowd. It's like he's looking for someone but can't find them.

It could well be fear of further punishment from the terrorists but, as far as Daniel can gauge, Double M isn't looking at the terrorists, he's looking at the hostages.

The woman who was with Double M is at his side, so it can't be her that he is looking for. It is only when Double M's eyes rest on the woman who was talking with the bartender that they stop searching.

The smile that spreads across the wrestler's face tells Daniel everything he needs to know. Some might have figured that Double

M was just pleased to be alive after a failed attempt, but Daniel knows better. He knows Double M and has watched him for years.

In his wrestling days, Double M was the champion of the underdog. When a minor character was on the receiving end of a beat down from several other wrestlers, it was always Double M who'd come rampaging to their rescue.

He'd wade into the fight and battle to protect the underdog. Sometimes he'd succeed, and sometimes he'd achieve nothing more than a pounding for his troubles. Regardless of this, he came to the rescue of so many, that self-sacrifice grew to be expected of him.

Double M was also a master of distraction. He'd walk halfway down the ramp that led to the ring and pause when his presence was known, or he'd emerge from the crowd and walk around the ring. With their opponents distracted, the underdogs would then have the chance to regain their breath or launch a surprise counter-attack.

For these reasons, he was loved by the fans and his transition to the WFW's CEO had been accepted without complaint. The way he still carries a threat level to any of the current wrestlers is just another reason he commands respect.

When Double M had beaten his chest, Daniel was sure the wrestler would be killed for his stupidity in warning the terrorists that a big man was about to do something. He'd expected to see a gun pointed at Double M and a red spot appear on his body.

The fact it hadn't happened that way was significant. By beating on his chest and slapping his thigh, Double M had given the terrorists a deliberate warning and allowed the one he was targeting a chance to prepare. Therefore, the response could be measured. It was a gamble but, if the expression on Double M's face was anything to go by, despite his injuries it had paid off.

Daniel scratches at his leg as he follows his train of thought. Double M appeared to have nothing to gain from a failed attempt attacking the terrorist with the tattooed neck.

At least nothing obvious, until his personality was factored into the equation. Daniel assesses what he knows about the wrestler:

Double M is best known for his supporting of underdogs and creation of distractions.

There wasn't a fight, which means there couldn't be an underdog.

His attempt must have been a distraction.

His reason for creating a distraction is a puzzle, until Daniel remembers that the bartender went to the men's room and has not returned. The terrorist who'd taken the bartender, along with four others, is the one whose neck is covered in tattoos.

Daniel smiles to himself as he realises that Double M had also noticed this, and did what he'd done to give the terrorist something other than the visit to the men's room to think about.

It is typical of the wrestler: distraction and self-sacrifice rolled up into one action. That it could have turned out to have a tragic end is something Double M will have considered, yet he risked his life anyway to give the bartender a better chance of escape.

The man goes up in Daniel's estimation. The slight he received upon meeting Double M is forgotten as he ponders on the risk the man had taken and the thinking behind it.

Double M wouldn't have wanted to go into the room with the crazy terrorist lady, but, from what Daniel had seen, everyone who cooperated came out of the office looking shocked, but more or less unscathed.

Double M must have another motivation: the greater good.

As Daniel looks at one of the terrorists, he realises he can clearly see the man's face.

Bad guys don't let you live if you've seen their face.

All the terrorists' faces are visible; none of them are wearing masks. The hostages are going to be killed before the terrorists leave.

He blinks his eyes and chews the inside of his cheek.

He isn't going to cry.

He is fifteen now, and big boys don't cry.

Chapter 26

Nathan grips the armrest and wonders what he's gotten himself into. The piste basher's lights are only picking out a roiling mass of snow. There is nowhere near enough visibility for him to have any idea of where they are. At best he can see no more than five feet in any direction.

For all he knows, they could be inches away from dropping over a steep cliff or riding up the middle of a wide corridor.

The cab of the piste basher stinks of stale cigarettes, staler alcohol, and is tinged with a hint of body odour.

In the normal course of events there's no way Nathan would have gotten into Knightly's cab, but, despite all the logical explanations running through his mind, he can't get past the feeling in his gut that something is terribly wrong at RidgeTop.

How Knightly is navigating the vehicle is beyond him. The older man sits in his seat with the nonchalance of a sunbather sitting beside a hotel pool, guiding the piste basher with a series of minute adjustments of its controls as it barrels up the gradient.

Like Knightly, Nathan is pinned into his seat by the upward angle, but there is no way he can match Knightly's seeming indifference to the fact they can't see more than five feet in front of them.

Their journey up-slope had begun with a gentle gradient that had gradually steepened. So far as Nathan can tell from the dials in front of Knightly, they are travelling at only a fraction below full speed. Every inch of their journey has been made to the soundtrack of a huge engine thumping pistons up and down. Knightly doesn't seem fazed by it, but Nathan knows he'll have a thunderous headache when he returns to the bottom of the slope.

'We'll be there in ten minutes.' Knightly plucks a cigarette from the packet on the dashboard and fumbles in his pocket for a lighter.

Nathan doesn't answer him. He knows the last part of the journey will be the trickiest. Access to the ski slopes leading away from RidgeTop is a five-metre-wide corridor, which has precipitous drops on either side. There are handrails and fences to protect skiers, but they won't be strong enough to stop the piste basher should Knightly make a mistake.

They crest a small bump in the slope and Nathan feels the piste basher take a two-foot lurch to the left.

A glance at Knightly shows him unconcerned. The cigarette hangs from his mouth, a curl of smoke rising upwards, and a half-inch of ash hanging, ready to fall in the manner of an iceberg calving from a glacier.

How Knightly knows where they are is a complete mystery to Nathan. It's as if he is navigating by instinct and memory. Maybe when they are safe and sound, and this is all over, he'll ask him; but, for now, he doesn't want to do or say anything that might distract him.

As Nathan sits, wondering if he is about to die, it's all he can do not to pick at part of the seat's armrest where the stuffing is poking out.

'Come in. Can anyone hear me?'

The voice is faint, but Nathan hears it.

He snatches at the walkie-talkie on his lap as Knightly throttles back the engines so he can hear better.

'Hello. Who's there? Over.'

'I'm at RidgeTop. Terrorists have taken the resort over. So far they've killed one person and maimed two others. Send help at once.'

'I'm Nathan. A cableway operator, who are you?'

'My name is Jake Boulder. Please, send help before anyone else—'

Rather than Boulder's voice, the last thing Nathan hears is gunfire.

He switches the walkie-talkie to a different channel and connects with the receptionist at RidgeWay as Knightly begins to turn the piste basher around.

Chapter 27

I duck behind the low wall and wonder where the gunshots are coming from. The last thing I want to do is get into a gunfight.

Not only am I not a good shot, but the noise is sure to alert the other terrorists to the fact something is up. As soon as the gunshots are heard, one or more of the terrorists will investigate. Although I don't want to take another life, this has to take a backseat: if a life must be taken, I'd rather it not be mine.

A more pressing concern is the sound of footsteps coming my way. It's the scuff of boots on concrete, which tells me the man with the gun was at the other end of the cable car station.

I have the submachine gun in my hands – as soon as I acquired the weapon, I made sure I knew where the safety catch was, and which position was off and on.

I hear the crack of a shot and duck instinctively. A reflexive action as the bullet would have hit me before I'd ducked.

Lots of ideas shoot through my mind.

Should I try standing and emptying the submachine gun's clip at him? Or dive out from the end of the wall and make a smaller target of myself? Maybe I should raise only the gun, and fire a few shots his way to allow me to find better cover?

In the end, I do none of these things, as a better solution comes to me.

I shrink back along the low wall, which acts as a barrier against people falling off the platform when alighting or disembarking a cable car, and find cover behind a packing crate.

It's not a particularly big crate, but it's a damn sight better than nothing.

A gun appears over the wall and stiches bullets along its length.

Rather than wait until he's shooting at me, I lift my gun and aim it at the hand and the arm I can see.

The clatter of my gun drowns out every other sound bar one. The terrorist's gun drops from his fingers as bright red spurts of blood arc from his arm and splash across the wall.

Before he has chance to recover his wits and reach for the pistol I expect to be on his hip, I'm upright and moving forward. I take in everything as I run towards him. His eyes are wide in shocked pain and he's cradling his right arm in his left.

His eyes widen further when I emerge with the submachine gun aimed at him.

I expect his life is flashing before his eyes, or some other cliché is at play; I'm sure he expects to die. I would if I were in his position.

He falters, caught halfway between pleading for his life and reaching for the pistol on his hip.

I make the decision for him and slam the stock of my submachine gun into his temple.

He crumples into an untidy bleeding heap.

As I did with his compatriot, I poke him in the eye to test consciousness. He's out cold.

A glance along the corridor tells me reinforcements aren't quite on their way yet, but I'm expecting them any second.

I drag the prone terrorist to the far end of the cable car station and relieve him of his weapons. Like the guy tied up in the beer cellar, he's got no personal effects on him. What surprises me most of all is that neither man has a radio earpiece to communicate with the other terrorists.

They must be using some kind of blocking signal that would interfere with comms as well as cell phones. The good news is, if he heard me radioing for help, he won't have been able to share that news with Hannah, or whoever is in charge of the terrorists.

As quick as I can, I return to the control desk and go to activate the cable cars.

There are no lights on the control desk, which makes me think for a moment that it's broken. For it to break down when there's a terrorist attack is too great a coincidence, so I check the basics. There's an isolation switch on the side of the control panel, and when I look at it I see it's in the 'off' position.

I flick the lever over and the control desk comes to life.

It takes me a couple of moments to find the right controls, but I manage to get the cableway running.

The last thing I do before finding cover is empty the terrorist's submachine gun at the back wall of the station. This blows out four windows and allows snow to billow in, but I'm not worried about the cold.

All I care about is creating a scenario that might make any investigating terrorists believe there's been an assault on the hotel via the cable car.

Chapter 28

Instinct tells Sharon that something has gone wrong for the terrorists. One of their numbers has come marching from the back of the hotel and gone straight to Fleming's office.

The look on his face is stern, but he is a picture of happiness compared to the female terrorist when she exits the office.

Sharon watches as the woman clicks her fingers and sends the terrorist and another man back along the corridor. Her first thought is that Boulder has been seen or heard.

It's obvious the two guys have been tasked with finding and, in all probability, eliminating the person they'd seen or heard.

Sharon's heels drum into the thick carpet as her frustrations at not being able to warn Boulder overtake her.

To her mind, he'll be helpless against the men. Sure, if it were a bar fight he'd have a chance, but an unarmed man should never triumph against two gun-toting thugs.

Another concern is that if they capture Boulder instead of killing him, there's every chance he'll be tortured for information. As much as she trusts Boulder, there is no way she expects him to keep her involvement secret.

Sharon can feel her skin crawl as she imagines the horrifying revenge the female terrorist will visit upon her.

Should it come to that, she plans to die fighting, and, if possible, snatch a gun so she can at least take one of the terrorists with her.

A quick death from a bullet would also be far preferable to a slow, screaming death. Sharon isn't prepared to let the woman put that knife to her breasts or shoot through any of her joints.

The female terrorist glares at all of her hostages then turns and stomps her way back to Fleming's office, as the man with the clipboard calls out another name.

Sharon pities the person whose name has just been called as they'll have to face an enraged terrorist.

Were it not for her certainty that the terrorists planned to kill them all, Sharon would doubt the wisdom of Boulder making his attempt to summon help.

Now two of the terrorists are hunting him, it seems his attempt has been a waste of time, its only purpose to hasten his death.

Chapter 29

From my hiding place I can hear someone coming my way. There's the rustle of clothing, and the brush of boots on carpet then concrete, as the person enters the cable car station.

I give the terrorist a moment to survey the scene I've created, and hopefully fall for my ruse, then go to peek around the packing crates I'm hiding behind.

When I hear a voice, I freeze.

There shouldn't be voices.

A terrorist by himself won't speak, unless he's calling for one of the two I've already taken out. Except he's not calling out, he's speaking in a low tone.

Therefore, there must be more than one person looking for me.

The problem is, I don't know how many of them are out there; there could be two or half a dozen.

A second voice answers the first. I can't hear what's said, but I can tell the accent belongs to someone from the Deep South. It has the distinctive drawled softness that makes it unmistakable.

I shift my head and peer through a gap between the packing crates.

Two terrorists are standing at the edge of the platform. They're both looking at an approaching cable car.

The one nearest me has his gun trained on the cable car, while the other is inspecting the station around him.

When he turns and puts his gun to his shoulder, I sense an unmissable opportunity.

With as much stealth as possible, I position myself behind the two gunmen and adopt a sprinter's crouch.

They are five paces away from me.

I'm confident I can cover that distance in two seconds at most.

They'll hear my footsteps as soon as I launch myself forward.

The first second will be taken up reacting to the noise and turning to look. The second will be used to assess the threat. In the third second they'll point their guns at the threat and open fire.

Three seconds will be too late for them.

On the other hand, if they react by opening fire, two seconds is a lifetime and will see their bullets tear me to shreds.

I tense. It would be easy to shoot them, but there's no telling how close reinforcements are. Plus, I've managed to take down two of their number without killing them, and I'd like to end this without another man's death on my hands. They might not respect the sanctity of life, but I certainly do.

I throw myself into a sprint and, at the last second before colliding with the nearest one, dip my shoulder to deliver what my high school coach would have called an excellent blocking tackle.

The man I hit falls forward into his buddy and the two of them teeter on the point of balance. Their arms windmill as curses fall from their lips.

I give them a shove and watch as they drop forty feet towards the snow-covered rocks below. Maybe the snow will be deep enough to prevent them breaking any bones; maybe it won't. While I have no desire to take their lives, I can live with breaking a few of their bones.

When I check for movement I don't see any, but that doesn't mean they aren't just winded.

I snatch a jacket from the cableway operator's cabin and head towards the edge of the platform. A steel ladder descends to the mountain and I plan to take it.

Not only can I check that both terrorists are out of action, I need to get away from this part of the hotel. I've been lucky so far, but that luck won't last much longer.

The metal ladder chills my fingers like nothing I've ever known. Every time I release one of the rungs I expect to leave behind a layer of skin.

I really should have searched for a pair of gloves, but I hadn't wanted to spend any longer in the cable car station than necessary.

As well as expecting company at any moment, I'm aware that I'm an easy target when on the ladder.

I get to the bottom and approach the terrorists with my submachine gun aimed at them. I'm ready to pull the trigger if they try to attack me in any way.

Neither is moving beyond the rise and fall of their chest.

I remove all their weapons, keep the magazines from their pistols, and launch everything else into the blizzard.

My next move is to use the duct tape I stuffed into a jacket pocket to bind and gag the two men.

One of them is conscious and his eyes reflect a blend of hatred and fear.

I don't give a toss how he feels about me. Maybe a few hours lying in the snow with broken bones will change his opinion – when he realises I could have killed him at any moment but have chosen not to, he'll conclude that things could have worked out a lot worse for him.

I'm tempted to drag the two men out of view from above, but decide against it. That I haven't killed them may well go in my favour should things end up going against me. Plus, the longer I'm below the platform, the greater my risk of being discovered. So far, the terrorists have all been armed with submachine guns, but if one appears with a rifle I'll be dead before I hear the shot.

There's also the fact that hauling bodies through the snow will be hard work, not to mention agonising for them. I choose to leave them where they are.

The snow that's cascading from the sky will soon cover them. It's already attaching thick wet flakes to me; I can feel the cold starting to pierce my clothing and my hair is dampening. The wind that's blasting the snow around is sapping any vestiges of heat from my exposed skin.

I skirt the bottom of the cliff until I'm among the concrete pillars that support the dining room. There are eight pillars, in two rows of four. Each pillar supports a cross-member, which in turn supports the heavy timbers of the dining room's floor and a balcony where people can watch others skiing.

As I make my way past the last two pillars, I feel my eyes being drawn upwards. I don't know why, but I find myself looking up at the tops of the pillars.

I've never seen explosives in real life before, but I've watched enough movies to know them when I see them. Each pillar is ringed with two straps of what looks like plastic explosives. A shiny detonator protrudes from each block of the plastic explosive and they're all linked with a yellow cord, which I assume will fire the detonators.

When the charges are triggered, each pillar will have a section blown clean away. The entire dining room and the bedrooms above it will collapse and fall to where I'm standing.

With everyone in the dining room, all the staff and customers will be caught up in both the explosion and the resulting collapse. With the sub-zero temperatures hampering rescue efforts, the odds of anyone surviving are too slim for even the most optimistic gambler to take a punt.

What the terrorists are planning is mass murder, bordering on genocide.

Somehow, I've got to get rid of either the explosives or the detonators.

The first thing I have to work out is how to get myself within reach of those charges.

Chapter 30

The beating in his chest is wrong. He knows it, and he knows how to treat it. Except he can't. He's left his next packet of meds in their suite. It was a deliberate act, done so he could go back for them and have a quick check of his emails without his wife knowing.

Now she's looking at him with that curious expression she has. The one where she's assessing him and waiting for him to tell her something she already knows. Lily might be acerbic and unloving, but she's not a fool.

'Take your meds, Leslie. They will help you.'

Leslie shakes his head. 'I left them in the suite.'

'I thought you might.' For the first time in years he sees a sparkle in her eye. 'You do things like that so you can spend five minutes with your precious computer.'

There's no censure in her voice, just a bland statement of facts. Her words give Leslie hope. A glimmer of expectation that she's not only worked out his ploy, but has counteracted it. He wouldn't put it past her to have put a pack of his heart meds in her purse to be produced when he claimed to have forgotten them. If that is the case she'll have them on her, and he'll get the meds that will ease the uneven beating of his heart.

The doctor had told him about a heart valve that didn't always work as it should. His diet of fried food had copped the blame, along with his age and the stress of his job. Once he'd found out that he could be treated with daily meds, he'd stopped paying attention to the doctor and let his mind wander back to the deal he was working on.

'Does that mean you've got my meds in your purse?'

'No. I've thought about carrying your pills with me a thousand times, but I never have.'

'Why not?'

Leslie knows she will think nothing of thwarting his plans. At one point during their life together, the only time they had spoken to each other was to yell accusations of skulduggery, but they'd moved past that and settled into a world of mutual acceptance.

Lily lays a tender hand on Leslie's arm. 'The way I see it, you sneaking off for a quick look at your computer is better than you getting stressed about not being able to go and look at the infernal thing. You could say that, to me, it's the lesser of two evils.'

As he digests her words, Leslie begins to understand the deep love and concern that has fuelled Lily's actions. She's played him, but for his benefit, not hers.

As always, she's referring to his laptop as a computer. He knows, in her mind it is a device that computes, therefore, it is a computer. She is the same with cars. Over the years they'd had Mercedes, BMWs and a whole host of other brands, but they'd always been referred to as cars. He'd reference the brand of their cars and she'd refer to them as yours or mine. It is her way and he knows she is too old to change now.

What he doesn't expect is for her to rise to her feet and look down at him with determination. 'Where did you leave them?'

'On the desk.'

'Beside your computer?'

Leslie nods. The meds were left there so he didn't forget to take them when he was at his laptop and there is no point pretending otherwise.

He watches as Lily rises to her feet and walks to the nearest terrorist.

'Excuse me. My husband needs his heart meds from his room.' She hands over the keycard for their room. 'Room 107, the meds are on the desk next to where his computer was before you took it. If you don't get them for him, he'll go into cardiac arrest and will die. His name is Leslie Trouseau, not that his name should matter to you.'

The guard looks over his shoulder towards the guy with the clipboard.

He comes over and the two men exchange a few words.

The man with the clipboard takes the keycard from Lily, walks away, and passes it on to another of the gunmen.

Five minutes later the gunman returns and hands a packet of meds to Lily.

With two of the tablets doing their stuff, Leslie puts an arm round his wife's shoulders and weighs up what has just happened.

It's a small detail in a bigger picture, but it's the first time any of the terrorists have shown anything that might be construed as compassion. From his judgement of people, he doesn't believe compassion is high on the terrorists' list of concerns.

Getting him his meds must have some value to them. The only reason he can think of is they haven't finished with him yet, and they need him to stay alive.

His first visit to the office was traumatic enough, the last thing he wants is to have to repeat it.

It's not a thought that sits well with him, but as there's nothing he can do about it, he puts the meds in his pocket and tries to remain calm.

Chapter 31

I know I have to remove the explosives, but I have no way of reaching them. There are ladders in the maintenance shed but that doesn't explain how the terrorists managed to fit them.

The obvious answer is that they got one of the ladders and tossed it when they were finished.

Rather than waste time sneaking up to the maintenance shed, I try and find the ladder the terrorists used.

I can't see much, and if the ladder has been laid on the ground there's every chance it's buried under the falling snow. As I move around I'm dragging my feet through the snow rather than taking proper steps.

My dress shoes and thin trousers offer no protection against the cold. My feet are soaking and feel as if they have frozen solid, but compared to the numbness in my fingers they're in good shape.

I've stuffed my hands into the borrowed jacket's pockets to try and combat the numbness, but it doesn't work in any way that's noticeable.

The snowstorm rages around me. Regardless of the direction I'm facing, the wind seems to blow the snow in my face. The fact there's no visibility beyond a dozen or so feet, gives me the feeling that I'm existing in a frozen cocoon.

I've never been troubled with claustrophobia before, but right now, I feel isolated by the limited visibility I have. It's like there are shifting shapes, being pulled back and forth by the howling wind. My eyes are slitted against the blizzard and when the extent of their range is shortened by a gust of snow, I can't help but feel like the world is closing in on me.

Regardless of the tricks my mind is playing on me, I have to press on with looking for a way to disarm those explosives.

After searching for a couple of minutes, my right foot bangs into something in the snow.

I bend down and use my useless hands to paw in the snow. A few unfeeling swipes reveals the silver shininess of an aluminium ladder.

Within a minute I have the ladder hauled out of the snow and propped against the nearest pillar.

Before setting foot on the bottom rung, I do my best to make sure none of the terrorists are creeping up on me, but all I can see is swirls of snow, so I step onto the ladder. It sinks at least a foot into the snow, so I bounce my weight on it until it doesn't sink any further.

Step by step, I climb the ladder until I'm face to face with the strap of explosives. They are held on with duct tape. A strip of tape has been wound round the pillar twice to hold the blocks of explosive in place.

The wind is howling around my head and the gusts of snow, coupled with the icy air, are peppering my face and seeking out every possible way they can to chill my body further.

The pillars are ten inches square, and each side I can see has two blocks of explosive strapped against it.

I'm sure the pillars are made with the best grade concrete and are heavily reinforced, but there's no way they'll withstand this amount of explosives.

As I'm peering through the snow at them, I realise I don't know how to disable them. My common sense tells me that removing the detonators will neutralise them, but it doesn't tell me if this will cause them to detonate. Another option is to disconnect the yellow cord, but again, I don't know how to do that without triggering an explosion.

If I'm wrong, not only will I kill myself, but everyone else in the dining room twenty feet above my head. It's a huge responsibility, yet I know that leaving the explosives in place will condemn them all to death.

Because I've managed to get word out about what's happening here, there may be help on the way, but if the terrorists find themselves backed into a hole, and in need of a distraction, there's every chance they'll blow these charges. Therefore, this is a risk I have to take.

I figure that removing the detonators is the lesser of the evils I'm facing, so I place my numb, trembling fingers on the one in front of my face and gently exert enough pressure to remove it from the block of explosive.

Chapter 32

The fact the pair of terrorists who were sent along the corridor haven't returned, doesn't go unnoticed by Sharon.

The other terrorists have also noticed. Sharon has seen their glances at the corridor and paid attention to the changes in their body language. Where they were relaxed but vigilant earlier, they're now keyed up and vigilant.

Their feet are shifting, and their eyes take a dance round the room before returning to the corridor. Guns are gripped that little bit tighter and there are constant, reassuring checks that the additional weapons on their hips are in place.

Sharon hopes that Boulder has managed to elude the terrorists sent to hunt for him. Their continued absence can be explained by either them not finding Boulder or finding him and currently battling with him.

Maybe he's even managed to get the jump on them. As much as she wants to believe that, she knows it isn't a hope she should cling to. After all, Boulder is just an ordinary guy up against what appear to be well-trained soldiers.

The last of the customers have been escorted into Fleming's office, and the staff are now all stationed at one side of the room, with the customers at the other.

Sharon works out the terrorists must have finished whatever they needed the customers for. What she can't figure out, is why they're still here.

Her best guess is that the terrorists have identified each customers' next of kin and sent ransom demands. If that isn't the case, she can't work out what their motive is. While the customers are all very wealthy people, and in some cases famous, it isn't like any of them are political figures so there is no political pressure that can be applied.

One reason could be that the terrorists are bartering for the release of certain political or high-profile prisoners against the safe release of the people in this room, but that doesn't seem likely either. Had the terrorists been of a different ethnicity, she would have believed their motives lay in that direction. Every which way she looks, it always comes back to one thing: money.

A glance at the watch on her left wrist tells Sharon the time is twenty to midnight.

In twelve hundred seconds a new year will be born. Around the globe, people will get drunk, fall out, make love, and celebrate the occasion with their loved ones.

The bitter pang of regret stabs at Sharon. While the rest of the world is partying, here she is, interrupted from working her backside off by a gang of gunmen led by a psychotic bitch.

Not for the first time this evening, Sharon curses her luck. It is bad enough being held like this, but not being able to relieve some of her stress with a cigarette is a grievous insult that has left her nerves jangling.

Sharon looks up to see the female terrorist has emerged from the office. Her expression is one of controlled fury. She's on the edge and is fighting to maintain her composure.

When she was calm, she was cold and dangerous; now she's angry, Sharon's terror has escalated several levels.

The woman's eyes scan the terrorists, and narrow when they don't find what they're looking for. Sharon knows she is looking for the men she sent up the corridor, knows their failure to return will enrage her further.

She watches as the woman speaks to the guy with the clipboard, and sees him point to four of the terrorists.

The woman gives a sharp nod and turns to address the crowd. 'Some of you may have noticed that one or two of my colleagues have left this room. Do not be fooled into thinking our numbers are dwindling. They are merely preparing for our exit. Those of us who remain are more than capable of quashing any rebellion you may try and make. Trust me when I say this, from now on, my men have orders to shoot anyone they feel is a threat.'

The woman spins away and joins the four terrorists pointed out by the guy with the clipboard.

Sharon can't hear what the woman is saying to them, but she doesn't need to. They will be getting orders to find their colleagues, and if their colleagues are dead they'll be after Boulder.

While the spiel the woman had delivered to the crowd was measured, there had been no masking her fury.

Chapter 33

'There's no way I'm calling for a SWAT team on your say so. You could have been talking to anyone up there – a damned kid, yanking your chain to impress his friends.'

'Then what are you going to do?' Nathan plants his hands on the desk and glares at the cop. 'I've told you that we've been told of terrorists holding people at gunpoint. One person has been killed and two maimed. Will you take your head out of your ass and start protecting and serving, or do I have to go to the press before you'll do your job?'

'And what are you going to tell them? That you've heard a garbled message? Or that you're jumping at shadows?'

'I'll tell them everything I've told you. That an employee of RidgeTop Resort has put in a report that terrorists have overrun the facility and killed one of our customers. I'll also tell them the police aren't acting upon this information.'

The cop returns Nathan's glare with an intensity that makes the cableway operator drop his eyes. 'This employee, who are they? Have they been with you long? What do you know about them?'

'His name is Jake Boulder. I don't know him well, but he's polite, friendly enough, if a bit withdrawn. He's only been here a couple of weeks, but he seems like a stand-up guy.'

Nathan casts his eyes in the direction of Attwood as the cop speaks into his radio and requests information on Boulder. The resort manager looks anywhere but at Nathan. It's clear he doesn't agree with the cop, but Nathan can tell that his threat to go to the press has him as worried as the cop.

One of the manager's key responsibilities is protecting the resort's good name. If Nathan follows through with his threat, it is possible the adverse publicity will cost the company millions – and him his job. Nathan doesn't envy him, but a bit of support from his boss wouldn't go amiss.

When his radio crackles into life, the cop puts it to his ear. Nathan can't make out what's being said until the cop thanks the person at the other end and returns his radio to its clip.

'Seems like your man, Boulder, has a habit of attracting trouble.' He points out of the window towards RidgeTop. 'How many people can those piste bashers carry?'

'Two plus a driver.' Nathan speaks from recent experience.

'Is that all? How many of them do you have?'

'Four.' It's the manager who answers. 'That's all we need.'

'So, we can get eight men up there.' He pulls a face. 'My sergeant is sending a dozen tactical cops from Montpelier. Is there no way we can get more men in them? Sitting on knees, standing, anything would do.'

Nathan has a flash of memory. 'The Ridge Rambler.' A few years ago, the company ran night tours up the mountain and they adapted a tracked trailer into a makeshift coach. It was basic at best, but the Ridge Rambler had proven popular with tourists who wanted to experience the beauty of the snowy mountain on a starlit night. The best of it was, it had four rows of three seats; therefore, it could take the dozen tactical cops with ease, as well as having room for their equipment.

To make things even better, it was Knightly's piste basher that had pulled the Ridge Rambler.

'What's that?' The cop's face is full of confusion.

'A trailer the piste basher can tow up the mountain. It has seats for twelve. It'll be cold, but it'll get them up there.'

'Then it'll do.' The cop looks at his watch, then at the resort manager. 'They'll be here in an hour. Can you have the thing ready to go, along with a full schematic plan of the resort and any other buildings up there?'

'Of course. Nathan, you deal with the Ridge Rambler; I'll sort out the plans.'

Nathan nods at his boss and reaches for his jacket. He's acutely aware that Knightly will be less than ecstatic at being disturbed to take a second unscheduled trip up the mountain.

Knightly's ire is a small worry, it's a quarter to midnight, which means it'll be quarter after one by the time the tactical cops have arrived and travelled up the mountain to RidgeTop. With two maimed and one dead already, there could be a lot more casualties before the terrorists are stopped.

Chapter 34

I slide the final detonator from the last block of explosive and use my knife to saw through the duct tape. Once I have the eight blocks wrapped up in the duct tape strap, I sheath the knife and descend the ladder.

It's a long time since I had any feeling in my fingers and toes, but I'm not finished out here yet. The explosives have to be hidden – when they don't go off, the terrorists are sure to come looking for it.

I look down and see something that makes my heart stop. Through the flurries of snow, I spy a terrorist creeping his way along the pillars towards me.

As he gets closer, I can make out that he's holding his gun at gut height and the barrel is pointing my way. He's so intent on catching me by surprise, he hasn't yet registered that I've stopped moving and I'm looking his way.

I'd slung my submachine gun over my shoulder and positioned it resting against my back, so I had both hands free to deal with the explosives. This leaves me with a sheathed knife, and a gun that's stuffed into my waistband underneath a huge jacket. A jacket that's hi-vis; I stand out like a beacon. Having said that, the terrorist is wearing black and he's just as visible in the whiteout as I am.

By the time my frozen fingers withdraw the pistol and fumble their way inside the trigger guard, he'll have had enough time to walk across to the ladder, climb up it, and put his pistol to the back of my head. The same goes for bringing the submachine gun round to where I can aim and fire it.

Even if I had either gun to hand, I wouldn't fancy my chances of shooting him before one of his bullets could tear into my flesh.

I take a step up the ladder and drop the bundle of explosives down the side of the pillar where he can't see them.

My right hand goes against the pillar and my left grabs the ladder's top rung; I give an almighty push with my right hand and a hard pull with my left.

As I do this, I throw my bodyweight right to left.

I'm now arcing through the air, twelve feet above him, as the ladder falls anti-clockwise with me at its head.

I see his gun start to lift as I fall towards him.

His reactions are too slow.

At the last second, I haul down on the ladder and curl myself into a ball.

The ladder misses his head, which was my intended target, but it slams into his shoulder with a metallic clatter as I flump down into the snow.

I'm on my way to my feet a second later. My right hand arcing upwards to deliver a ferocious uppercut.

I connect with him at the same moment the vicious clatter of panicked gunfire rents the air.

The terrorist jerks and twitches as the bullets slam into his back.

My hands wrap themselves around his submachine gun and yank it from his grasp as I duck behind the nearest pillar.

I don't know where the other gunman is, although I'm aware he knows where I am. I have to move, have to get myself away from him.

The problem is, the odds that I'll run into him are pretty much fifty-fifty.

I force my numb fingers to grasp the submachine gun tight, and thumb the safety catch into the off position, the rate selector to fully automatic.

Almost everything I know about guns has been learned from books I've read. Not manuals or anything like that, just good old-fashioned thrillers with a resourceful hero or a clever detective.

From what I can recall, from many hundreds of books, submachine guns like the one I'm holding can empty their entire magazine in a matter of seconds.

This is a worry, but I'll just have to restrain myself from clamping down on the trigger. Rather than trying to evade the terrorist, my plan is to do the opposite of what he expects.

With a deep breath inside me, I whirl out from behind the pillar and charge in the direction I'd heard the gunshots coming from. I know my opponent will be jumpy – he's already shot his buddy by mistake.

With luck, he'll either freeze and allow me to shoot him, or pull his trigger before he's had a chance to take aim. As well as fire rates, my reading material has also taught me that submachine guns are notoriously inaccurate.

I burst forward with my gun held sideways so its recoil will stitch bullets right to left, rather than pull my aim above the terrorist's head. My feet are dragging through the snow and there's no way I can call my progress a run.

He's six feet away.

The knee-deep snow is slowing me down and making me a much easier target.

The terrorist registers my laboured movements and I can see him adjusting his aim.

My gun spits a trail of bullets and two strike his gut.

He fires my way as he falls to his knees and I feel something slam into my arm as I dive at him.

My shoulder crunches into his gut and drives him from his knees on to his back. His gun arm flails outwards, the trigger staying depressed until a clicking sound indicates there are no more bullets to come.

He's down with two gut shots. Laid where he is, he'll be lucky to survive until the police eventually come, and he'll be in agony during every minute that passes. Then he'll have to be rescued and transported to a hospital. Sure, he'll get a jab to knock him out and relieve him from the pain, but the way blood is gushing from him, he'll probably bleed out in the next few minutes.

The possibility that he may well freeze to death before the police come is another factor to consider; lying out here, with a couple of gunshot wounds, hypothermia won't take long to set in.

As much as I'm feeling the cold, he'll have it worse when he's unable to move to generate any body heat.

In theory, it'd be easy to put a gun to his head and spare him the pain, but I'm not willing to play executioner. Yes, I may be the cause of his eventual death, but that was in a 'kill or be killed' situation.

Deep down I know that's an excuse I'm using, to give my conscience an easier time, but it's something Doctor Edwards has reinforced – so I run with it.

I remove his weapons, lay them out of reach, and gather up the eight bundles of explosives.

There's a narrow ravine that runs alongside the ridge, which gives the resort its name, it's as good a place as any to dump the explosives, so that's where I toss them.

I go back to the moaning terrorist, see the tightness that agony has created on his face, and decide to be merciful. If he's the ex-soldier I think he is, he'll know about bullet wounds. He's got two in his lower gut. The bullets will almost certainly have pierced his intestines, along with other organs such as his kidneys, liver and spleen. If his intestines have been nicked, sepsis will kill him if blood loss doesn't.

He'll know all this. If he's ever been in a proper gunfight, there's every chance he's seen people who've been gut-shot. He'll have heard their screams, listened to them begging for help and heard their cries growing weaker. On more than one occasion I've read about soldiers who would always try to put a bullet into someone's gut at the start of a battle; their thinking being that the injured man's cries would unnerve their enemy. For all I know, he could be the kind of soldier who employed that kind of barbaric thinking.

I retrieve his pistol, remove the cartridge, and drop all the bullets bar one into my jacket pocket.

When I lay the pistol on his chest, pointing at his head, he understands what I'm *not* saying and gives me a nod of thanks. He knows he's dying, and I've given him the chance to go on his own terms.

Dying men have nothing to lose and I may well be mistaken with my diagnosis of his injuries. If that's the case, he'll want to use that bullet on me. Another consideration is he'll want to exact revenge for taking his life.

In light of these unsavoury ideas, I back away with my gun trained on him until I'm confident I'm out of the pistol's range. I'm wrong to think he'll try and exact vengeance, as his hand never goes for the pistol during my retreat.

I leave him to his fate and start to make my way back to the areas where I can hide out better and have access to the resort. I may have disabled their explosives, but these terrorists have to be stopped.

I'm passing the final pillar when I hear a single shot.

Chapter 35

I open the door of the maintenance shed and creep inside. It's empty and is shrouded in darkness. That doesn't bother me, darkness is good – welcome even.

I've holed up here for two reasons: number one is I'm frozen and need to regain some feeling in my feet and fingers; number two is I need to speak to Nathan again to find out if he's alerted the cops, and if they're coming.

When I pull the door shut behind me, there is not a shred of light. Thankfully, I know Ed, the maintenance man, has a touch of OCD, and he keeps his gear in a uniform and regular way.

I rifle through his winter clothing and find a better jacket than the one I'm wearing, along with a hat and several pairs of gloves. The first pair of gloves I try on are more like mittens, and while they'll restore heat to my fingers, they're so large and cumbersome there's no way I'd be able to hold a gun, let alone thread a finger through the trigger guard.

My next search is done on hands and knees as I grope around looking for some suitable footwear.

My fingers latch on to a pair of boots. I kick off my shoes and remove my socks to wring the water from them. It doesn't make sense to put wet socks into dry boots, so I slide my bare feet into a pair of Ed's boots.

My toes butt against the tips of the boot long before I can get my heel in. I press down with considerable force to no avail; my feet are just too large for these boots. I source another pair but they're the same size and also useless.

With a grimace, I put on my sodden socks and frozen shoes. I pull on the thin gloves, cradle the submachine gun in one hand – the barrel pointing at the door – and retrieve the radio from my pocket.

I remove my uniform vest and white shirt. The left sleeve is sodden with blood but, although it's painful, I can still use my arm. I cut both sleeves from my shirt and toss the bloody one to the floor. The good one I use to fashion a bandage for my injured arm.

I've been lucky: the bullet has done nothing more damaging than gouge a trail of flesh from my bicep. As much as it hurts now, as time passes I know the pain will increase.

With my sleeveless shirt back on, I shuck my way into Ed's jacket and do up all the zips and buttons. It's far warmer than the hi-vs one, although its scarlet colour is every bit as noticeable.

I turn on the radio and, with the volume switch at its lowest setting, press the call button and say Nathan's name.

He comes back to me within seconds. His voice is full of concern and I'm already thinking he's a man I'd like to buy a hefty amount of beer for.

'I'm here, Boulder. How's it going up there?'

'I've incapacitated four terrorists, and …' I don't want to tell him two of the terrorists are dead because of me. I don't know who he's with and whether they'll charge me with homicide.

'And?' Give Nathan his due, he picks up on my reluctance to self-implicate and gives me an out. 'It's just me that can hear you.'

I add a case of bourbon to the beer I intend to buy him, but, while I feel I can trust Nathan, I don't know who else is listening in on this channel, so I choose my reply with care.

'Two others are no longer a worry.'

Maybe the snow will bury their bodies until spring. I plan to be elsewhere by then. Somewhere warm, somewhere with multiple ways in and out, somewhere that has a police station close enough to deter bad guys from doing bad things.

'Good. There's a tactical team on its way. They're coming up the slope in a piste basher. ETA one fifteen, or thereabouts.'

I bid him goodbye and think about what I've just learned. The cops will be here, in force, in less than an hour and a half. Therefore, I have plenty of time to hole up and keep myself safe.

The problem with hiding out is twofold. First off, I can't abandon the two hundred or so people I've left in the dining room. Hannah is bound to be getting angry about the guys I've taken out so far, and there's a chance she will take out her anger on her hostages.

A second, more personal concern, is that she'll be looking to nullify the threat I'm presenting, because of the men she's lost so far, and she'll increase her efforts to find me.

Places where I can escape from the snow and the cold will be top of her list. As nice as it is to be where it's warm and dry, I can't stay here for much longer.

I decide to stay put for five more minutes, to give my hands and feet a chance to thaw, then I'll make my next move.

As I sit with the gun pointed at the door, my thoughts turn to the men who've died because of me. I didn't know either of the terrorists and, in the greater scheme of things, I know I should feel no great remorse for their deaths.

That both of them were trying to kill me, and neither of them had technically died by my hand, doesn't assuage my guilt. They are dead because of me and that is something I'll have to live with.

Once again, I find my thoughts turning to the conversations I've had with Doctor Edwards since I left Casperton. His counsel has always been wise and, while he's made me admit to personality traits I've tried to stifle, I've learned the benefits of talking to him.

When I opened up to him about Taylor's death, and the depth of my feelings for her, he fell silent and left me to stew before finally pointing out that my guilt was a natural reaction and, while I should feel some responsibility, I was wrong to accept all the blame as others were far more culpable.

While this makes sense on a technical level, I can't escape the fact that Taylor was killed because she'd followed a decision that I'd made.

I can, however, find solace in the doctor's insistence that the experience has changed me, and I no longer see myself as judge, jury and executioner. I can't help but wonder if he would revisit his statement after tonight's events.

So far, I haven't resorted to murdering anyone, but the night is still young, and I know I'll do whatever it takes to make sure everyone in the dining room is alive to see the sun rise.

As I stand to leave, a memory of my conversation with Nathan nags at me. There was a foreign sound halfway through him telling me about the tactical team coming. If I didn't know better, I'd say Nathan had released the button on his walkie-talkie. He couldn't have though, otherwise he'd have been cut off.

When I think about it, I realise that either one of the terrorists was listening in, or the police were. Either way, I'm glad I didn't admit that two of the terrorists were dead thanks to me.

I peer out of the window and look for shapes moving through the snow. When I find none, I prepare myself for the cold and tease open the door.

Chapter 36

The faint sound of gunfire was heard by everyone in the dining room. The customers all exchanged glances; the terrorists showed tight grins.

It's obvious to Daniel that the gunfire involves the bartender, but he doesn't know whether he's the one being shot or doing the shooting.

He keeps his eyes on the terrorists, rather than the customers and staff. He's afraid a shared look with Double M, or the server who was talking with the bartender, will draw suspicion.

His mother is clinging to him hard enough to cause discomfort, but he doesn't complain. Her embrace is reassuring for them both. They've always been close. Without his father, they'd been each other's world for as long as he could remember.

It was Mom who'd read him bedtime stories, driven him to football games, and become his best friend.

He'd always missed having a father and, now he is older, he can't understand why his mom hasn't looked for anyone else. She is an attractive woman and he's seen men hitting on her without success on more than one occasion.

When he'd plucked up the courage to ask her why she'd never had a boyfriend, she'd given him that beaming smile of hers, told him that he is the only man she wants in her life, and added that she still loves his father and no other man could replace him.

Daniel knows all about his father's death; he even watched the video of the crash on YouTube while at a friend's house. His father was a NASCAR driver. While leading a race at Martinsville Speedway, his car had blown a tyre and he'd lost control. The car had careered across the track, collided with two others, and flipped up into the protective netting.

All the netting did was throw his father's car back at the pack of cars that were pursuing him. Two cars had slammed into the roof of his father's car at a hundred miles an hour, flattening the roll cage and crushing his father.

Daniel had read the reports of his father's death and learned how his mom had sued the tyre manufacturer and won an eight-figure settlement.

As much as he loved his mom and the luxurious lifestyle she gave him, he'd give every last cent of the money away if he could play ball with his father just once.

All boys idolise their father and Daniel is no different. Because he's never known the man he has no memories of him, meaning the idolisation has never been tempered by human frailties. He's never had to deal with his father's depressive tendencies after losing a race, nor has he witnessed the times his parents had shouted and screamed at each. There had been no broken promises or harsh words delivered in anger. All those familial let-downs and eye-openers have been absent from his life. Just like his father.

He pulls his mother close and strokes her hair. 'Don't worry, Mom.'

Daniel sends his eyes around the room one more time and finds the terrorists still keyed up, but not quite so much as they were ten minutes ago. He can tell they're confident that their men have triumphed.

The only way he'll know for sure if the bartender has managed to get away and call for help, will be if there is more gunfire. He hopes there is: the bartender was a good guy, and he doesn't deserve to die.

Chapter 37

The terrorist with the clipboard walks across to where the customers are, looks down at the clipboard, says a name, and points towards the manager's office.

Sharon doesn't know the reason for this, but she recognises the customer to be the person who was called first when they were all taken to the manager's office the last time.

Try as she might, she can't find a logical explanation for a second visit to the office, other than to provide proof of life to the person paying the ransom. Therefore, the customer would need taken to the office to speak with them.

If that's the case, the terrorists must have a way to communicate with the outside world.

Sharon has seen one or two customers trying to send secret messages with their cell phones, only for their faces to register disappointment. Blocking cell signals is an obvious move that the terrorists were bound to have made, but she applauds the courage of those who've tried to summon help.

What interests Sharon as much as the couple who've been taken to the office, are the faces of the other customers. All of them show dejection and anger; most have resignation too, as they contemplate their own fate.

She revises her thinking and begins to question the idea that the terrorists are actually kidnappers. There's too much anger on the customers' faces for that theory, so she revisits the idea that it's about money and looks for a different angle.

What she can't work out is how the terrorists are getting money from people when they are stuck up here. There's no doubt in her mind that collectively the customers are wearing jewellery worth hundreds of thousands of dollars, but there hasn't been one attempt by the terrorists to retrieve any. Nor have they gone around collecting wallets and billfolds.

Had they done that, the credit cards they'd have collected would have given them fantastic spending power, yet they haven't bothered.

This realisation leads her to think their purpose may have a payoff that isn't finance based. Which brings it back to a political motive.

Whatever it is, Sharon is on constant alert waiting for the right opportunity to strike back. The gunfire she's heard doesn't bode well for Boulder, which means she is the only person here who's had anything like the training the bad guys have.

As manager, Kirk Fleming should have been reassuring his staff and calming his customers, but he's been worse than useless. His brother Patrick is every bit as ineffectual. Yes, his job as security manager is more to do with making sure the customers feel safe, but other than identifying a chambermaid who'd stolen a necklace from a customer's room, she's never heard of him doing anything that could be classed as protecting the resort and those inside it.

She knows it's unfair to point the finger at him this way but, as security manager, Patrick should have anticipated this kind of threat and taken measures to ensure it couldn't happen, or if it did, that there was at least a way to alert those at the bottom of the mountain.

Whether it was a regular call or message didn't matter, so long as there was a protocol, the authorities could be alerted and they'd have a hope of being rescued.

The same applies for a secret alarm button. One on the manager's desk and another under the reception counter would suffice.

Once pressed, a call could be made from the bottom of the mountain to check whether or not the alarm was genuine. If that call wasn't answered, the request for the cavalry could be sent out.

There is no doubt in her mind that when all of this is over, those measures will become commonplace at all resorts like RidgeTop.

If she survives, maybe she can find a role as a security consultant herself. With her military background she'll be able to assess the security at resorts and give specialist advice on how to protect not just the customers and staff, but also the reputations of the various resorts. It has the potential to be a good business and she'd be able to charge enough to finally clear the debts her useless ex-husband has saddled her with.

Sharon knows in her heart that surviving the night is unlikely, but with Boulder on the loose at least they have a chance.

As she shifts to a more comfortable position, she vows once again that if she's going to die tonight, she'll die fighting.

Chapter 38

I skirt around the edge of the maintenance shed and half-trudge, half-wade my way past the control booth for the ski lift. So far I've seen nothing but snow and buildings.

On one level, I'd like things to stay that way; on another, I've a very specific mission in mind and, as such, I'm looking for something in particular.

What I'm looking for shouldn't be hard to find. It's large enough and there's only one place it can be.

Sure enough, I see the blurred shape of a helicopter sitting on the helipad. Like so many of them that land here, it's large enough to carry cargo and a number of passengers. It's the kind of twin-rotor craft favoured by the rescue services and the military.

The make is unimportant, as is everything else about it apart from one detail: the man sitting in the cockpit.

His presence confirms it's the terrorists' helicopter. Had it belonged to anyone else, he would have been rounded up and held in the dining room or dispatched and buried in the snow.

He's alive and well, and would appear to be relaxing. Having to stay with the helicopter won't be the most pleasant of tasks as he's bound to be chilled to the marrow, but it'll be a better option than having to threaten people at gunpoint.

He will, of course, be the pilot, which is why he's been left out here. Should anything happen to him, the terrorists would be trapped on the mountain.

I'm not sure how he plans to fly away from here, but I reckon that he and Hannah have devised a safe option. Maybe the helicopter's maximum flying height will see them clear the top of the mountain, or perhaps there are compass headings they can take that will keep them out of danger – even if they are flying blind. I would imagine the helicopter had landed here before the snowstorm got too heavy.

Whichever it is, I'm sure there will be a detailed plan for the terrorists' escape.

That's why I'm here: it's my plan to disable the helicopter in the most permanent way. With no escape route available to them, the terrorists are far more likely to surrender when the police get here.

However, the presence of Mr Pilot means I either have to either take his life or remove him from the helicopter before I start playing with fire.

I'm wondering how to get him out of his seat when I see something move out of the corner of my eye.

There are a pair of terrorists patrolling the area. They're looking everywhere, examining every possible hiding place.

I don't have to be a rocket scientist to work out who they're looking for.

As I slink further behind the ski lift's control booth, watching them approach, I pay attention to the way they're moving.

They're covering each other at every step, making it virtually impossible for me to ambush them.

I'd tried a suicidal charge once and gotten away with it, the only cost to myself being a flesh wound, but I know I can't use that tactic again. I won't be so lucky a second time, especially if there are two people shooting at me.

I don't have a lot of time to find a new hiding place, or formulate a plan of action, so I retreat to the far end of the structure and climb the stairs until I'm in the control booth.

It's a bare, uncluttered space with glass windows on all four sides. There's nowhere to hide apart from behind the control desk.

As soon as I've ducked into a crouch, I curse myself. The flashlights used by the terrorists are bound to pick out the tracks I've left in the snow. By coming into the control booth, cornering myself is all I have achieved.

I need a new plan, and I need it in a hurry.

Chapter 39

I reach up to the control desk and turn the key to power it up. Next, I move the gearing lever from neutral to reverse.

The normal movement of the lift sees the chairs slide alongside the control booth to a level area where passengers can dismount, before the cable goes around a horizontal wheel and sets off down the mountain for the next load of passengers.

When I'd rounded the booth, I had to dodge one of the chairs. I press the button that sets the gears into motion and hope my plan works. I hear nothing, which could be good or bad.

I charge down the stairs and around the corner in time to see the two terrorists grappling with the chair, which is pushing into their backs. They hadn't heard it coming due to the storm and the fact that the ski lift is powered by electricity.

As I run at the terrorists, I assess the threat levels they each present, as well as which man offers me the best opportunity of striking a telling blow.

The man nearest to me is the shorter of the two and the chair is banging against the back of his head. He's ducking to avoid it, while his taller companion has bent himself at the knees to allow the chair to pass clear over his head.

As the taller one has taken the wiser option, he's more of an immediate threat, so I concentrate my attention on him first. Because there's two of them, I have to take one out and be ready to fight the other by the time he's let the ski chair past and got himself re-orientated.

I charge forward and launch into a dive that sees me grab the rail at the front of the ski chair. My weight and momentum thrust it backwards as I throw my legs underneath it. The rear edge slams into the top of the shorter terrorist's head with a thump that causes a spurt of blood to fly upwards until it's swallowed by the blizzard.

This is an unexpected bonus, but I'll take it. Sometimes, you have to accept a spot of good luck. When fighting armed terrorists, I won't just accept good fortune, I'll buy it dinner and make sure it gets home safe.

My feet land exactly where I've aimed them: right in the centre of the taller man's chest.

He flies backwards until he's sprawled on his ass.

He shakes his head as he tries to recalibrate his brain.

I release the chair and run at him. A glance to my right tells me the shorter guy isn't a threat. He's out cold. I don't know whether he's stunned or dead but, as he's not reaching for a weapon or clambering to his feet, he's of no concern to me.

The taller one has sat up by the time I get to him, and he uses crossed arms to block the kick I aim at his face.

It's a good tactic, but this isn't the first time I've been in a fight.

I lean my weight back and plant my foot on his chest.

He can't help but be levered onto his back.

I shift my balance onto my right foot so all my weight is on his chest. My left foot is arcing at his head when he slams a fist into the back of my knee.

My leg buckles. I don't want it to, but I can't do anything about it as the tendons take the kind of hit that decides their fate for them.

The kick I aim at his face is way off target as I fall backwards and flump into the soft snow.

I try to slam my heel towards his head but he's already on the move. His hands are clawing at my body as he clambers over me.

A fist slams into each of my cheeks and then my mouth.

I can taste blood and feel a tooth loosen, but those are minor details. He's on top of me and has weapons. I need to change the narrative of this fight before it comes to the kind of sudden end that involves him getting the better of me. Should that happen, I'm a dead man. The terrorist will either kill me outright, or he'll take me inside and Hannah will make me suffer before she kills me.

Neither option appeals so I writhe around, trying to buck his body off me while attempting to grab his wrists.

I manage to get my hands round his left wrist.

He realises what I'm trying to do and reaches backwards with his right hand.

Whether he's reaching for his knife or his pistol doesn't matter, either one will kill me.

I pull his left hand away from his body and try bucking him that way.

He braces himself against my efforts, which is what I'd expected him to do.

My next buck throws him the way he's leaning. I twist my grip and force his arm to my left and his right. He doesn't have time to correct his balance before I've got him falling towards the snow.

He extends his right hand to break the fall, which means he's not reaching for his weapon any more.

So far, so good.

As he leans, unable to move either way, I twist his forearm behind his back. It'd be easy to get him in a painful armlock and pin him to the ground but, while that move works well with drunks, this situation requires less finesse and a tad more brutality.

When his forearm is pointing straight across his back, I plant my left hand on his elbow and yank his hand up and away from his body. The movement is akin to that of a mechanic loosening wheel nuts.

He screams in agony as the cartilage and tendons in his elbow are torn apart by the unnatural movement. I dare say some bones break as well, but that's his problem rather than mine. I might not plan to kill any of the terrorists, but after seeing how they intended to kill everyone at the resort, I have no compunction about breaking them a little.

I release his arm to grab his weapons and toss them out of his reach.

My next move is to slam punches into his temple until his howls of pain stop.

I rise to my feet mindful there may be another ski chair coming my way.

There isn't, so I cross over to the shorter guy. He doesn't react when I push a finger into his eye, so he isn't conscious.

He could have irreparable brain damage or may just be out cold; there's nothing I can do except neutralise the other terrorists and let the emergency services pass their judgement on him. My fingers are too numb to check for a pulse, but when I stare at his chest I can see it rising and falling.

Rather than leave the terrorists lying in the snow to freeze to death, I drag each of them into the control booth.

It's a struggle getting the taller one in there, but I manage. He's starting to come round as I get him there, but another punch to the temple solves that.

When the two men are laid side by side, I pull the roll of duct tape from my pocket. There's only a foot or so of it left, which isn't enough to bind them both.

A quick stab to their hearts, or a slash across their throats, will make sure they're neutralised, but I'm not yet ready to resort to murder again. I hope I never am.

To make sure I don't have any trouble from them, I pick up the short one's right leg and lay his foot on the taller one's chest.

A stamp on his shin makes sure he's out of the game.

I do the same with the taller one's left leg.

As I'm closing the door to the control booth, I realise I should have replaced my dress shoes with their boots. I could go back and get a pair from them but, while I have no compunction in breaking their bones if it prevents them from coming after me, I'm not cruel enough to exacerbate their injuries by pulling off boots from broken legs.

Chapter 40

With the two terrorists dealt with, I turn my attention back to the helicopter. I'm convinced it's key to the terrorists escaping the resort. Part of me wants them to have the facility to leave, but a greater part of me knows if they decide to go they won't leave any of their hostages alive.

It's my intention to disable the helicopter, thereby shutting off their escape route. If they can't leave they'll be less likely to murder their hostages. If they're faced with a stark choice between going down in a hail of bullets or limiting their crimes when faced with a police SWAT team, my thinking is they'll pick the wise option and accept a life in jail.

Maybe Hannah and one or two of her closest aides will make something of a stand as ringleaders, but if they do that, I reckon they'll want live hostages.

I know I could be well off target, but until the cops get up the mountain I'm the only one who can put even the slightest dent in their plan.

What their plan actually is, I'm still unsure. All I know is it involves every one of the resort's paying customers, as they were all being taken into the office. I'd like a bit of time to sit and think about what the terrorists are up to, so I can try and work out what their plans are, but that's not going to happen for a good while – if ever.

The helicopter sits dark and malevolent in the snowstorm. I can see the shape of the pilot sitting in the cockpit. He'll be cold and bored. Whether he's armed to the teeth or carrying nothing more dangerous than a flight plan doesn't matter. I have to presume he's got the same weapons as the other terrorists. To think any other way would be naive and little more than suicidal.

I circle the helicopter keeping enough of a distance from it that it's a shadow in the snow. I'm sure it'll have doors to allow passengers and cargo in and out, but I'd be surprised if they weren't locked.

When I consider the number of terrorists who've come looking for me and haven't returned, it's fair to assume Hannah will be taking all precautions necessary to protect her interests. A key one of these being the helicopter.

I need a ruse to get the pilot out so I can take him down. I'd also like to spend a few minutes questioning him about his flight path. Wherever Hannah wants him to fly, there must be a way the terrorists can land and get away without detection from the law enforcement agencies that will be going after them.

This has to be the most crucial part of their plan, for I don't believe they're on a suicide mission. Hannah is too smart not to have figured out a way to get herself and her troops to a place of safety when their mission is over.

If I can find out where they're due to land, the police can also mop up any getaway drivers that may be waiting for them.

I'm thinking of ways to get the pilot out of the helicopter when he does the job for me.

He climbs out, takes a quick look around, and wanders across towards the maintenance shed. Rather than head for the door, he stands at the sheltered side and arranges himself in the universal stance men adopt when facing a urinal.

As opportunities go, it's gilt-edged and far too good to pass up. I sneak up behind him, slowing from a crouched run to a brisk walk. With every step I take I'm afraid the crump of my feet on the snow will give me away, but the howling wind covers my approach and allows me to sneak up on the pilot.

He goes to turn round so I introduce his temple to the butt of my pistol. My pistol is happy at the meeting, his temple not so much.

He staggers a little and mumbles something incomprehensible. I didn't put maximum power into the blow as I want him conscious. He's a little stunned but that won't last long.

To further the effect of his brain rattling around inside his skull, I grab the front of his jacket with my left hand and draw his face onto my forehead.

Headbutts are a primitive form of fighting, but they're sure as hell effective. His nose is busted, which means his eyes will be watering and he's now blind and disorientated. A minute ago he was taking a whizz, now he's in a state of confusion and is about to be in a world of pain.

My knee slams into his groin. It's not what you'd call fighting fair, but he's an armed terrorist. I could just as easily have put a bullet in the back of his head, but that would have been homicide.

The funny thing about homicide is it makes people uncommunicative, and I need the pilot to talk.

It's also illegal, immoral and just plain wrong.

I repeat the knee to the crotch. It's not necessary as the fight has gone out of the pilot, but I want him to understand I'm more than happy to hurt him.

He crumples to his knees and I accept his inability to move as an invitation to frisk him. He's got a pistol holstered at his waist, but otherwise he has no weapons. What he does have though is a packet of cigarettes and a lighter.

It's a filthy habit and one I managed to quit several years ago. In light of the evening's events I'm tempted to have one for old times' sake, but the idea disappears as soon as I realise I'm re-enacting the cliché of the condemned man being given a last cigarette.

I stuff them in my pocket for later. In the right hands, cigarettes have more uses than just being a nicotine delivery system.

Give the pilot his due, despite the agony of his crushed groin, he's trying to mount a counter-attack. He wraps his arms around my legs and tries to drag me down into the snow with him.

A solid punch to the side of his head dissuades him.

I take a step back and kick his shoulder, causing him to fall face-down.

Now he's where I want him, I put my pistol at the back of his knee and pull the trigger once.

He'll never walk again, without a stick, and I'm pretty sure he'll never pilot another helicopter, but that's not something I can worry too much about. If he'd been unarmed I'd have been less inclined to cripple him; although, I'm now of the thinking that every terrorist I encounter must be neutralised, and as I'm not killing them, I have to make sure they can't come after me.

His agonised howls are whipped away by the wind, but I don't need to hear his screams to know how much he's hurting.

When I place the pistol against the back of his other knee he stops howling and starts begging.

I ask him a series of questions and he answers them without hesitation. My dominance has been established and he knows full well he's powerless against me.

What he tells me explains an awful lot and, in a weird way, I find myself respecting Hannah's ingenuity and bravery, while despising her cold-hearted nature.

To save him from any more agony I crash my pistol into the side of his head, and then go through his pockets.

I don't find any keys, which means at least one of the helicopter's doors is unlocked.

I leave him to be covered by the falling snow.

Chapter 41

Sharon does as she's told and assembles with the rest of the waiting staff. The female terrorist has her gun to Fleming's head and is asking him if all staff are present. She can see the little knots of people that represent each department and knows it's Fleming's way of giving an accurate count.

It's only a matter of time before he realises it's Boulder who is missing and gives his name to the terrorists.

While she doesn't like the manager in any way, the man is being put in an impossible situation. Fleming can't be expected to gamble with his own life to protect Boulder, a guy he's only known for a couple of weeks.

Therefore, Boulder's identity will soon be known to the terrorists. The question that's puzzling Sharon is how will that information be of use to them? With all the communication signals blocked they can't find out anything about him, and if they are able to contact him, they'll also be able to shoot him, meaning the information is useless to them.

That they're asking the question tells Sharon there must be a reason. Maybe they plan to look at his personnel file to see if he's ex-military or ex-law enforcement.

This indicates to Sharon that Boulder's still at large, that the terrorists who've been sent after him haven't found him.

Sharon almost dares to hope that Boulder has gotten away, until she sees Fleming looking at the bar staff. His face tightens and his lips clamp together.

The female terrorist sees this and screws her gun against his ear with enough force to push his head to the side.

Fleming's mouth opens and a few words spill out.

Sharon can't hear what he's said, but she doesn't need to, to know what they are. The smug triumphant smile on the female terrorist's face tells her everything she needs to know.

Some more questions are put to Fleming and they're answered with short sentences interspersed with the odd shrug.

Fleming is sent back to his seat as the female terrorist marches towards his office.

A minute later she returns holding a thin file.

Sharon doesn't think the file will be of much use to the terrorists, Boulder has always been guarded about his past. She'd had a few conversations with him, but he always ducked her questions about his background.

All she'd learned was that he'd moved to Utah when his mother remarried, and that he'd found work tossing drunks from a bar. His lack of knowledge about TV and films had been explained away by his love of reading.

Sharon had felt an instant kinship with him when they'd talked books. His knowledge of crime and thriller novels dwarfed hers, and she loved that he'd asked about her favourite reads and then recommended similar books that he thought she'd enjoy. She'd tried a couple of his recommendations and had been captivated by the stories.

Like her, he'd read right across the genre, taking in police procedurals, thrillers, historical fiction, and novels about ordinary people thrust into extraordinary situations.

That's how she feels now: like a character in a story. The arc of her narrative isn't hers to control, it's in the hands of others. Tonight, the female terrorist is the author and Sharon's fate is in her hands.

If there's as little in Boulder's file as she suspects, the next obvious move is to put the gun back against Fleming's head to find out who Boulder is friendly with.

Sharon knows hers is the only name that will feature. She's the only one Boulder had allowed to get anything like close to him, and she suspects if it hadn't been for the fact they are both weegies – as

Glaswegians are known – and avid readers, she would have been kept at the same arm's length as everyone else.

What little she does know about Boulder won't help the terrorists, but Sharon doesn't plan to give up that information easily. Every minute she keeps her mouth shut is a minute the terrorists are dealing with her and not looking for Boulder.

She doesn't know how she can be so sure, but she's certain the fate of all the customers and staff of RidgeTop Resort lies in his hands.

Chapter 42

Itry the helicopter door that the pilot exited from and find it's unlocked. When I climb in, I go pistol first in case there's someone waiting to ambush me. The pilot said there wasn't, but it's better to play safe than trust a man's word when you've just kneecapped him.

It turns out he was telling the truth as the helicopter is empty.

The cockpit is festooned with knobs and levers that mean nothing to me, but I find the one I asked the pilot about right where he said it would be.

There's a stale smell in here that tells of anticipation and men jacking up their nerves ready for battle. It's the stink of a locker room, and I'm sure there were ribald comments and a certain amount of mickey-taking as they made their way here.

Hannah's presence may have curtailed their comments to some degree, but soldiers are soldiers the world over, and all of them have a bawdy, black humour they use as a coping mechanism. For all I know, Hannah could be worse than any of her men.

I pull the prescribed lever and make my way into the rear of the helicopter where I find the wingsuits the pilot had told me about.

Their escape plan is a simple one. They'd fly the helicopter straight up, until they reached five thousand feet, and then set a course for Montpelier. With the highest point of Vermont being less than four and a half thousand feet, they wouldn't have to worry about crashing into a mountain.

Then it would be a case of using wingsuits to carry them from their jumping point over Roxbury, to where their getaway vehicle was located near Brookfield.

The helicopter's automatic pilot would fly it over Montpelier and onwards until it ran out of fuel.

I don't know a lot about such things, but there's every possibility the terrorists in their wingsuits wouldn't be large enough to be picked up by anyone manning air traffic control stations. Maybe a military grade radar would detect them, but I'm guessing Hannah's plan doesn't involve anyone looking for them until long after they've made their getaway. Hence the explosives, which would have eliminated all the witnesses.

In case my plan gets interrupted, I remove the knife on my hip from its sheath and use it to slash at each of the wingsuits that are arranged in the rear of the helicopter. There's also a box containing what appear to be wrist-mounted GPS sets. This makes sense as the terrorists would need some way of homing in on their destination.

Whichever way I look at it, donning wingsuits and leaping from the helicopter in the middle of a snowstorm shows each terrorist has the proverbial nerves of steel.

It also shows a lot of planning, which tallies in with what I have already worked out. Hannah and her cohorts must have a definite goal in mind, which again makes me wonder what was going on in the office.

My next move is to grab the map and flight plan from the cockpit and make my way outside the helicopter.

When I've found the fuel cap, pulled it back and removed the screw top, I roll the map into a tube and stuff it in the opening. I'm sure there's a valve of some kind in there to prevent fumes coming out, but I poke and prod until the valve is fooled into thinking the helicopter is being refuelled.

The smell of the aviation fuel is like nothing I've experienced before. It reminds me of gasoline, but more potent. It's like gasoline's bigger, angrier brother.

My intention at this point was to light the end of the map, but I realise the folly of that before I blow myself up with the helicopter.

A quick change of plan sees me dashing back to the maintenance shed where I fumble around in the dark until I find what I need.

I take a length of timber and tape the packet of cigarettes to it. Next, I wrap an old rag around the cigarettes and pick up a can of gasoline.

The can of gasoline isn't as heavy as I'd like it to be, which means it's about half full. There's maybe two to three gallons in it, which should be more than enough for my purpose.

I return to the helicopter and splash half of the gasoline over the map. Next, I make a trail of gasoline from the ground below the fuel cap and the map, until I have travelled around ten feet.

The last half pint of gasoline in the can gets poured onto the cloth I've tied over the end of the stick.

If the cloth burns away, the cigarettes beneath it will carry on burning.

When I've added another ten feet to my distance from the helicopter, I pull the pilot's lighter from my pocket and flick the wheel.

Its sparks ignite the makeshift torch in my hand. The sudden brightness is blinding for a moment, but I don't have a lot of time to allow my eyes to adjust.

I use an underarm throw to send the flaming torch to the end of the gasoline trail.

It rotates once before landing in the snow.

My throw is off and the torch lands three feet from the end of the trail; it's obvious I haven't allowed enough correction for the wind. Either that, or the thick layer of snow on the ground has absorbed enough of the gasoline to dilute its flammability.

I now have to decide between making another torch and trying again or going to the existing one and dropping it on the trail of gasoline.

As I stand there, trapped by indecision, I feel an extra hard gust of wind.

It must have blown some gasoline fumes towards the torch as there's a flash and the gasoline trail ignites. There is a fair chance that the snow will prevent the gasoline from reaching too high a temperature, but so long as it burns it'll do its job.

The row of flame shoots forward until it's underneath the helicopter.

When I see the flames start to climb, I turn on my heel and dash for the cover of the maintenance shed.

There's a huge boom and, all of a sudden, the flow of air changes direction. Instead of fighting to run into the wind, it's at my back, picking me up and throwing me forward. It's no longer cold – the air propelling me is heated like a super-charged summer breeze.

I know I've landed in a snowdrift, but there's little I can do about it. My ears are ringing, and every last scrap of air has been removed from my body.

Chapter 42

Daniel hears the explosion and reacts the same way as everyone else: he flinches, afraid for his safety, then he looks to his nearest and dearest for reassurance they're unhurt, and finally, he looks in the direction of the explosion.

Four of the terrorists are running towards the back of the hotel with their guns drawn. There's no clue as to what has caused the explosion, but the terrorists' reaction is a sure indicator that it's not part of their plan.

Therefore, it must be something to do with the bartender who slipped away earlier. Daniel hopes he's got a good hiding place as the four terrorists looked murderous when they ran out of the room.

Try as he might, Daniel can't imagine what could have caused the explosion. He wonders if it's the fuel supply for the generator that powers the resort, but he soon dismisses that as there's power for the emergency lights.

He's still puzzling over the explosion when one of the terrorists returns and goes straight to the woman who's in charge of them.

The terrorist says a few words to the woman and she screws up her face in anger. There's a potted plant near where she's standing and she delivers a vicious kick at it, toppling the plant over.

As it rolls, she aims a few more kicks at it until she regains control of herself.

The way she's so angry means the explosion has had a profound impact on her plans. Daniel considers what it might be, until he remembers how he got here.

The ride in the helicopter over the mountains had been super cool, even if his mom had sat staring ahead on the few occasions she'd opened her eyes. His arm still has the bruises from where her fingers had gripped him. It was a small price to pay, as she'd been brave enough to confront her fear of flying just so he could take the helicopter ride.

They'd got here by helicopter, which means the terrorists could have arrived the same way. Their helicopter must also have been their escape route. This explains why the woman is so angry. Now the terrorists are trapped at the resort, the same way their hostages are.

While the hostages are held by the terrorists, the terrorists are isolated because of their location. The remoteness and inaccessibility of the resort that started off working in their favour, was now a factor against them.

Daniel isn't sure whether this is a good or a bad thing. Now the terrorists' escape route has been cut off, their plans will have to change if they are to get away with their crime. He figures this may be a good thing, that it will make them leave sooner than they'd intended so they can get away before morning comes and the people at the bottom of the mountain raise the alarm after hearing nothing from the resort.

So far as Daniel can work out, the only way the terrorists can get down the mountain now is to ski. In the current snowstorm, it would be stupid to try, but the more he thinks about it, the more he realises that if they wait until first light, and take it carefully, they may be able to slip away.

The storm is supposed to peter out during the night. He knows this because the one thing everyone focuses on at a ski resort is the weather. There are concerns there'll be too little fresh snow, and worries there will be snowstorms that make it unsafe to go on the mountain. The wrong temperatures, or type of snow falling, can increase avalanche risks, and if the mountain is deemed unsafe, everyone has to hang around waiting until conditions improve.

As much as there are things to do in the resort, everyone is here to ski, and that's why there is such an interest in the weather.

Daniel doesn't like the idea of the terrorists hanging around until first light, but as he can't figure out another way for them to leave the mountain, he knows he has to accept the situation and deal with it.

The man with the clipboard ushers the woman towards the office and turns to face the crowd.

Daniel's blood chills when he hears his mom's name called out. What had happened in the office the first time was bad enough, but now the woman terrorist is so angry anything could happen.

As he walks forward with his mom he gives her hand a squeeze. His intention is to give her reassurance, while also warning her that she has to comply. He knows the fact that she'd do anything to protect him is a given, but she is also headstrong and more than a little stubborn.

If the woman terrorist pushes her buttons the wrong way, there is no telling how far his mom will dig her heels in.

Chapter 43

The walkie-talkie in my pocket buzzes static at me. I thought I'd turned it off, but my frozen fingers must have failed to twist the tiny knob all the way to the off position.

After the helicopter exploded I forced myself to move – to get myself to a position where the flames weren't stealing all the oxygen, to put some distance between me and the area that was lit up by the fire.

I could have made my way back into the maintenance shed, or the control booth, but I wanted to find somewhere less obvious.

I'm now holed up underneath the raised deck of the resort. I've clambered up the rocks and found myself a dark space where I can hide until the tactical police team arrive. With the billowing snow causing drifts around the resort, and the darkness under here, the only way the terrorists will be able to find me is if they come specifically to search this area.

Because of the whistles and howls produced by the wind, and the fact that visibility is no more than a dozen feet at best, I'm confident I can stay hidden as long as is necessary.

There is sure to be a backlash from the terrorists now I've trashed their helicopter, and the last thing I want to do is make it easy for them to find me.

By my reckoning, the police will be here in a half hour or so, and I'm quite comfortable with the idea of spending a half hour crouched on a rock shivering. I'll be cold, there's no question about that, but I'm more than happy to handle a spot of discomfort if it keeps me alive.

It's not just the terrorists I'm keeping away from. When the police get here, they're going to be pumped up, jumpy even.

They'll be expecting resistance. I'm covered in blood, half frozen, and armed with as much firepower as any one of the terrorists. This makes the odds of me being shot by the cops rather higher than I'd like them to be. Friendly fire is a real threat, and when I do expose myself to the cops, I won't be carrying any weapons and my hands will be as far north of my head as it's possible to get them.

With the terrorists still at large, there's no way I'm going to relinquish my weapons just yet though.

I hear a crackle of static again and reach for the walkie-talkie in my pocket.

When I pull it from my jacket I have to force my fingers to grip it with enough strength to depress the call button. 'Nathan?'

'My name isn't Nathan. Your name, however, is Jake Boulder. You're a bartender with a most interesting history. You're also a former doorman who keeps finding himself in trouble. Trust me, Boulder, blowing up my helicopter was the stupidest thing you've ever done.'

The voice coming through the walkie-talkie belongs to Hannah. There's no mistaking the hint of French accent or the surety with which she speaks.

How she's identified me isn't hard to work out. A gun pointed at the head of one of the kids in the room would have gotten someone to tell them who was missing.

While Sharon portrays herself as a tough cookie, it's an act everyone can see through. If it was her who gave Hannah my name, I bear her no ill will. She's done what is best for her and those she can protect, and that has to be admired.

When all is said and done, Hannah and her cohorts knowing my name won't change the situation. They still won't know where I am. All they'll know is that I was tending bar at RidgeTop.

I quickly realise the mistake in my thinking: Hannah had said I kept finding myself in trouble. This means she knows more about me than I tell people.

The information isn't hard to find if you know where to look. In her shoes, I'd have gone to the personnel files to learn as much as I could about the person I was up against.

My file will have details of my employment history and my home address. A two-minute search on Google with my name and home town will have brought up results that detail the trouble she's speaking of.

Those parts of my life aren't a secret, I just prefer not to talk about them because they're what set me on the path that turned me from a doorman to a stone-cold killer. I left Casperton to escape the man I'd become and to try and find the Jake Boulder I used to be. It's why I took the job on RidgeTop.

Hannah will now be aware that I've killed before, that I'm not the kind of man to walk away from a fight, and that I'm nobody's fool.

I also realise she must have a way of accessing the Internet that isn't available to any of the hostages. Maybe she's just unplugged the Wi-Fi router and plugged a laptop into the wall, or perhaps she's got a fancy satphone that allows her to surf the web.

'So, you know my name. What's yours?'

The line is the kind I'd use on a pretty girl in a bar, and I don't for one second expect that she'll tell me her real name, if she gives me a name at all. She's opened up a line of dialogue and I'm curious as to what she's after. She's bound to be less than happy with what I've done to her helicopter and the men I've either disabled or killed.

In her place I'd be desperate to nullify the threat to my plans.

'My name isn't important. What's important is that you have become a nuisance to me. I want you to stop being a nuisance. Therefore, I am proposing you stay holed up wherever you are until I've left, and I won't start shooting hostages.'

I'd bet my life savings she won't keep to her word. The presence of the explosives tells me that she plans to kill everyone. As callous as it sounds, it's better that a couple of hostages are killed rather than all of them.

Hannah suggesting I hole up somewhere is also indicative of her intentions. Someone hiding is often much easier to find than a person who's moving around keeping a watch on all areas.

Should I follow her instructions I'd be playing into her hands. On the other hand, I'd already found my hiding place before she radioed me. She couldn't know that though.

There must be another reason for her wanting me to hole up for a while.

It's as I look at the walkie-talkie in my hand that I make the connection.

She's contacted me on the walkie-talkie, which means she has one, and if she's heard my conversation with Nathan, she'll know the police's tactical team are on their way and that their arrival is imminent.

That's why she wants me holed up. She's planning a reception committee and doesn't want me to attack it or warn the tactical team.

'You got a deal, lady.'

It's a lie that's every bit as large as the one she's told me. I have every intention of warning the cops.

I thumb the control of the walkie-talkie and try to raise Nathan on a different channel.

Five times I speak his name as I try each of the walkie-talkie's other five channels, before I give up and try the first channel again.

I'm more than aware I'm gambling with the life of at least one hostage by trying to contact Nathan in a way Hannah can overhear, but I have to do what I feel is best for the majority rather than the individual.

I say what I have to say and listen with my breath held to see who replies.

'You're wasting your time, Boulder. I've had one of my men install a signal blocker.' She gives a contented little laugh. 'It's a clever piece of kit, we can set the distance it blocks radio signals and leave a zone in which communications can still be made. It's currently set at fifty feet, which means you're very close.'

Hannah's words leave me colder than any snowstorm. If she's telling the truth, the police are heading right into a trap, and if she's lying, she's trying to flush me out.

I decide to give Nathan five minutes to come back to me, and if I don't hear from him, I'll have to try and ambush the welcoming committee.

Five minutes pass, and so does a sixth.

When I clamber out from my hiding place, I'm cold, stiff, and more than a little nervous about my chosen course of action. None of that matters, my logic that the good of the many outweighs the good of the few has to apply to myself as well as others.

I make sure the submachine guns in my hands are ready to fire and start trudging my way to the top of the resort. The snowstorm's intensity has remained, which means I'm working in an isolated bubble that keeps me ever fearful of shapes appearing out of the snow. The billowing swirls make constant changes that throw all kinds of shapes at me.

With every step I take I expect to encounter a terrorist, or to feel the slam of a bullet hitting my body.

Chapter 45

As I head towards the resort my mind is firing on all cylinders. I'm rehashing my brief conversation with Hannah, and second guessing my assumption that she'd overheard me talking to Nathan earlier. I'm also wondering how I can warn the tactical cop team if I see any signs of an ambush being laid.

It's as I pass the control booth that both questions are answered. Through the swirling snow I see the outline of a warning sign. I passed the sign earlier and remember its brief but poignant message.

The sign warns of the avalanche risks, and alerts skiers of areas they should avoid if the avalanche siren is heard.

If I can use the siren to give the SOS code, the cops will know there's something up. As plans go it's a good one, and should work, apart from one flaw: the controls for the siren are in the resort itself. Specifically, they are in the ante-room used by the professional ski-instructors. To get access to the controls, I'll have to sneak back into the resort and make my way to the ante-room.

The problems don't stop there. I've heard the siren ring out on more than one occasion. Its very purpose is to make a lot of noise and it's exceptional at its job. As soon as I trigger the siren the terrorists will hear it.

Hannah will figure out my plan at once and will despatch someone to silence it. Just because she doesn't know where the controls are located won't matter. It'll take her no more than a few seconds to put a gun to someone's head and get the information.

With luck, I'll have a whole minute between switching on the siren and someone arriving at the ante-room with a gun full of bullets bearing my name. Without luck, it could be thirty seconds, which means I'll barely have time to ring out my SOS before I get company.

Either way, I don't want to be trapped in a room with an armed terrorist outside the door. The ante-room has only one door and no windows. If I'm caught in there I'm as good as dead. Being realistic, I know I'll have enough time to set off the alarm and make a run for it. Anything subtler than that will be akin to signing my death warrant.

There's no doubt in my mind that I have to do it, though. Somehow, I have to warn the tactical cops they could be walking into a trap.

Other than side doors and emergency exits, there are only three ways into the RidgeTop Resort. The first is via the cable car station, the second is the door that leads onto the top of the ski slopes, and the third is via the decking that leads alongside the hotel to the balcony in front of the dining room.

I'm sure all the smaller doors will be locked from the inside. This makes sense at the best of times, and if Hannah's expecting a police attack, she'll be sure to have made life awkward for them. Therefore, there are only three doors I have to consider.

Accessing the resort via the cable car station is possible, but, if there's anyone waiting for me at the top, they'll be able to put a bullet or several in my back as I climb the ladder I used to escape the resort in the first place.

I'd seen the balcony doors being locked from the inside, which means I'd have to announce my arrival by shooting out the glass. With there being at least six terrorists guarding the hostages, I'd be dead before taking two steps into the building.

The main doors seem like the better option, but in reality, that's like saying facing a tiger is preferable to a lion. One man would be able to guard the cableway station by staying hidden. So long as he keeps the cableway mechanism inactive, all he has to do is see who is stupid enough to climb the ladder and shoot them at his leisure.

The main entrance is a different proposition: it's not cluttered with anything. Off to each side there are drying rooms with steel cage lockers where ski equipment can be stored. Once you get ten feet inside the doors there's a second corridor bisecting the one that leads from the doors to the social areas.

If a terrorist or two were to lie in wait a few feet along this corridor, they'd be able to cut me down with ease. There's also the worry of which way I should look. If I choose wrong, I'll be exposing my back to them.

I doubt I'll be quicker on the draw than them, or more accurate with my aim, but it would be nice to have the option of at least returning fire.

I move away from the resort so it's a vague shape in the darkness. Its outside lights are the only thing other than the gradient to help me navigate. I'm making damned sure I don't walk into an ambush that's been laid for me.

As I crest the rise to the level area where the helipad is, I'm at least thirty feet away from the nearest building, which is the control booth for the ski chairs. Like the resort, it's just a dark shape in the whiteout. Unlike the resort, it doesn't have any lights to guide me so I have to make sure I keep it in my sight.

My legs are aching from the exertion of wading through deep snow, and while my feet feel as if they've frozen solid, my thighs and calves are burning. My hands are as cold as my feet and, although I'm not out of breath, I know my heart is beating faster than usual. Fear may well be a contributor to that phenomena, but I tell myself it isn't, and my heart is pounding because I've just trudged up a mountain through two feet of snow, wearing nothing but indoor clothes.

The cold is fast becoming my enemy as much as the terrorists. My fingers don't move with anything like the speed they should and, if I didn't know better, I'd expect to see diving boots where my feet are supposed to be.

When I get a little further, I see the glare from the smouldering helicopter, which I can use as a navigational beacon.

From the light thrown out by the burning wreck, I can see the helicopter is now a twisted mess. The explosion has flipped the aircraft onto its side and there's not a mechanic alive who could make it fly again without replacing at least ninety per cent of its parts.

I keep the helicopter's fire on the limit of my sight as I circle round until it lies in a direct line between my position and the front door. This part has been easy. The next won't be.

When I look beyond the helicopter all I can see are dark, indistinguishable shapes. From my time at the resort I know what most, but not all, of them are.

I circle round further and approach the door from the side that doesn't lead to the slopes. It's bordered by a rugged rock face, which forms the picturesque ridge that gives the resort its name. There's nothing near the rock face that can be used as cover due to the fact it's been left bare in a magnificent display of nature's beauty and strength against the elements.

The problem with using that route is that some of the areas I'll have to cross are illuminated by the glare from the helicopter and the resort's outside lighting.

If I'm to have any success against the terrorists, stealth and subterfuge are my best weapons.

I retreat a few paces, strip off my jacket and lay it on the ground. Now I've removed it I realise how much it's kept me warm. Next, I take off the burgundy vest that's part of my uniform and drop it on the jacket. I add my shirt to the pile and remove my T-shirt. I pull the shirt back on and fumble with the buttons. It takes a half dozen attempts before my numb fingers get the first button closed, but I keep going until all bar the collar button is fastened.

The T-shirt gets pulled part-way over my head until its neck surrounds my face.

With a white shirt and T-shirt covering the upper half of my body, I blend into the snowstorm a lot better than I did when I was wearing the bright red ski jacket.

By the time I've taken a dozen steps I'm wondering if I've made a mistake in shedding the quilted jacket. I've been cold before, but never quite as cold as this. There isn't a part of my body that feels anything other than frozen. My arms are the coldest part of my body as my shirt is sleeveless from where I'd treated the bullet wound I picked up under the balcony.

I push the cold from my mind, if not from my limbs, and keep going.

I make it to the rock face without incident, and it's as I'm moving forward in a low crouch that I see a shape moving by the resort's door.

My stance becomes statuesque as I halt all movement that isn't shivering and watch the shape. It moves left five or six paces and then the same distance right, before turning left again.

There's no doubt in my mind it's a guard, patrolling back and forth to warm himself against the elements.

A quick glance at my watch tells me I have no time to do anything but go on.

I wait until the guard is walking away from me, progress forward four paces, and then stop.

Chapter 46

Every time the guard walks away from me, I move forward another few paces and crouch to hide the dark trousers I'm wearing. I'm on the fifth repetition of this when the guard stops halfway along his route and turns to the door. I'm close enough now to make out the shape of his body and can observe his movements in far greater detail.

I halt at once, and, when I see three more shapes join the first one, I ease my way to the ground until I'm lying prone in the cold, wet snow.

Of the three terrorists who've emerged from the resort, two are carrying automatic rifles and the third is carrying a large cylindrical object on his shoulder.

This must be Hannah's welcome committee.

I've seen enough action movies to work out that the cylindrical object is a rocket launcher of some description. It could fire rocket propelled grenades, or some other kind of missile, but that's a moot point. Whatever it fires will decimate the tactical police team or destroy the piste basher and kill its driver.

It's bad enough that cops could die in the line of duty, but the idea of innocents being slaughtered makes me hate Hannah and her gang even more.

It's obvious to me that Hannah is a psychopath of the highest order; what she did to Debbie Boitoult showed that, and everything she has done since has only reinforced my opinion of her.

Human life means nothing to her, she kills and maims without consideration for anything other than the negative effect it will have on others. Now she's identified a threat to her life and liberty, she's organised what will become little more than a turkey shoot.

The men who're under her control are little, if any, better. Every time I've seen her give an order it's been carried out without question or hesitation. Each of them are killers and, while I don't know their end game, they must stand to gain a hell of a lot to take the risks they're taking.

Whether it's a financial, political, or ideological goal they're after, doesn't matter any more. All that matters is that they're stopped.

As I watch them from my prone position, the three new men advance past the guard. The two carrying assault rifles are moving with tactical acumen, advancing and then covering each other, along with the man carrying the rocket launcher.

Every corner they round sees them lead gun first, before they sweep the new area and then wave the others forward.

In a way it's flattering to me that three of them have been sent, but the increased watchfulness of their actions will be a serious deterrent to any attempts I make to disrupt their plans.

The way they're going about their business, it's unlikely I'll be able to get the jump on them without getting shot again. They're armed with assault rifles, whereas the best weapon I have at my disposal is a pair of submachine guns.

While I'm no expert on guns, I know that soldiers carry assault rifles for distance shooting, and submachine guns for close up work like clearing houses of enemies. In my amateurish hands the submachine gun is no match for the assault rifles.

This leaves me two options.

One is to rush them, guns blazing, hoping for three lucky shots, and the other is to warn the tactical team of the terrorists' presence before they get within range.

The first option is suicidal and would require me to kill the terrorists, and the second is a lot harder because of the guard patrolling outside the main door.

As much as it goes against my instincts, and the desire not to have any more murders on my conscience, I know if I'm to stand any chance of success in saving lives, I'll probably have to kill at least one of the terrorists before this ordeal is over.

I could rush the guy at the door and take him down with a burst from the submachine gun, but that would alert the welcoming party, which means I'd be gunned down where I stood, or trapped between the terrorists both inside and outside the resort.

Neither of these options appeal so I try to think of another way to warn the tactical team.

If I can get access to the drying rooms, I'll be able to grab bundles of skis and send them down the slope. Whether or not it would work as a warning is debateable, but it would at least make the cops proceed with more caution. The counter point to this is not knowing where the cops are, or how they're approaching. If they're travelling the last few hundred yards on foot, skis coming at them out of the darkness could hit them; at the pace they would be sliding downhill, they would smash any limb they collide with.

I wait until the guard resumes his patrolling and back away until I'm at the other side of the helicopter again.

An idea is forming in my mind, but it's neither clever nor safe. The needs of the many still outweigh the few, so I have little choice but to follow through with the idea to its conclusion.

Chapter 47

The woman and the teenage boy emerge from the office and, like those who'd gone before them, they look shocked by what they've experienced. It's the second time they've been in there, and despite giving herself a headache trying to work out what's going on, Sharon can't see the terrorists having an agenda that doesn't involve kidnapping.

They'd been in there longer than any other couple, and while they both appear to be unharmed, the psychological toll of what they'd endured can be read on their faces and told in their body language.

The boy is trying to look after his mother, who looks to be catatonic and has to be guided to her seat. To Sharon, she looks on the verge of a breakdown, and she understands how the woman has been affected.

Mothers all have the same instinct: namely the protection of their young. They nurture, educate and guide their offspring through life. Their instincts have them ready to catch at any moment, to place a hand on table corners as their toddler approaches, and, while they accept there are some situations beyond their control, they do all they can to prevent their child being exposed to even the minimal of risks.

For a mother to have a child with her when being threatened by terrorists must be the worst kind of torment imaginable. The simple threat of harm to the child wouldn't even have to be spoken to coerce the mother. It would hang like a Damoclean sword, twisting in the charged atmosphere. Its very presence enough to ensure instructions were followed regardless of how unpalatable they may be.

The woman has endured all this and more. Her expression tells of utter defeat, of a future so bleak as to be undesirable. The woman still has her child, but if her body language is anything to go by, everything else in her life has been destroyed.

Sharon hopes the woman's survival instinct kicks in before depression takes hold. When someone is as devastated as the boy's mother appears to be, every miniscule obstacle becomes insurmountable as negative thoughts dominate and turn all mental energy into a series of self-doubts and recriminations.

The boy seems to be a good lad. Where most kids his age are all rolling eyes and snotty hormones, he's bright and considerate of others. His manners are impeccable and he's a son any parent would be proud of.

The Powell girl is a different entity, so far as Sharon is concerned. Every time the girl speaks her voice is laden with disdain. Whether addressing her mother, a member of staff or another customer, she's been rude and acted as if those she was speaking to were inferior to her.

Sharon has seen the trait on many occasions. For those who've never had to work for it, great wealth often came with a sense of egotistical superiority. Their lives are a succession of having their every whim pandered to, and the deferential treatment received from those hanging on their coat tails gave them an over-inflated sense of worth.

These people are rude and obnoxious for sport, they threaten people's jobs to get their own way, and boast about how they bullied a defenceless person who was facing struggles they've never had to imagine, let alone comprehend. The girl is like that, and Sharon predicts an unhappy life for her.

The girl is pretty enough to suggest there will be no shortage of potential suitors when she enters the dating scene. Her family's wealth will make her question every man's motives. She'll wonder if they are interested in her or the trust fund she undoubtedly has. If the girl makes the mistake of falling for someone who's after her money or social status, she'll become wary of being hurt again.

Regardless of how the girl will act when she grows up, and how the boy's mother will be in the next few hours and days, Sharon wants them to live long enough to find out.

Since Boulder's escape she's noticed that the number of terrorists has decreased – some have gone off and never returned. While it's possible they have been given other tasks now the hostages are being compliant, the increased stress on the face of the female terrorist, and the way she sought out Fleming to help her identify Boulder, makes Sharon believe that Boulder has taken some of them out.

The huge explosion will have been his work too. It had shaken the building and added to the woman's stress.

As much as Sharon wants Boulder to be unhurt, she knows the odds are against him. She wants to help, and now he's depleted the number of terrorists, there are fewer guards watching over them.

She slides the steak knife she'd palmed back inside her sleeve and rises to her feet. Two of the kitchen staff are asking for the toilet and she wants to join them.

It isn't that she needs the toilet, it's more of a way to give herself an opportunity to strike back. The knife in her sleeve isn't the deadliest weapon she's ever held, but if she can plunge it into one of the tattoos adorning the guard's neck, she'll be able to grab his submachine gun and the pistol on his belt.

Sharon makes to go for the ladies' again, which will draw the guard out of sight of the other terrorists. Once he is down she can make her escape and find Boulder. Together they'll stand a far better chance of beating the terrorists.

'Hey, use the men's room.' The guard takes a half step to the side so he is in her line of sight.

'I thought we'd got past that.' Sharon takes another step towards the powder room. 'I need to go there.'

'I don't care. Use the men's room.'

Sharon steps a half pace forward until the guard is within striking distance. 'Please?'

The guard's eyes narrow as he assesses her, his Adam's apple bobs as he swallows, the movement making the wolf tattooed on his throat appear to snarl.

With them being visible to other guards, Sharon knows if she attacks the guy standing in front of her, she'll be gunned down in seconds. Rather than provoke the situation any further, she turns to head back to the men's room. Her plan has failed and therefore she must rethink things and find another opportunity.

The noise she hears behind her is unmistakeable. Once you've heard someone cock a submachine gun, the sound never leaves your memory. The last time she'd heard the sound was in Afghanistan, but those were different times. She was in love with the major and was desperate for both of them to do their tour and return home unharmed. They had, and now she was hearing that metallic snap again.

'Put your hands behind your head and lace your fingers.'

Any hint of normalcy has gone from the guard's voice. His tone is now cold and business-like, so Sharon does as she's told. The very fact she has to obey an instruction grates on her, but she knows she must suppress her independent nature, otherwise it'll get her killed.

The hard point of a muzzle presses against her spine. 'Walk to the manager's office. Make one false move and I'll shoot you where you stand.'

As Sharon walks to the office, her mind juggles the risk of taking action and dying, against being handed over to the terrorist's boss. The woman is a stone-cold killer who no doubt has some vicious punishment in mind.

She feels the muzzle dig into her back, as a pair of fingers slide the knife from her sleeve. A second later, the point of the knife jabs her in the back – not hard, just enough to break the skin and inflict pain.

Every step she takes towards the office is accompanied by another jab from the knife. As frightened as she is about what the woman may do to her, Sharon isn't ready to quit yet.

Her jaw stiffens as she prepares herself for whatever punishment the female terrorist decides to mete out.

As she's pushed through the door, she's doing everything she can to replace her fear with anger. Terror will see her crumble, rage will strengthen resolve and fortify her determination.

Chapter 48

The music is loud and there are throngs of people half her age dancing and hanging out in groups, but that doesn't stop Ivy Boulder from forging her way through the crowd like an ice breaker.

She's leaving a trail of sharp glances behind her from the people she's jostled or scolded out of her way.

A drunk man slurs 'Happy New Year' at her and spreads his arms wide for a hug. She brushes him aside without a care for his feelings and arrows in on her target.

Alfonse Devereaux is her son's best friend, and if anyone knows why Jake hasn't been in touch with Hogmanay greetings, he will.

He's surrounded by a group of people who're half familiar to her as Jake's circle of friends, but rather than worry about embarrassing her son, she marches up to Alfonse and demands that he tells her why Jake didn't call her at midnight.

From the week they moved to Utah, and Jake had been landed in a new school, he'd been friends with Alfonse. The quiet, bookish lad was an immigrant the same as Jake and, while Ivy didn't know the full truth, she knew Alfonse and Jake had initially traded protection for academic help.

The knowledge her son is – and always has been – a fighter, is something Ivy has long since grown to accept as part of his nature. She doesn't like this facet of his personality, or the amount of time she spends worrying about the day he gets himself into a fight he can't win, but Ivy can live with the knowledge that one day her son will take a beating so long as it doesn't leave him with life changing injuries.

A greater concern for her is, sooner or later, Jake will get himself into trouble with the law. He's been more than lucky to have avoided prison for the escapades he's gotten himself into, and she knows in her bones that his luck is due to run out.

'I don't know, Mrs B. I haven't heard from him either.'

'What do you think he's up to?'

When Alfonse stands and takes her arm, Ivy lets him steer her to a place where they can talk without shouting in each other's ears.

'He might well be working.'

'What?' The last time Ivy had heard from Jake, he was working for a fast food chain in Idaho. 'Flipping burgers at this time of night? Don't you be giving me none of your bull, Alfonse. You're a grown man now, tell me what's going on and don't think you're helping Jake by lying to me.'

'Sorry, but I thought you'd know. He's got a job at a ski lodge. He's working as a bartender, and as it's New Year's …' Alfonse lets the sentence hang and Ivy understands what he is getting at.

There is no guile on Alfonse's face, just bemusement that she didn't know where Jake is and what he's doing. Ivy doesn't really blame Alfonse, it's Jake's responsibility to keep her informed of his movements, and he's failed her. Since he'd left Casperton, his calls were infrequent at best, and he'd been guarded when questioned about how he was.

'So, his poor mother is the last to know as always. Sometimes I wonder what I've done to deserve being treated the way he treats me. Night after night, I toss and turn, wracked with worry about my only son and what does he do? He moves round the country at will without updating me.'

'That's enough.' Alfonse's words hold no malice but there is a stern look on his face that Ivy has never seen before. 'Jake is trying to find himself. You saw the mess he was in before he left town, he'll be working, or doing lord knows what, but what he won't be doing is getting himself into trouble. He hasn't told me much about how he's feeling, but I've read between enough lines to know he's carrying a butt load of guilt. When he does get in touch, do him the courtesy of listening to what he doesn't say, as much as what he does. And never forget.' The way Alfonse is wagging a finger under her nose is infuriating her, but Ivy manages to curb her instinct to grab the digit. 'Jake needs our support right now, not a million and one questions, not a guilt trip every time he calls. If he needs time to find himself before he comes home, so be it, let's just make sure he wants to come back to Casperton.'

Ivy pushes her way past Alfonse then turns back. Never, in all the years she's known him, has he spoken to her with such frankness. In his own, respectful way, he's telling her to stop nagging at Jake and allow him space.

Alfonse is a good man, but he's not a parent, he's never had to raise two kids single-handed. He's never had to answer questions about why daddy left, nor has he had to explain a million and one things to a wide-eyed child, and he's missed out on the all-consuming worry that having children can engender.

'Your words are noted. Now, can you tell me where my son is, please?' Ivy regrets the ice in her tone, but Alfonse's lecture has ticked her off, and there's no way she can let anyone speak to her like that without retaliating.

'He's at a place in Vermont. Some hyper-exclusive ski resort called RidgeWay, or RidgeTop, something like that.'

'So he's in a ski resort and he's working the bar. Tell me, Alfonse, how well do you think that is going to work out?'

Other than his fighting, the biggest worry Ivy has about Jake is his binge drinking. It's not often that he drinks, but when he does, she knows he loses days at a time.

If he's in constant proximity to alcohol, there's little doubt in Ivy's mind that he'll be faced with a temptation he's unable to resist. All it will take is for someone to piss him off a couple of times and he'll be reaching for the nearest bottle. Then he'll fail to turn up for work and that will lead to one of two scenarios: he'll be sacked, or his boss will go looking for him. Neither will help Jake's quest to find himself.

The idea that Jake hasn't contacted her or Alfonse because he's working is a welcome one, as is the idea that he's hooked up with a woman for the night, but she doubts the latter. Against all his usual instincts, Jake had fallen for someone, and when she died because of his father's cowardice, Jake's fury betrayed how deeply he'd loved her.

'Mrs B?'

Ivy collects herself from her thoughts and looks at Alfonse. His cell phone is in his hand and his expression is grave.

He holds the phone so she can see the screen.

It shows a search result for RidgeTop Resort. That is all well and good; like the decent soul that he is, Alfonse has searched for the place Jake is working at so she can see it for herself.

It is the second listing that explains the look on his face. The listing shows a news report: RidgeTop Resort is the scene of a suspected terrorist attack and the police and FBI are in attendance.

Ivy presses her thumb against the second listing and waits a few seconds until the page loads.

So far, there are no confirmed casualties, but initial reports suggest that one of the hostages has broken free and alerted the authorities.

As she digests the news, she reads the report a second and third time, looking for her son's name. It isn't there, but she knows trouble is attracted to Jake the way flies are drawn to dung, and if he is at that resort, he won't be sitting quiet, hoping for a peaceful outcome. His nature will compel him to fight back, to do whatever he can to scupper the terrorists' plans, and basically put his mother into an even deeper state of concern than usual.

Ivy knows she should be proud of Jake and the way he always tries to do the right thing, but she's afraid he's bitten off more than he can chew this time, and it's all she can do not to crumple to the ground in floods of tears.

As much as she loves her son, a tiny part of her hates him for the way he keeps her in a constant state of worry.

Chapter 49

Try as she might, Sharon can't prevent her knees from trembling. It's all she can do to keep her face neutral and the fear from her eyes. Feistiness is in her nature and there's no way she is prepared to cower before the female terrorist. To do so would give the other woman the upper hand and show her respect.

Whatever happens, Sharon refuses to give the terrorists even the slightest advantage.

When she's pushed into Fleming's office, there is a couple facing the female across the resort manager's desk. Beside her, one of her men is sitting in front of a laptop, which has a tablet connected to it by a lead that has multiple tails, each featuring a different type of connector.

The female terrorist jerks a thumb at the couple and glares at Sharon and the guard with the tattooed neck. 'This better be good.'

The guard says nothing until the couple have left.

'I think she's connected with the guy who's running around out there.'

The female terrorist's eyes narrow as she lifts a pistol from the desk and points it at Sharon. 'Why do you think that?'

'When she went to the can earlier, she insisted on going to the powder room instead of the men's room. Said she needed sanitary products. I figured that while I was trying to watch over her and the others, I missed one of them going back to where the hostages are. Seems like she was distracting me while he made his escape.'

'I see. So, you're telling me that you fell for her distraction?'

'I guess so. I couldn't watch both ways.'

Sharon sees the pistol's aim transferred from her to the guard. The look in the woman's eyes is arctic in its coldness, and Sharon is expecting her to pull the trigger.

'Your mistake has proven costly to the operation. Therefore, it's only fair it becomes costly to you. Your payment has just been reduced by one third. I trust this is agreeable to you?'

'Yes, ma'am.' The man's tone shows disappointment and resignation, but Sharon doesn't detect even the slightest hint of dissent.

'Leave us now. If you want to redeem yourself, and go back to a full share, bring me Boulder's head. It doesn't necessarily have to be attached to his shoulders.'

The pistol's aim returns to Sharon.

'I'm innocent. Your man is an idiot who can't count. This Boulder guy you're after, I'm nothing to do with him.'

The bullet that slams into Sharon's left arm doesn't strike the bone, but it has enough impact to jerk her backwards. The pain is instantaneous as a series of nerve endings do their job and inform her brain of the injury. She can still move her arm and, while it hurts like hell, she knows the real pain will come later when her body stops dumping adrenaline to deal with the injury.

When she turns to face the terrorist, she has her right hand clasped over the bullet wound to stem the blood flow.

'Do not lie to me. I find lies incredibly tedious. I have seen Boulder's file and the picture it contains. He was sat with you before he escaped. My man is probably correct in that you created a distraction so Boulder could escape.' The terrorist rolls her eyes. 'Men are weird creatures. If I'd told him to skin you alive, he'd have done it without question, but you intimate you're on your period and he becomes all awkward.'

The conversational tone that the female terrorist is using scares Sharon more than the gun that's pointed at her. It would appear this is the woman's normal; she's not angry or showing any of the signs of wanting to exact retribution that Sharon had expected to see.

The barrel of the pistol points at a chair and bobs twice, so Sharon takes a seat. She wants to protest her innocence further, but doesn't want to risk catching another bullet. The first had inflicted pain without doing any real damage, but there is no telling where the next one will strike.

Rather than provoke the woman, Sharon keeps her mouth shut and waits for her to speak again.

'You're tough. Other than a yelp when I shot your arm, you've not made a sound. I dare say I could torture you to get the information I want, but to be frank with you, as much as I would enjoy it, something about the way you're holding your head tells me you'd rise to the challenge and wouldn't talk. You're sitting there, probably expecting to die. I'm certain you're expecting me to hurt you some more. I'd like to find out just how tough you are, but I don't have time to waste on you, so we're going to cut right to the heart of the matter. I have three questions I want answers to: one; who is Boulder? Two; why did you help him? Three; what other plans do you have to strike against me and my colleagues?'

Sharon doesn't speak until the female terrorist walks round the table and presses her gun against Sharon's forehead. The barrel is still warm from the first shot and Sharon can feel it burning her skin, but that's the least of her worries.

'Go ahead, kill me. You were right, as soon as your man brought me in here, I've been expecting to die. Pull the trigger; I'm not going to answer any of your questions.'

As brave as her words were, Sharon hears the fearful catch in her voice.

'You know, I believe you'd rather die than talk.' The woman turns to the man in front of the laptop and speaks a few words to him in a language Sharon recognises as French.

The man leaves the room and, after a minute or so, Sharon hears shouting and protestations.

When he returns he's got the three children with him who're customers at the resort. The smart boy is the first into the room and he's trailed by the Powell girl and her little brother.

The man stands guard at the door while the woman trains her gun on the girl.

'I'm going to count to five. Then I'm going to shoot her. Maybe I'll blow her brains out, or perhaps I'll put a bullet into her lungs. Can you picture the frothy blood spilling from her mouth as she breathes her last? Or the splatter of her brains on the wall? On the other hand, I could put a couple of shots into her gut. Bad way to die that, it's slow. Maybe her wailing in agony and crying for her mother will loosen your tongue.'

As much as she wants to resist the terrorist, Sharon knows she has a moral duty to protect the children rather than Boulder. 'I'll talk, provided you let the children go now.'

'No, you'll talk now.' To emphasise her point, the terrorist racks the slide on her pistol.

The girl shrinks back, whimpering as she tries to hide behind the smart boy. To his credit, he stands firm and allows her to cower behind him. The terror on their young faces is awful to see and there's no way Sharon can, in good conscience, maintain her silence. She knows when she's beaten, she just hopes what she tells the terrorist is so inconsequential that the information is of no use to her.

'Jake Boulder is working here as a bartender. He used to be a doorman in Utah, and when I looked him up online, I saw he got mixed up in a couple of investigations and ended up killing a serial killer or two. I helped him because you're not wearing masks, which leads me to think you're going to kill us all. There are no other plans to attack you and your men. So far as we're concerned, Boulder is our only hope.'

'Very good.' The woman points at the man by the door. 'Get them out of here.'

Sharon tries to remain impassive, but the agony of her arm is twisting her face and covering it in sweat. A part of her wants to tell this woman what an evil bitch she is, how inhuman her words and actions are making her, but there's no point. Either the woman knows and doesn't care, or she's such a psychopath that she feels nothing for anyone. The question is, what will happen to her, now the woman has the information she wants?

'You do know you won't get away with your plan. The police and the FBI will track you down and put you on death row for what you've done.'

'I think not. The state of Vermont hasn't used the death penalty since 1954.'

'You keep telling yourself that. Whatever you're up to, you're not doing it for nothing. The mass kidnapping, plus the murders you and your team of douchebags have committed, will count as a federal crime, and as such, they can overrule the state.'

'You seem well informed.'

Sharon gives a nonchalant shrug, glad to have prickled the female terrorist. 'I'm well read, that's all.'

'Are you now?' The female terrorist grabs a hardback book from a shelf and swings it at Sharon's injured arm. 'Well read this.'

Sharon tries to protect herself as the spine of the book slams into her arm, but the impact still causes her to squeal in pain.

Time and time again the terrorist swings the heavy hardback at Sharon's face until the Glaswegian passes out from the repeated blows.

Chapter 50

I crouch down and try to shrink into the roof. After making my way back from the main entrance, I'd circled round and picked up the trail of the welcoming committee.

As I expected, they've found a vantage point that lets them see the various ski slopes.

The place they've chosen to spring their ambush is the decked walkway that leads out to the balcony at the end of the dining room. They've smashed the lights, so they'll be hidden from the approaching cops, but I'm able to see their dark silhouettes against the falling snow.

Once I'd determined where they'd set up station, I ducked back and found the ladder that affords the maintenance man access to the roof.

With the design of RidgeTop Resort similar to that of a Swiss chalet, the roof has a steep pitch, which would be impossible to climb were it not for the snow guards that stick out at right angles to the tiles beneath.

The snow guards are designed to prevent the slippage of snow on the roof and, rather than the usual one or two rows, RidgeTop Resort has snow guards every four feet. It makes sense that they've more than doubled the required amount as it wouldn't do their reputation any favours to have wealthy customers caught beneath a deluge of snow that has slipped from the roof.

After cresting the roof's ridge, I made a slow climb down the opposite side until I was stationed above the three terrorists.

They have no idea I'm here, and while I'm confident I can shoot at least two of them before they realise where I am, I'm not ready in my mind to make a deadly ambush. If the police have heard my warning messages, or have managed to listen in to the conversation between Hannah and I, there's every chance they'll have aborted their original plan and come up with another.

They may also have enough guile about them to sneak the last few hundred yards up the hill and ambush the terrorists.

It's a welcome thought, and one that I'd love to become a reality.

I strain my ears and focus all my attention on listening for sounds of gunfire, or the roaring engine of a piste basher; nothing beyond the howl of the wind is audible, but it doesn't stop me concentrating.

If I wasn't listening like this I'd be worrying about the cold that is numbing my body. I'm still in my whiteout mode, although I've realised that, if I'm going to ambush these guys, I could have kept my jacket on and benefitted from its protection.

My eyes are on the terrorists below me and I have my submachine guns resting on the snow guard in front of me. I have my hands cupped in front of my mouth so they're getting warming breaths on them – there's no feeling in my fingers but they work when I tell them to bend or straighten.

A glance at my watch tells me the tactical team should be here by now. This renews my hope that they've either called off this plan or have added a decent layer of stealth to it.

My hopes are dashed when I see the terrorists below snap to attention. The one who's carrying the rocket launcher flips up what I assume is a sighting mechanism.

I strain my ears and hear a dull roar.

It must be the piste basher, which means the tactical team are about to come into view.

When I look down the slope I see a flash of lights fighting through the snow, as the noise of the engine gets louder.

I pick up the submachine guns and check their safeties are in the off position.

I'm now torn between two choices: I can ambush the terrorists before they spring their trap, which means I'll be facing three of them alone, or I can wait until the piste basher comes into view and use its distraction to aid my own attack.

What I know about rocket launchers can be written on the back of a stamp with a marker pen, but from what I've seen in the movies it takes a few seconds to aim one and, with a moving target travelling uphill in a snowstorm, I figure the guy firing it will take at least ten to twenty seconds to get his aim right.

That's more than enough time for me to stand and strafe the men below. It will also show their intent to murder, which is enough of a salve for my conscience to allow me to use deadly force.

The guy with the rocket launcher puts his eye to the sight, so I rise to a standing position with my feet braced against the snow guard.

I'm taking aim when I hear a whoosh and see a trail of smoke leave the rocket launcher. The way it curves off to one side, before being swallowed by the snowstorm, doesn't bode well for those in the piste basher.

The way that the terrorist had only pointed the launcher in the general direction of the piste basher, tells me the missile was either locked on to its target or it is heat seeking. After its slog up the mountain, the piste basher's engine will be more than hot enough to attract the missile's sensors. I figure their only hope is that there's a large tree between them that will act as a barrier. It's a forlorn hope and not one I cling to.

My fingers squeeze the triggers of the submachine guns I'm aiming at the three terrorists. Killing them is little more than an act of revenge. I could rationalise it as self-preservation, now it looks as though our rescuers have been slaughtered, but if that were the case I'd be scared. The one thing I'm not at this moment in time is frightened. My blood is pulsing though my veins and there's a redness at the edges of my vision. All thoughts of cold have vanished from my body, as have the feelings that I shouldn't act as judge, jury and executioner.

Chapter 51

The submachine guns kick and writhe in my hands, but I manage to control them enough to aim them at the terrorists. Two of the terrorists do that weird flailing dance you see in the movies when someone overacts being shot. That the terrorists aren't acting means the people in the movies have got it right, although it's never looked that way to me.

It's the guy with the rocket launcher and the guard on his right that I've hit. The third guy is standing dumbstruck, he's turning around, looking into the snow for the hidden shooter who's taken out his buddies, when my submachine guns click on empty.

My fingers are too numb to fumble about changing a magazine, so I leap off the edge of the roof towards him.

He's only a couple of yards away, and there's enough of a height difference between where we're standing for me to cross those yards in the air. His attention is still on the snow but he's turning towards his colleagues as I close in on him.

He's lifting his gun and I can see the frightened expression on his face.

My gun may not have any bullets – I've tossed one and lifted the other above my head – but as I drop beside the terrorist I bring it crashing down on his skull.

The impact creates a sickening crunch and jars the submachine gun from my hands.

He's reeling, his eyes are dazed, and this is the kind of opportunity fighters like me always make the most of.

When your opponent is in the state of disorientation the terrorist is experiencing, they're never more than a blow or two from being knocked out. His brain will be reverberating inside his head. There may be hairline fractures to his skull, or even an area that's been smashed in.

I doubt the latter has happened, though, as he's still vertical.

My hands grasp his gun and wrench it from him. It would be easy to turn the gun on him and blast away, but the beast inside me that's reddening my vision has a more primal idea.

I toss his weapon to one side and throw a punch at his jaw. The blow sends him staggering backwards but he stays on his feet.

A second punch follows the first and, when this one doesn't drop him, I grab his lapels and drag him onto the hardest headbutt I've ever delivered.

He drops to his knees, where he sways but doesn't topple.

A part of me admires his resilience, another, larger part, is glad of it. I want him to be tough, to be hard to put down. If that's the case, I can unload my anger onto him and make him feel real pain before I finish him off.

While he's still dazed, I strip him of his other weapons and send them over the balcony so they're out of his reach.

As I'm turning, ready to deliver a blow that will keep him in his current state, I feel a pair of arms wrap themselves around my legs, and a shoulder collides into my hip.

I fall backwards and feel his weight as he swarms over my body. His punches are aimed at my face, so I duck my chin onto my chest and use one arm to try and protect myself while the other mounts a counterattack. The bullet wound I'd picked up earlier howls in protest, but it's only a flesh wound, so while my arm hurts like hell, I can still use it.

I've been hit harder, but his desire to stay alive is powering his arms, so while he's not delivering the best of punches, it's fair to say that in his current condition he's giving it his best shot.

Had I not landed the first few blows, I'm sure he'd be hitting me with a lot more power and precision.

Rather than trying to land a punch on his head or throat, and risk my aim getting deflected by his swinging arms, I go for a different target.

When you're on your back with an opponent on top of you, it's as near as dammit impossible to punch upwards with enough force to rock the other fighter. This is because you can't draw back your arm far enough to gain a decent amount of momentum.

On the other hand, there's plenty of room to swing a more lateral punch.

I snake out my right hand, until it's pointing northwest compared to the rest of my body, and swing it downwards in an arc, lifting it as my hand curls into a solid fist.

My knuckles slam into his side just above his hip. I'm not sure whether the blow has landed far enough back to be a proper kidney punch, but it knocks a little more of the fight from him.

I give up using my left arm for defence and use it to grab his left wrist.

This time when I repeat the punch my left arm is pulling him across my body, exposing a large area to my right hand.

I throw three more blows and then buck him off me.

I don't plan to clamber on top of him after showing him how to get out of the situation, so I roll the other way and bring myself back to standing.

I'm sure when I have time to put a hand to my face I'll feel a mass of swelling and a broken nose, but self-examination can wait until later. This is the one positive side effect of being so cold.

The terrorist is on his hands and knees in front of me.

One well-placed kick at his head will end the fight here and now, but I'm not finished punishing him yet.

My kick breaks at least three of his ribs and lifts him two inches.

His arms buckle and his head slumps down to the snow, but his hips are still raised enough to make his balls a target that's too inviting not to swing a foot at.

He screams in agony and rolls onto his side.

I grab one of the stalactites hanging from the eaves and give it a vicious jerk.

It comes loose in my hand leaving me holding a ten-inch stiletto.

I thump the sole of my shoe into the terrorist's shoulder so he's laid on his back. The skin covering his throat doesn't offer much resistance to the stalactite, and neither does his Adam's apple or his larynx.

When I turn my back on him, frothy blood is spilling from his throat and running into his collar. He's got a minute to live, maybe ninety seconds if he's unlucky and his will to stay alive drags out his suffering.

With the three terrorists taken out, I turn my attention to the piste basher.

As I peer through the snow, the only sign of it that I can see is a yellow glow flickering in the distance. My subconscious heard an explosion when I was shooting at the terrorists, but if the rocket had missed its target, I'd be staring down the barrel of a cop's gun by now.

I leave the balcony and set off towards the piste basher. Not for one second do I think anyone has survived the rocket blast, but there's no way I can take the chance that someone has, and I've left them to die by not checking.

Chapter 52

When he hears his name, Leslie pulls himself to his feet with the help of a table. The night has gone on a lot longer than he's used to. As a rule of thumb, he's in bed by ten thirty and asleep within five minutes.

His days start at four thirty when, after a light breakfast, he opens his laptop. The three hours before Lily comes down offer him far greater peace to work than his office does. There's no ringing phones or knocks at the door to distract him, just the muted strains of Bach or Beethoven.

For him to stay up until midnight is a stretch, to go past one in the morning has sapped what little strength his frail body possesses. Regardless of his own poor health, he offers a hand to Lily and helps her to her feet.

He knows what will happen when they're taken back to the office. As soon as the first person to have been shepherded into the office was taken in again after midnight, he knew that he and Lily, along with every other one of the hostages, would be called upon for a second visit.

The only hostages who've not been escorted into the office are the staff, and to Leslie that makes perfect sense. With all relevant respect, the staff aren't important or wealthy people; therefore, they are of little or no worth to the terrorists.

The customers, on the other hand, are all people who enjoy a certain status in life. They have money or power; in most cases they have both.

Whether terrorists kill or extort people for political, religious or financial gain doesn't matter to Leslie as he walks to the office with his wife's hand clasped in his. He knows what they've already had from him, and he has no choice but to give them the same again.

The way he had been forced to do as instructed rankled him, and went against all his principles, but when the muzzle of a pistol was placed against Lily's temple, he'd caved and done their bidding.

A part of him knows that every hostage's visit to the office has played out the same way, with two exceptions.

He might not like his wife very much at times, and the love he feels for her is more like the one he has for his siblings, but he cares enough for Lily to abandon his principles rather than his wife.

The office is the same as it was the last time he was there, with one notable exception.

Where the female terrorist had been calm and in control earlier, there is now a palpable change to her manner. She is strung out and there's a different set to her jaw. Previously it was determined, now it juts out with an angry challenge to every target her eyes land upon. The hand that's holding the pistol has white knuckles and, even to Leslie's untrained eye, she looks as if she's about to have a psychotic meltdown.

Leslie follows her arm and takes the seat she is pointing to and prepares to follow her instructions again.

'Are you going to do as you're told?'

'Yes, ma'am.'

As craven as his compliance may be, Leslie doesn't want to provoke the female terrorist. He reaches forward and starts to do her bidding.

A significant part of him is cursing her for the way she's forcing him to act against his will. Not only does following her instructions go against every one of his principles, but he also knows that once this is all over, the events of the evening will affect many hundreds, possibly thousands, of people.

Despite all this, he can't stop himself from admiring the woman's ingenuity in not only coming up with the scheme but finding the right people to help her execute it too.

Chapter 53

It's not hard to see where the piste basher is; the flames licking at its body make a most effective beacon.

As I wade through the knee-deep snow towards the stricken vehicle, I make sure that my hands are above my head. If any of the cops have survived the blast they will be mighty pissed and more than a little trigger happy.

I've claimed an assault rifle from one of the two terrorists acting as guards for the guy with the rocket launcher. I've strapped it to my back so it's out of sight until I can establish my credentials.

Walking downhill in this fashion, through deep, cloying snow, isn't easy – especially when I'm wearing dress shoes – but I manage to get within a hundred yards of the piste basher without slipping and landing on my ass.

Now that I'm close, I call out as I approach the wreckage. I don't see any signs of life, but if any of the cops have survived, they've probably found cover and will be lying in wait for terrorists to arrive. In their position, it's exactly what I'd do.

As I'm covering the last twenty or so yards, the vague shapes of the machine become clear.

The piste basher has been ruined by the explosion, which has ripped apart the area where the cab would sit above its mighty engine. Behind it, what looks to have been a trailer converted into an alpine-style tour bus, is decimated above its tracks. Its sides are thin aluminium sections topped with Perspex and it's covered with a Perspex sheet, which must be to allow its passengers to see the stars on a moonlit night.

The flames from the piste basher are throwing weird shapes around while illuminating the trailer enough for me to look inside.

Not one of the bodies I can see silhouetted in the trailer is moving. The Perspex has been more or less shredded away to nothing by what I imagine was shrapnel from the explosion.

I call out my name and announce I'm not a terrorist as I circle the vehicle.

I also make a point of mentioning I have an assault rifle strapped to my back. The last thing I want is for a hidden cop to see it and consider me a threat.

The more I walk round the piste basher, the less I worry about getting a bullet in my back. The trailer has twelve seats and each one of them has a body slumped on top of it.

Those in the rear look as if they're sleeping, but when I reach through a hole in the Perspex and nudge the nearest one to me I get no reaction.

I take a step towards the front of the trailer and look back at the man I nudged. His face is more or less unmarked, but there's a thumb-sized chunk of metal protruding from his throat. The man next to him carries similar wounds, and as I move further towards the front of the trailer the injuries worsen.

The men in the front row have borne the full force of the explosion and the shrapnel it created. They're missing limbs, and in one case, a head.

Even as I'm trying to comprehend the horror of what I'm seeing, my brain is firing off at tangents. Part of it is fanning the flames of the MacDonald blood in my veins, which in turn is creating all kinds of murderous feelings, while another, more practical, part is taking in the straps that are holding the men to the seats, and seeing the logic of them in a vehicle that is designed to go up even the steepest of slopes.

The heat from the fire would be welcome to my frozen body were it not for the fact that its source has spelled death for a dozen brave cops, and the man whose job it was to drive this behemoth.

To warm myself by its flames is wrong on every level. I'd rather freeze to death on the mountainside than warm myself on what's nothing more than a pyre.

The final part of my brain is troubling me with thoughts I'm all too familiar with. These are ideas I've carried too far, for too long. The feeling that people have died because of me and my actions is back with a vengeance.

This time the guilt is telling me that my ideals are wrong, that I should have killed the three terrorists before they had the chance to fire the rocket launcher, that my inaction had cost thirteen men their lives.

Whichever way I look at it, I know if I'd acted sooner they'd still be alive. By staying my hand until I had what I felt was just cause for the execution of the terrorists, I'd condemned all the men travelling on the piste basher and its trailer to death.

I force the guilt from my mind and use my anger as a stimulant to power my legs as I turn and head towards RidgeTop Resort.

The time for being reactive has long passed, as has the idea of taking down the terrorists without killing any of them. From now on, I plan to use whatever methods I can to ensure the safety of the hostages.

With the cops out of commission, it'll be an hour or so before their superiors in the valley bottom give up hope of them returning and call for another team. From there, it'll be an hour for them to get to the valley, plus another hour or so to travel uphill.

That's provided they even try coming this way again.

If they do, the soonest they'll be here is three hours. Three hours after that, the first wisps of daylight will be showing, which means there's a strong possibility that whoever is in charge of the cops won't act until daylight. They'll be wondering if the piste basher has had an accident, or if the terrorists have forced the tactical team into a standoff by aiming their guns at the heads of the hostages.

The police won't want to act without new information, that they've already done so much on my say so is little short of a miracle.

So far as I'm concerned, three hours is far too long to leave the hostages in Hannah's hands; six is unthinkable. She's planning to murder them all, and even though I've dismantled her bombs, she has enough firepower to gun them down.

My breath is labouring as I trudge my way back up the slope, but I don't care about being breathless, I have a rifle in my hands and I'm looking forward to pulling its trigger.

For the first time since spotting the three terrorists leaving the resort, a different part of my brain speaks to me.

It's the limbic system that is talking to me, telling me there's danger ahead.

I know how the so called 'sixth sense' works: it's all to do with experience, coupled with details that are absorbed by the subconscious rather than the conscious brain.

The details trigger a search-engine-like trawl through the brain's experiences and known facts until it's sure of itself, and then it warns the rest of the body.

Right now, my sixth sense is screaming at me to be careful, that there's a danger on the slopes that isn't anything to do with the conditions or the risk of avalanche. It's telling me there's a hunter out there and I'm its prey.

Chapter 54

The pain is worse than anything she's experienced before, including childbirth, but that doesn't worry Sharon. To her the pain is welcome, it tells her she's alive and, despite the beating she's taken, there's no lasting damage to her head.

If the crazed terrorist had broken her skull, Sharon knows she'd either not be feeling anything, or her head would be aching a lot more than it does.

From what Sharon remembers of the beating, the book wielded by the female terrorist had been slammed into her face rather than her skull.

Even through her agony, Sharon is aware of the other woman's intent. As she'd done with the singer, her brutality had been aimed at inflicting psychological as well as physical pain.

Where she'd cut the singer's chin and rested her knife underneath one of her breasts, the terrorist had chosen to ruin Sharon's looks.

It didn't just speak of a cold ruthlessness, but also an inner vanity. For a woman to do such a thing, she had to be heartless – that much was a given – yet, so far as Sharon was concerned, the woman's attacks were most likely fuelled by the things she most feared.

Therefore, looks are important to the terrorist. The threat to the singer's breast also speaks of personal fear. Nobody wants to lose a part of their body, but breasts are by and large a part of the human body that are often removed for medical reasons. They're also tampered with for cosmetic and egotistical reasons, but that won't be the case with the woman.

For her it is all about fear.

Sharon couldn't help but surmise that someone close to the terrorist had a horror story to do with losing their breasts, and because of this, an irrational fear has settled in her mind. It's irrelevant whether or not her mother had a mastectomy that got infected, or didn't cut out all the cancer, a chink in the woman's armour has been exposed and Sharon knows what lies beneath. The terrorist's vanity is her Achilles heel, and while Sharon doesn't yet know how to make the most of that fact, she's at least got the advantage of knowing one of the woman's weaknesses.

So far as her own injuries are concerned, Sharon isn't bothered about lasting effects. Her face is a white-hot ball of agony, but she can breathe, and one of her eyes opens enough to let her see the person crouched over her. During her time in Afghanistan she witnessed the injuries caused by IEDs, bullets, and other weapons of that most vicious of wars. She'd met up with comrades who'd been invalided out of the army and had found a way to cope with their disability.

Sharon is self-aware enough to know that looks are superficial, that what matters is the person beneath, and she possesses enough self-confidence to have never worried about her own looks.

What's of far greater concern to her is there's been no indication that Boulder has raised the alarm, and it's been a long time since any of the terrorists left to go after him.

'Jeez, Sharon, are you okay?'

The speaker is one of Sharon's fellow servers, she can't remember her name, but that's nothing new. The youngsters who take jobs here seem to change every week or two, so she's long given up trying to memorise who they are. Sweetheart, darling and honey are perfectly good names for either sex, and though she doesn't like to admit it, Sharon's aware she's old enough to use them whenever she chooses.

The question is a stupid one. Sharon's face has been smashed in and, while she's alive, she's a long way from being okay.

'Aye.'

The one word answer costs her dearly. She didn't know until now, but speaking a word that is nothing more than a letter tells her that her jaw is broken.

The server misunderstands Sharon's answer and reaches a hand forward.

'Does your eye bother you? Here, let me open it for you.'

The touch on Sharon's closed eyelid is gentle, but to Sharon it feels as if molten metal is being poured over her face.

She bats the girl's hand away and resorts to a hand signal the girl can't fail to understand.

When she lowers her finger and focuses on the girl she sees nothing but anguish.

Despite her pain, Sharon can't stay angry at the sorrowful girl, so she twists her hand until she's got a closed fist and a raised thumb.

What's nagging at her is that she knows she spotted something when she was in the office that had given her a clue as to why the terrorists were meeting with the customers. The fact her brain won't let her remember what she saw is frustrating, but right now she needs to focus on staying conscious.

Chapter 55

Rather than head back up the slope the way I came down, I've made my way across to the safety netting that borders all the ski runs. My reasoning for this is that I've left a trail for the terrorists to follow, and if there is someone out here hunting me, I'm not going to walk right into them.

I'm about a quarter of the way back up the slope when my limbic brain stops whispering in my ear and raises its voice to a shout.

I halt and swing the automatic rifle from side to side as I peer into the billowing snow.

My eyes don't find any human shapes, so I rotate until I've scanned every compass point. I still don't see anything, but my brain hasn't stopped shouting.

My granny in Glasgow would call it a 'fey feeling', and I'm wont to agree with her assessment. The old Scottish term is more than apt for the impending sense of doom that's enveloping me.

I'm aware I may well be jumping at shadows or the swirls of the snow, but my instincts are telling me there's a threat to my life. I'm back in a cocoon of isolation and, because of that, I'm unnerved. I don't want to overreact, but every few seconds another shape created by the whirling, shifting snow makes my heart leap, and my arms swing the automatic rifle towards an imagined threat.

I'm effectively going back to the resort, risking my life, in an attempt to save the other hostages, so it's not the danger that's spooking me; it's the unknown, and the claustrophobia that's being created by the darkness and the snowstorm. If the guard from the resort door had heard the gunfire, he'd had two options. The first: coming to help his buddies, and the second: going to get help.

If he'd gone with the first option I'd be dead by now, as he'd have arrived while I was fighting with the last member of their welcoming committee. So either he hadn't heard, or he's on his way down the slope with one or more of his colleagues.

There's no way of knowing what he did or didn't hear, but I've learned to trust the warnings my limbic brain gives me, and that's why I'm moving with every scrap of caution I can inject into my trek back to the resort.

Every step I take, I sweep the rifle's barrel through a one-eighty arc.

For the next ten yards I see nothing but snow and the unmistakable outline of one of the mighty pine trees that flank the ski runs. As much as the safety netting does, they delineate the ski runs, while also adding to the beauty of the environment.

I keep moving, torn between the need to get back to the resort before the terrorists kill any more of their hostages, and the urge to listen to the warnings my brain is shouting at me.

When I reach the first corner of the slope, I pause long enough to do a three-sixty turn, but again I see nothing that resembles a human being.

I set off again. With every yard I cover without incident, the more I convince myself that my fey feelings are mistaken and I'm jumping at shadows.

I'm inclined to point the finger of blame for my jumpiness at the cold. It's seeped into every part of me now and, as much as the slog uphill is strenuous enough to shorten my breath and get my heart pumping, I've been out in the snowstorm for so long that my limbs are chilled to the bone.

My ears, fingers and toes all feel as though they've been clubbed with a mallet, and there's a woolliness to my thinking I've never experienced without being drunk.

There's nothing much I can do about the cold, so I keep going. When I get back to the resort I can swap my sodden clothes for whatever I can find in the maintenance shed. Getting out of the wet clothes will help me, but only to a point. The decision to shed the padded waterproof jacket now seems like a stupid mistake. I don't know enough of the signs to recognise if I'm getting hypothermia, but it's got to be a possibility – as has frostbite.

These concerns aren't something I can do anything about until I get back to the resort, get out of the cold and find some dry clothing.

I follow the fencing for another hundred yards. I'm not too familiar with the exact layout of the ski run, but I judge that I'm maybe within a hundred yards of the run's starting point.

My arms are still sweeping the rifle through its arc, but I'm not sure I could pull the trigger if I saw someone, and the rifle seems to have quadrupled in weight since I picked it up.

'Drop your weapon.'

The instruction is shouted into my left ear as a pistol is pushed into my right.

I go to do as I'm told, but my hands are so cold I have to shake them before they'll release the rifle. Rather than get shot, I warn the man with the pistol what I'm doing.

The fact he's caught me means I'm going to die. Either by his hand or he'll take me back to Hannah. All he has to do to finish me off is pull his trigger once.

As much as I don't want to be taken back and handed over to Hannah, I plan to obey his every command – the longer I'm alive, the more chance there is that I'll have an opportunity to escape.

If I were a betting man, I'd figure my odds of surviving the rest of the night are somewhere around a million to one.

'Walk.'

The shouted instruction is accompanied by a firm jab to the back of my head with the pistol.

I'm still facing uphill, so that's the direction I go.

Every time I slip a little he jabs at me with the pistol, but I'm too cold to feel any of the pain he might be inflicting on me.

It's obvious he's lain in wait until I've come up the slope and stepped in behind me. How I missed him is a matter for another time; right now, every brain cell I possess is bent towards getting me out of this situation.

The ground levels out a little and I know we're cresting from the ski run to the level area at the resort. This means I'm less than fifty yards from the resort and he's less than fifty yards from getting help.

Something hard and metallic slams into my head with enough force to stun me.

'Don't give me an excuse, buddy. Much as I want to see you screaming in agony, begging for death, I'm quite happy to kill you right here.'

I don't answer him. I just keep trudging forward as slowly as I dare.

Chapter 56

Nathan slams the door of his control room and looks at the police captain and the resort manager; neither man looks happy at the situation and Nathan shares their sentiments.

The press having arrived is a complication none of them wanted, but that's the least of their worries as it was inevitable the press would show up at some point.

They haven't heard from the tactical team since they set off. This was part of the plan, lest their communications be intercepted, but they're twenty minutes overdue for arrival at RidgeTop Resort: as soon as they had made contact, Roger Knightly was supposed to radio down to let them know they'd arrived and that the rescue mission was underway.

Having seen their serious faces and the equipment they were carrying, Nathan was convinced they'd succeed in their mission against the people who've taken over the resort. Each man was grim and taciturn, completely focused on their last-minute weapons check. Their eyes were clear and bore the intense concentration of those who had battle experience.

Every one of them wore winter camouflage clothing and they were carrying enough weaponry to stage a military coup.

Just looking at them, Nathan had felt confident they'd triumph. Except they were late checking in.

With no GPS transponder on Knightly's piste basher there is no way of knowing where they are. The police captain had voiced his doubts about Roger's ability, falling silent when the resort manager told him he was wrong.

Nathan can tell the captain isn't convinced that Knightly hasn't gone off course or been delayed, but he's kept his opinions to himself so far.

Time and again the reporters bang on the door of the control room, but Nathan had twisted the key over to keep them out. Their presence is a nuisance that everyone could do without.

Olly Attwood is a decent enough man, even if he always puts the needs of the business ahead of any other consideration. He's a company man through and through: a confirmed bachelor, he has no life outside his work, and his habit of working sixteen hour days during the entire ski season is known to every employee. Nathan knows he will be as worried about the adverse publicity as he is about the danger to those who've been taken hostage.

Captain Ogden is a brute of a man with an upper body that reminds Nathan of a rodeo bull's front shoulders. The square cut to his silvering hair accentuates the image, and it doesn't take much imagining for Nathan to picture the captain as the kind of cop who bulldozes his way to a result using brawn rather than brain. The man's rank might give him authority, but it is his physique and personality, not his status, that makes him the alpha male.

Even the battle-hardened men of the tactical team had shown him a deference that spoke of respect and admiration rather than lip service to his rank.

The control room is too small for a man of Ogden's size and intensity to pace back and forth, but that doesn't stop him doing it. Attwood has brought them all here to draw the press away from any of RidgeWay Resort's customers.

'At what point do you give up waiting to hear from your men and admit that they've befallen misfortune?'

Ogden whirls at the question from Attwood, but Nathan can see the fire in him cool as quickly as it has flared. From the way he scowls, Nathan is sure the captain has been thinking the same thing and he doesn't like his thoughts. Whether he likes it or not, it's a valid question that needs answered – in his own mind at least.

The captain glances at the digital wall clock. 'In another twenty-five minutes. If we don't hear from them by then, it's time to look at plan B.' He shifts his eyes to Attwood. 'And before you ask, I'm still working on plan B.'

'I'm sorry, Captain, but that's not good enough. With staff included, there's almost two hundred people up at RidgeTop, you've got to do something to save them.'

'And what would you have me do? Send them up in a cable car so they can be shot to ribbons? Maybe you think I can parachute some men in? Tell me, Mr Civilian Hotel Manager, how do you think that will end? If I send twenty men to do that, five will miss the target by a half mile, another five will injure themselves on landing, and the other ten will be lucky not to sail right into an ambush. I wouldn't presume to tell you how to do your job, don't try and tell me how to do mine.'

Nathan is surprised at the way Attwood has stood up to Ogden. He's never seen the man deal with confrontation in such a positive manner. 'Surely there's something you can do, send another team up in a piste basher?'

'Say I had another team at my disposal, do you have another trailer? Do you know what's happened to the first team that went up the hill? Until we know what's happened to them, I'm not risking any more lives on foolhardy whims. For all we know, they could be buried by an avalanche, or the machine has broken down or been driven into a crevasse, or maybe, just maybe, those men are up there doing what they're paid to do and risking their lives so the people who've been taken hostage are returned home safe. You've seen the way the snow is falling, it's got to be twice as bad up there. As well as fighting the terrorists, my men will have to wade through at least a couple of feet of snow. I respectfully suggest you shut up and wait for my men to do their job.'

Attwood falls silent, but his expression suggests he's still expecting the captain to come up with a solution.

Ogden points at Nathan as he backs away from the door. 'You. Unlock that door and open it wide.'

Nathan does as he's told and, as soon as the door opens, Ogden is on the move. By the time he reaches the door his strides are long and determined. The three members of the press don't stand a chance of halting his progress as he barges his way through them.

To Nathan, everything the captain has said makes perfect sense.

Like an expectant father waiting for the sound of a wail outside a delivery suite, there's little they can do until they hear from the people dealing with the situation.

Nathan isn't religious, but he considers saying a prayer for all the innocents at RidgeTop Resort.

Chapter 57

There have been a few occasions in my life when I've wished I could turn back the clock and have a second chance to do things a different way. If I had that opportunity now, I'd be travelling up the other side of the slope and I'd be free of the man with the gun at my back.

I know with a certainty that brooks no argument, if I let myself get taken inside the resort, not only am I a dead man, but I'll die in agony as Hannah takes out her anger on me.

However, reading is my main source of entertainment – crime and thriller novels in particular – and when you've read as many thrillers as I have, you can't help but osmose some of the techniques that the characters use to get themselves out of perilous situations.

One particular book I've read has stuck with me more than others. The lead character is the kind of idiot who keeps getting himself into situations where he has a gun pointed at him. The various ways he escapes are so laughable that I watched a few online videos. By the time I put down my tablet, I'd wasted two hours checking to see if the character's ways of disarming aggressors holding weapons against him were recommended techniques or something the author had made up. My conclusion was an even split between the two.

I can't remember the exact details on how to deal with someone pointing a gun at my back, but the basics are still in my head.

I'd be more confident if my limbs weren't numb; if I didn't suspect the man behind me had been trained by a military instructor, I'd fancy my chances a whole lot more.

Every second I spend worrying is a second less to act before it's too late.

I pretend to slip a little so he puts the gun against my back to push me forward.

He makes the mistake of complying. I can now feel the gun pressing against my back, about two inches to the right of my spine. Its position, along with the way he'd ground it into my right ear, tells me he's right handed.

I whirl counter-clockwise, hoping against hope I can move quickly enough when encumbered by the snow.

As I turn, my left arm sweeps up over his gun arm, and snakes into a position where my forearm is applying upwards pressure on his elbow, while his forearm is trapped by my armpit. He can pull the trigger all he likes, but his pistol is six inches behind my back.

My right arm curls inwards so my elbow can crash against his jaw with as much force as I can put behind it.

I hear the snap of his jaw breaking and go to lift my right knee into his groin.

My knee collides with his thigh, so I give his jaw another crack with my elbow.

There's no questioning the man's toughness, so I drop my right hand and throw a punch at his groin.

I don't get a perfect connection but it's good enough to double him over.

Even as his knees are buckling I can feel him trying to turn his pistol so he can take a shot at me.

To counteract this, I wrench his gun arm into an arm bar and drive my right elbow down onto his with every scrap of strength I can call upon.

His elbow doesn't stand a chance.

I snatch his gun from where it's buried in the snow, put it to the back of his head and force my forefinger to pull the trigger. It's not hard for me to end his life, considering his crimes, but it takes one hell of an effort to curl my finger.

The single shot kills him outright and he plunges face first into the snow.

When I roll him over to relieve him of his other weapons, I see his neck is ringed with tattoos.

I'd expected him to have more than just a pistol and a knife, but part of me isn't surprised. I'm pleased to find he's stuffed my pistol into his waistband as well.

He'd captured me with stealth, not force; his way was to sneak not charge.

I appreciate he has mimicked my tactics – it's a sign of respect, even if he hadn't realised it.

So far as his death is concerned, I feel nothing. The second he stuck his gun in my ear was the moment he signed his death warrant. After that, we were locked on a course that would see us engage in a fight to the death.

I could have spared his life and kneecapped him, but he would either have died a slow, agonising death from exposure, or his cries for help would have been heard and alerted his comrades.

How he died is neither here nor there, but the other terrorists must not know what state I'm in – that cannot be allowed to happen.

I know I need to act, but I also know I need to look after myself as well.

My next destination is the maintenance shed so I can once again pillage some warmer clothes.

Ed's range of clothing isn't what you'd call good for stealth, but what it lacks in camouflage it more than makes up for in warmth.

I switch my shirt for a thick padded jacket and remove the T-shirt from my head and toss it in a corner.

My rummaging reveals a set of quilted coveralls that have a distinctly unhealthy smell to them. I don't care what they smell like, so long as they keep me warm. I whip off the jacket and pull on the coveralls over my shoes and trousers. As I fumble with the zipper I can feel the coveralls reflecting my body's internal heat back at me.

The jacket goes on over the top of them.

The next thing my search uncovers is another woolly hat. It's ratty, dirty and has a smell that makes the coveralls seem like a floral bouquet, but it'll replace the one I lost during one of the fights and it'll keep my head warm; that's good enough for me.

My new outfit may be second-hand clothes that stink like a rotten skunk, but the way they're warming my body makes me feel as if I'm dressed like a king.

My new clothes don't allow me to keep my weapons anywhere handy, so I find a couple of pieces of rope and tie one around my waist as a makeshift belt. It's tighter than I'm comfortable with but I can stuff the pistols between it and my clothes. As holsters go, it's not going to win any style points, but it serves its purpose.

My next move is to cut a two-foot length from the other piece of rope. This gets stuffed into my jacket pocket as it'll come in useful should I want to strangle someone from behind.

I find a pair of gloves but they're heavily padded, and when I try them on I find I can't feed my finger through the pistol's trigger guard.

As much as I'm tempted to cut off the glove's forefinger, I don't. Should I get into another fight where punches are thrown, I need to know every blow will deliver the maximum effect.

For the time being I keep them on, but I know that when I leave this shed, the gloves will be off in every conceivable way.

Ever since the fight with Tattoo Neck, I've been considering what my next move should be. It would be suicidal to charge into the resort with guns blazing. At best, I'd only manage to kill one terrorist before I'd be gunned down.

With only two pistols as distance weapons, I need to come up with a different plan to the one I had when I was heading up the hill with a rifle in my hands.

It's a bit of a gamble going back to where I'd left the welcoming committee, but I know there should still be an assault rifle there. If I can find that, my arsenal will be a lot deadlier.

I peel the gloves from my hands and grasp the door handle. My hands are now twice as compliant as they were, but they're still a long way from normal.

It's as I'm swinging open the door that a new plan comes to me.

The plan hinges on me finding a better weapon than a pistol, but if I can do that, I should be able to put Hannah on the back foot for a change.

Chapter 58

Ivy scowls at Alfonse and tries to believe that Jake isn't at the resort that has been overrun by terrorists. No matter which way she looks at it, she knows that, if there's trouble, Jake will be mixed up in it.

She knows her son has a way about him that draws conflict. Ever since his first day at school he'd been in one scrape after another. There is no badness in him, just a point-blank refusal to back down from any challenge. He'd squared off against boys three and four years his senior on more than one occasion during his schooldays. He may have lost a few fights, but he'd never surrendered. Nor had he learned how to avoid trouble.

On most occasions, he'd be standing firm on his principles. Alfonse was a target for schoolyard bullies until Jake had stepped in. Others had been protected by him as well and, if he saw the slightest injustice, he'd step in to right the wrong and restore what he believed was balance.

However, she also knew there were times when he was spoiling for a fight and nothing other than a punch-up would sate his urge.

In her more reflective moments, she accepted that some of his demons were created by the way his father had abandoned them, and some were created by her. She knows she's not the greatest mother in the world, but she's done the best she could by her children and she's proud of them both.

The days after Cameron left had been the hardest of her life. He'd left her with two children under five years old and no source of income. She'd had to work three jobs to make ends meet. Had her mother not been able to look after the children, Ivy would have ended up on benefits, which for her would have been the ultimate sign of failure.

They didn't have much for the first few years, but what they did have had been bought with money she'd earned. Taking benefits would have been the easy option, but Ivy wasn't one to accept handouts from any source; they were her kids and therefore her responsibility. It was down to her to put food on their plates and clothes on their backs.

A month after Jake had turned twelve she met a man who changed her life. Neill Boulder was a relaxed guy with an easy laugh and a quiet confidence.

When he'd asked her to marry him and move to Casperton, she'd said yes without hesitation. A new life in a warmer clime had always been her dream, and as much as Glasgow was part of her soul, she'd begun fearing for Jake's future. There was no doubt he was smart enough to get a good job that would see him earn a decent wage, but what kept her awake at nights was his growing propensity for fighting.

Glasgow was full of hard men and the last thing she wanted was for her son to get sucked into that culture. While his morals and principles would prevent him from seeking out a life of crime, sooner or later he'd go to defend someone, or correct some situation he'd perceived as wrong, and find himself up against one of the hard men. When that happened, he'd either get the pasting of his life, or he'd win and draw the wrong kind of attention to himself.

At the time there were many small gangs in Glasgow, but they were all affiliated to one of the two crime firms who ran the city. Every one of these gangs employed hard men as their muscle and, should Jake best one of them, retribution would be sought.

An even greater fear for her was that the gangs would entice Jake into their world. Threats against herself and Jake's sister could be used to manipulate him, and once he'd done a job or two for them, they'd have enough on him to use blackmail to keep him under control.

The proposal from Neill couldn't have been timed better, and Casperton was too small to be of interest to crime gangs of any size. By the time Jake had got himself fully integrated into the local society, he'd had enough punch ups to establish his position in the town's pecking order and had found a job that kept him out of trouble.

'Mrs B, look at this, will you?'

When Ivy peers at the screen she can feel the blood draining from her face. Jake's name is in the police report as the person who'd raised the alarm about the events at RidgeTop Resort.

Jake had told her that Alfonse could get into any database, but until now she hadn't believed him. She'd always thought he was embellishing things and mocking her. Computers aren't something she understands, beyond online shopping and basic searches, but here, in front of her eyes, she can see that Alfonse has tapped into the Vermont police's computer and is accessing their communications about the suspected terrorist attack.

There are lots of other communications, but none of them are important to her. All that matters, is that her son is in a situation where terrorists are present.

She knows her son, and not just in the way a mother normally knows their child. She has a deeper understanding than most. The knowledge of how far he'll go to protect others is the greatest burden she carries, and the fact he's laden with guilt and grief means he'll be compelled to fight back against the terrorists.

Details on the terrorists are sketchy at best, but that doesn't reassure her. In her mind, there are dozens of gun-toting bad guys facing off against an empty-handed Jake.

She hasn't seen her son since he left town after the business in New York, but there's no doubt in her mind that he won't have undergone a personality transplant in the months that have passed.

'What will become of my boy?'

The question is a rhetorical one, but Alfonse takes her hands in his so she looks up at him.

'Jake will do what he will do. Knowing him, he'll find a way to take those terrorists out. What it'll be, I have no idea, but, Mrs B, I trust him to find a way.'

'And if he doesn't?'

Alfonse looks away. When he speaks, Ivy has to strain to hear him. 'Forgive my honesty, but if he can't find a way, I think he'll die trying rather than quit. He couldn't protect Taylor, and in his mind, saving the hostages' lives will atone for some of the guilt he feels about her.'

Ivy doesn't reply.

She can't.

Not because she thinks Alfonse is wrong.

But because she thinks he's right.

She'd wanted him to tell her something, anything, else. Instead, he's confirmed the worries she's been harbouring since hearing of the attack on the mountain.

She knows Jake will put his life on the line for others and, while she admires his courage, she can't get her head around the fear that her son may already be dead.

Chapter 59

Ileave the maintenance shed behind me and creep through the snow. After being ambushed by Tattoo Neck I'm more cautious than ever. The extra level of caution slows down my progress, but I'm comfortable with being a little slower if it keeps me alive.

My first destination is the decking that runs out to the balcony – the more weapons I have the better. Plus, what I do or don't find there will let me know how much the terrorists know.

If the bodies of the three terrorists have been moved, and their weapons are gone, I'll know Hannah has sent someone out to look for them. On the other hand, if their orders were to remain outside in case of further rescue attempts, it's possible that she's unaware I've taken them out and I'll find them lying where they dropped.

When I get within sight of the first part of the decking, I give the whole area a slow, careful scan. It's hard to look for movement when snow is billowing and swirling around, so I scan more than once before crossing the open area at a slow trot.

I press my back against the wall of the resort and check both ways before moving along the decking.

There are three large mounds halfway along the decking. They're semi-covered by the falling snow, but there's no mistaking they're human shapes. I slide my feet through the snow until one of my feet bumps against something.

I thrust my hands down and retrieve the rocket launcher. With it stood against the wall I continue dragging my feet along until they bump against something else.

This time my hands emerge with an assault rifle.

I brush the snow from the three bodies and find two more clips of ammunition for the rifle.

As I'm bent over the third body, I notice a smaller mound in the snow. In the half light, from the outside lights that the terrorists didn't smash – I'm not sure why they're working when the electricity has been cut, but I figure they double as emergency lights that will work in the event of a power failure – it looks to be about two feet long and one wide. When I brush the snow from it, I find an ammunition case.

I haul it from the snow and take a quick look around me before reaching for the clasps. There's no one about so I open the case's lid and reveal a pair of rockets for the launcher. They're encased in moulded padding, but that's not what's got my attention.

Their presence is what's gripped me. I'd come here looking for an assault rifle, and I'd have been more than happy to get one. Instead, I've gone one better and not just got the rifle, but also a rocket launcher, and ammo for them both.

I don't yet know how the rocket launcher can be of use to me, but I'm glad it's in my hands and not theirs.

I remove one of the spare rockets from the case and slide it on the end of the rocket launcher. It glides down and there's a soft thunk when it's in position. I lift the launcher up so I can examine it in the faint glow.

There's a safety catch and a trigger, but I don't see any other controls. I had expected it to have some complicated mechanism that required a series of actions to activate it, but when I think about it, that doesn't make sense. When used in a combat situation by army grunts, it needs to be as simple as possible to use.

Now I've got it prepared, I can start to execute the next part of my plan.

I prop the rocket launcher against the corner of the resort wall and peer round the timber cladding.

The man patrolling outside the front door is still pacing back and forth. Other than the falling snow there's not a scrap of cover in the thirty yards between us.

There's no way I can use stealth to sneak up on him; all I can do is ambush him, so I wait until he walks towards me and, as soon as he turns, I dash from where I am and head straight for him.

I'm gambling on a couple of things: that I can get close enough to shoot him before he hears me coming and turns his gun on me, and that there are no other terrorists waiting just inside the door.

The thick layer of snow coupled with the howling wind muffle my approach, but he's at the end of his route by the time I'm within five yards of him, so I squeeze the trigger on the assault rifle.

It spits bullets and I have to wrestle with it to keep it trained on him.

I see him jerk backwards, and then his head snaps to the side.

He slumps in a heap, but I keep running towards him.

I skid to a halt and reach down to grab his collar with one hand and his rifle with another.

It's a struggle, but I manage to drag him until the resort's main entrance is only just visible through the snowstorm and lay him on his back.

My next move is to untie the laces of his boots.

I haul him into a sitting position and press his shoulders forward until I can tie the laces of his left boot around his right wrist. Once both of his arms are tied to his boots, I claim his weapons and retreat to get ready to put the next part of my plan into action.

When I reach the end of the decking, I tease my head around the corner and see what I'd both hoped and expected to see.

The sliding glass doors that form the front wall of the dining room, and provide easy access to the balcony, are not just closed, but their curtains are still drawn.

This makes the first part of my plan a lot safer.

I face the wall of glass and raise my automatic rifle. I've checked the clip and there's around twenty bullets remaining.

It takes around two seconds for the twenty bullets to smash every pane of glass. While the glass will be toughened, and have a shatterproof membrane attached, it's not designed to deal with small projectiles travelling at several hundred miles an hour.

Chapter 60

Daniel lifts his head and stares around him. Like him and his mom, everyone else in the room had pressed themselves to the floor at the sudden burst of gunfire.

One of the terrorists had opened fire in retaliation, but thankfully he'd aimed at the windows behind them rather than at the hostages.

Now the terrorists are huddled in a tight bunch and the woman has left the office to speak to them.

Even though Daniel can see she's strung out, it looks like she's calming down her men.

He watches as she takes a gun from one of them and inches her way along the wall; she teases the curtain back just enough to let her peek beyond it. Her head shakes, and she marches back across the room. She points at two of her men and sends them towards the end of the room where the broken windows are.

Daniel looks at his mom and sees the fear in her eyes. He knows she's nowhere near as tough as she makes out – he's known for a long time, although he's never let on to her. To tell her he knows would shatter what strength she does have. Despite his tender age, he's aware that some illusions have to be believed by the conjuror as well as the audience.

When he turns and looks at the windows he can see the curtains flapping in the breeze. The temperature in the room has dropped several degrees already, and with the windows appearing to be smashed it'll soon get a lot colder.

As he's looking at the curtains he notices something odd about the ceiling. Right along the first six feet of the ceiling, there is a series of pockmarks in the wooden panelling. He's sure they weren't there before, which means they're a result of the gunfire.

This makes him think about who'd fired at the windows from outside, and why.

The obvious answer is that it's someone coming to their rescue, but he doesn't know who that someone could be. So far as he can work out, the only candidate is the bartender. If the police were involved then the gunfire would have been followed up with an attack of some kind.

Daniel knows from his experience of playing online games with his friends that storming a building works best when there's a distraction of some kind. That's what he figures the police would do, but there's no sounds of gunfire coming from the opposite end of the building, indicative of a follow up attack; therefore, it must be the bartender who'd shot out the front windows.

The position of the pockmarks in the ceiling suggest to Daniel that the bartender had kept his aim high to avoid killing anyone in the room.

That one of the terrorists had reacted by firing at the windows is telling. It shows at least one of them is nervous about what's happening, and Daniel has already noticed that several of the terrorists have left the room without returning.

Daniel's not sure whether it's good or bad that the terrorists are on edge. On the one hand, they might well decide to cut their losses and make their escape while it's still safe to do so, but on the other, the longer they stick around, the more chance there is of their brutality continuing, or even increasing.

The more he thinks about it, Daniel realises the effect that shooting out the windows has had.

The terrorists are now under attack, and although the woman had looked to see if she could spot whoever was attacking them, she can't have seen anyone as she'd shaken her head.

Daniel has to hide his smile at the fact the terrorists are now being terrorised. It's the most perfect of ironies and nothing less than they deserve.

Chapter 61

I rush to the front of the hotel as fast as the snow allows me and get ready for a group of terrorists to come running out. So they don't immediately see me, I keep myself tight against the building and wait either for bodies to appear, or for them to start shooting at the man I've sat in front of the entrance.

If they appear, I'll shoot them. If they stay back and shoot at their comrade, I'll know when they're coming and, as such, I'll be prepared for them trying to sneak out.

I'm comfortable either way, but my preference would be for them to come rushing out in a tight knot. Then I'll be able to attack them before they're even aware of my presence.

My heart is pounding in my chest and I know it's nothing to do with the short dash from the balcony.

At times like these the human body fills itself with adrenaline, as part of the natural fight or flight reaction. As much as I'm keyed up and ready for the next battle, a part of me is screaming that I should get myself out of here as it's more than a little probable that I'll die in my attempt to save others.

I don't listen to that part of my psyche: running away doesn't solve anything. If it did, the world would be populated by nomads as the entire population upped sticks for greener pastures at the first sign of trouble. My own experience of leaving town can't be described as positive. Everywhere I've been, I've carried my troubles with me, and were it not for the fact that my presence endangers those I care about, I'd have given in to my homesickness months ago.

Nobody emerges from the resort's main entrance.

The same nobody refuses to take a shot at the terrorist I've trussed up.

It's possible they can tell he's one of their buddies, but I'd made sure to drag him far enough away that the snowstorm would shield his identity and leave him appearing as nothing more than a shadow.

I give it another minute or so, and then turn my head to check my rear. If they've fooled me, and exited the building via the shot-out windows and doors that lead to the balcony, they'll be able to ambush me from behind.

There's no sign of any movement in either direction so I revise my thinking and stay where I am.

For the next five minutes I keep my back pressed against the wall and swivel my head left and right.

Nobody comes out of the main entrance or around the corner from the decking.

This tells me a number of things. Number one is that Hannah or one of her lieutenants has a cooler head than I've anticipated. I'd expected them to react in anger or fear, and send a posse charging after me; that hasn't happened.

The second thing is that they've enough training to make sure their superior numbers work for them. From the military thrillers I've read, the odds are always with the force that has the greater numbers. This counts even more so when one force is storming a building held by their enemies. By far their safest course of action is to stay put and wait for someone to try and breach their way into the resort.

A third point is that they don't know who they're up against. It's possible they saw the piste basher explode but, as their men haven't returned after shooting rockets at it, they may well think the cops escaped unhurt and have taken out their buddies. My shooting the resort's front windows out will have reinforced their fears that they're under attack.

I already knew they were disciplined, but their non-reaction shows self-control.

It's possible they have escaped down the ladder leading from the cable car station, but I'm not sure where they think they could go.

Either they're going to negotiate for a helicopter to take them away, or they're going to try and sneak away.

To stand any chance of sneaking away they'll need to go a couple of hundred yards uphill, to the summit of the mountain, and then make their way down the other side.

That area is cordoned off due to the avalanche risk, but for terrorists looking to escape a police chase it'll look mighty inviting.

The next thought that enters my head isn't a welcome one.

If they're planning their escape, they'll be getting ready to make sure there are no witnesses left behind.

I don't know at what point Hannah plans to detonate the charge on the columns, but it makes sense that she plans to do it before the hostages have a chance to move away from the kill zone.

If she's in there with her finger on the detonator, she'll soon realise her charges aren't working. Once that moment is reached, she'll starting gunning down the hostages.

This line of thinking is most unwelcome; all I can picture is a row of terrorists firing their submachine guns into a crowd of bodies.

I check both ways again and start making my way back to the corner of the building. I left the rocket launcher there and I feel it's time it was used against the terrorists, instead of by them.

Where they'd got it from is beyond me, but I've lived long enough to know there's nothing that can't be bought, provided you approach the right people.

Chapter 62

Captain Ogden barges into the control room with the same force of personality he left with. His face is set in concentration as he faces up to Nathan.

'These cable cars, can they be controlled from either end, or do you have to work in synchronisation?'

Nathan isn't sure of the reason for the question, but figures that Ogden must have an idea of some kind if he is asking it. 'Either station can control the whole thing, but we always run with an operator top and bottom. The people who can afford to stay at RidgeTop expect to see us controlling the cars and, because they've got money…' Nathan gives a helpless shrug. 'Some of them think the cableway exists for their personal use, so we have to be on hand at either end. Over the years I've been here, I've sent customers cartons of cigarettes, suitcases they've forgotten, and, on a couple of occasions, hookers.'

The way Attwood rolls his eyes tells Nathan he is probably in line for a disciplinary hearing for that last admission, but he isn't worried. He's been honest with the captain and, as far as he's concerned, that's the most important thing.

'Can you tell if someone's trying to move the cars from the top station?'

'Definitely. If the brakes are on you can hear them protesting against the pull, and if they're off you can see the wheel turning.' Nathan points up at the huge wheel, which is suspended from the ceiling of the station. 'Plus, of course, you see the cars moving.'

'Right. Are the brakes on at the top?'

'Yes, they are. It's protocol to have the brakes on at all times when the cars are stationary.'

'Fair enough. I want you to release the brakes at your end. I don't suppose you can release them at the other end too?'

Nathan doesn't bother looking at Attwood before throwing the brake lever into the off position.

The resort manager has other ideas though. 'Why do you want the brakes off? Surely if they try and escape this way you'll want to be able to stop them?'

'I do indeed. But I also want to give the hostages an escape route. We don't know what in Sam Hill is going on up there, but if my men are doing their jobs, they may want an open route to evacuate people. Let's make sure they have one.'

Attwood fronts up to Ogden. 'Is that all you're doing? Giving the terrorists a possible escape route? Good God, Captain, what about the people who're trapped up there?'

'I've a little surprise in store for the morning, but trust me, I've had my orders from the chief of police. No more men are to be risked until first light. If the terrorists have any demands, they're yet to make contact. If they plan to kill everyone up there, then we're already too late.'

Attwood pushes himself forward from where he'd been leaning against the control desk and stands toe to toe with Ogden. 'This surprise of yours, I don't expect you to tell me what it is, but it had better include a helicopter gunship.'

Nathan watches as Ogden pulls a face, but the captain doesn't react quick enough to hide the flicker of surprise in his eyes. Therefore, a gunship is exactly the kind of surprise he's got for the morning.

With a helicopter gunship providing cover, an assault team will be given a great chance to land and then storm the resort. As Ogden has pointed out, the terrorists are yet to make any demands, so, theoretically at least, time is on their side.

Attwood isn't finished with his questions though. 'And what if it's the terrorists who come down? I'm not risking any more of my staff.'

For a moment, Nathan thinks the finger that Attwood is jabbing in Ogden's face will make contact, but he's glad his boss doesn't go that far. Maybe it's Ogden's physique that stops him, or perhaps his rank, but he has enough sense to make sure his finger doesn't touch the police captain.

'I wouldn't ask you to.' Ogden jerks a thumb over his shoulder at the public area of the cableway station. 'That's what they're here for.'

When Nathan looks at the station he sees a squad of men similar to those who clambered into the Ridge Runner. Each man is dressed in combat clothes and is carrying an automatic rifle. Another group of regular cops enter the station carrying what look to be armoured riot shields.

Nathan gives out a low whistle. 'I like how you think, Captain.'

Ogden glowers towards Attwood. 'It's a good job someone does. Tell me, how long does it take for one of those cars to get from top to bottom?'

'Fourteen minutes and thirty-six seconds.' When Nathan sees the amazed expression on Ogden's face he gives a shrug. 'There's a lot of long, boring nights in this job. You gotta amuse yourself somehow.'

Ogden leaves with a half chuckle rocking his shoulders, but there's no such levity from Attwood.

Nathan knows his boss will already be counting the cost of the attack in terms of lost revenue through a decrease in future bookings. He suspects Attwood will already be thinking of ways to limit the reputational damage and how to market the resort in the days and weeks to come.

To Nathan's mind this is a waste of time, as nothing can be decided until they know all the details of the attack.

Chapter 63

I've waited here long enough to realise that none of Hannah's men are coming out to where I am, so I revisit my earlier thinking and move on to the next plan. I'm not sure what letter of the alphabet I'm up to, or if I'm now on the second round, but such concerns have long passed me by.

If I'm going to progress with plan whatever, I have to do it now before I lose my nerve, or give the terrorists even more time to anticipate my arrival, and prepare all manner of traps and ambushes.

Rather than walk straight in through the main doors, I plan to use a little subterfuge, if not stealth.

I forge my way back to the corner of the building and take a careful peek around it. When I don't see anybody waiting to ambush me, I step around the corner and lift the rocket launcher.

It's heavy and unwieldy in my hands, but I've lifted greater weights, and anyone who's ever had to carry a drunk out of a bar will have experienced the worst kind of flaccid load imaginable. When working as a doorman, I've tossed, carried and knocked drunks out of bars on more occasions than I can remember.

Compared to tonight, those were halcyon days, when the worst I could expect was a ten-beer-hero with an array of badly thrown punches, and the prospect of a few bruises on my knuckles.

I don't put the rocket launcher to my shoulder, or try and aim it in any way, I just want it to hand for when I do need it.

There's still isn't anyone near the main entrance as I approach it, one crumping step at a time. When I'm a foot away from the point where I'll expose myself, I lean the rocket launcher against the wall and creep until my head is right by the open doorway.

I listen. Chatter, the striking of a match or the cocking of a weapon are what I'm listening for, along with footsteps. In an ideal world, footsteps and chatter are what I'd like to hear. They'd allow me to judge the number of opponents, along with any possible movements they're making.

I hear nothing but the howling wind of the snowstorm.

With no other option, I cast a quick look back towards the balcony and check there isn't a terrorist coming my way, and then turn so I'm facing the wall.

I bend at the waist, so my upper body leans left and then right.

My left eye passes the edge of the doorway for less than a half second, but I get enough of a look to see there aren't any terrorists waiting for me.

It feels as if the rocket launcher has gained another twenty pounds since I put it down, but I blame the extra weight on tiredness, and my body's inability to produce an endless supply of adrenaline.

The hour is late and, while I'm no stranger to late nights and hard work, the way I've been chilled, and have slogged up and down the ski slope, has sapped a lot of my strength and energy. The fact I've had to wade through snow for the last couple of hours has caused my energy resources to more or less vanish. Adrenaline has carried me this far and it's going to have to keep me going for a while longer.

The fact I'm so weary is yet another concern I have to push to the back of my mind; if I were fresh and rested, I'm sure I'd be a bit more confident about the course of action I'm about to take.

I creep into the main entrance. My eyes are flicking all ways, but I see no immediate threats.

This is a worry, I don't for one minute believe they've left the entrance unguarded. Unless the bullets I fired high into the windows at the front of the dining room have ricocheted off the ceiling and buried themselves in the terrorists, it doesn't make sense for them not to have a presence here.

Except it does.

They've been hunting me in small groups. I've taken those groups out.

They think they're under attack, either from me or a police tactical team. Therefore, they're now doing the smart thing and allowing Mohammed to come to the mountain.

The layout of the main entrance is a wide passage bisected at right angles by a corridor with doors leading from it. Ahead of me the passage leads to the customer suites, and the dining room where the hostages are being held.

There's a series of heavy doors between the entrance and the dining room – which keep the heat in and the cold out – meaning I can't be seen by anyone from that direction.

It would make an awful lot of sense for a couple of terrorists to wait ten yards along the corridor, ready to ambush anyone who enters.

The question is, are they to my left, or my right? For a fraction of a second, I wonder if they're on both sides, before I discount the idea. If they were on both sides of the corridor, shooting at someone in the middle, there's every chance the two teams would shoot each other.

What I need to do now is figure out which side they're on and a way to eliminate their threat.

The answer is a simple one.

I creep forward until I'm within ten feet of the corridor and release the assault rifle in my right hand. It hangs from its strap, bumping against my hip, ready to be grabbed should I need it.

The rocket launcher in my left hand gets hoisted onto my right shoulder and I give it a quick check to make sure it's ready to fire when I press the trigger.

All I need to do now is identify whether to fire left or right.

The fingers of my left hand grasp the ratty hat on my head and toss it into the middle of the corridor.

Gunshots ring out before the hat has even landed, and punch it to the left.

It makes sense for the terrorists to have taken up station on the right, from there they can cover attacks from both the main entrance and the cable car station.

I now know the terrorists are on my right and that they're jumpy – the speed of their response has shown as much, as they shot without realising what they were shooting at and gave away their position at the same time.

A more worrying concern is that they hit a small moving target within a second of it appearing.

Rather than dwell on negative thoughts, I take two steps to my left and point the rocket launcher right. I can see the first few feet of the corridor, but no more than that.

I'm not a hundred per cent sure I won't get caught by the explosion, but I've come too far to start worrying about the unknown.

I squeeze the trigger and take a couple of steps to the right, so the corner of the wall will give me some cover. The whoosh from the rocket launcher is immediately drowned out by a thundering explosion that pummels me with superheated air and pushes me backwards.

As soon as I can recover my balance, I drop the rocket launcher and run into the corridor with my hands clutching the automatic rifle.

I'm looking at the right-hand end of the corridor for signs of life, but it's a waste of time. There's nothing but utter carnage. Two bodies are slumped against the walls and there's the acrid smell of burning in the air, although I don't see an actual fire.

Chapter 64

An idea comes to me, so I make my way to the cableway station as fast as I can while still showing a reasonable level of caution.

I don't think there will be anyone ahead of me, but I have to make sure I don't have any nasty surprises. To run into a trap now would be careless, possibly fatal. My biggest fear is that the explosion will have been heard by everyone in the dining room.

It's one thing for the terrorists to have taken up defensive positions, but another for them to hold tight when they're under attack. So far, I haven't found any radios on the terrorists, which means they've no way of communicating with each other. Therefore, those in the dining room will have no idea whether the explosion has killed their men or the enemy. The last thing I want is Hannah sending some more of her men to investigate.

It's a gamble, but I aim the automatic rifle along the corridor and fire a short burst. My thumb flicks the rate selector to single shot and I fire off two rounds, three seconds apart.

I've wasted maybe ten rounds, but if I'm lucky they'll be fooled into thinking there's a firefight going on and their guards are still alive.

Rather than waste time waiting to see if my ruse has worked, I get to the cableway station and have a quick search. The men I pushed over the edge are still there, but the one I dumped behind the packing crates has gone.

I run back to the beer cellar and find that the man I'd left between the kegs has also gone.

There's nothing I can do about it now, but I curse my earlier thoughts of being merciful. At least two of the men I fought with earlier are back in the game and, while it was very noble of me not to kill them, I'm now wishing I'd crippled them the way I did the guys by the ski lift.

I expect that, if I get out of this alive, Doctor Edwards will have something to say about my escalating levels of violence, but when he asks, I plan to bat the question back at him to find out what he would have done in my position.

I push those thoughts from my mind and concentrate on the matter at hand. Any further terrorists I encounter will either be killed or disabled to the extent they can no longer offer even the mildest threat.

When I throw the drive lever against its stops, the cableway creaks into action.

I then grab the notepad and pen from the operator's control desk and start writing. My fingers are too cold to hold the pen properly, and this makes my writing childlike, but I do the best I can.

I have to drop the pen and grab the drive lever when a cable car hoves into view.

I don't bring the cable car to a halt in the correct place, but it's near enough for me to slide the door open and get inside.

It takes me about two minutes to scrawl everything I need on three sheets of paper, and another minute to find a roll of tape.

Before I return to the cable car I toss a glance along the corridor.

It's clear, so I dash into the cable car and tape my notes to the inside of the door. Not only do I have to get a message to those at the bottom of the mountain, I have to make sure I'm trusted by those who receive it.

I go back to the control panel and send the cable car on its way downhill.

When I first came to RidgeTop, my natural curiosity made me time the journey. It took fifteen minutes. Therefore, it will be at least thirty-five minutes before I hear back from Nathan, or whoever receives my message. That's fifteen minutes each way, plus a minimum of five minutes for them to compose a response.

In an ideal world, another police team will be waiting at the bottom and will come right back up, but I doubt that will happen. They'll be fearful of being picked off by the terrorists.

I could have let them know I'd stay and guard their approach, but the idea of sitting around for a half hour, while Hannah does goodness knows what to the hostages, doesn't sit well with my conscience.

'Boulder.'

I freeze at the mention of my name. It's coming from the radio I'd stuffed into my pocket and forgotten about.

As much as I want to get into a dialogue with Hannah, and tell her what I think of her, I don't answer. She can take from that whatever she likes.

A reply from me will tell her I'm still alive and give her the confirmation she's after.

'Boulder, we need to talk.'

I stifle the snarky response that's in my mind and pick up my rifle. I'd rather show her I'm still alive and active than tell her.

Chapter 65

The wind howling in from the smashed windows makes Leslie as cold as he's ever felt. He's got his back against an upturned table and an arm round Lily. They're huddled together for warmth but the only part of him that doesn't feel chilled is the part that's pressed up against his wife.

The longer this ordeal goes on, the more he believes he'll not see dawn.

His heart is troubling him, but he's keeping that information from Lily. There's no point in worrying her about a situation she cannot change.

He's just taken his meds and there'll be the usual ten minutes delay before they kick in and settle his heart.

Lily had raised one of her sculpted eyebrows when she saw him take the meds. He wasn't due any more until morning, but she hadn't commented on what he was doing. For once in their marriage she trusted him to do what he thought best.

Rather than waste time worrying whether or not his heart would survive the night, he distracts himself by puzzling over the actions of the waiting staff.

The one in her forties, who'd been beaten up, is being tended to by one of the younger ones. This in itself isn't unusual, he'd expect the same level of care for a colleague in any working environment. What is odd, though, is the way the younger one has stripped off her shirt so the older one can use it as a makeshift cloth to dab at the wounds on her face.

Had it been a male colleague who'd done that, it would have been unremarkable. The same thought would have carried had the younger woman worn a T-shirt or vest under her shirt.

The problem is, she doesn't. Therefore, there is very little chance she would have chosen to expose herself in this way just to provide a cloth for a colleague. When Leslie factors in the dropping temperature – since the windows were shot out – the likelihood of the act being solely about caring for a colleague shrinks even further.

Other than her bra, the girl is naked to the waist and Leslie can see her shivering from twenty feet away.

The only other reason he can think of for the girl to remove her shirt is that she is trying to distract one or more of the guards.

Them trying such an obvious tactic is a sign of their desperation and, while Leslie doesn't think for one moment that the guards will be naive enough to fall for such a simple ruse, he has to admire the bravery shown by the two women.

Should he be well enough to get to his feet when their moment comes, he plans to do whatever he can to help them.

Chapter 66

There's a lot to be said for Hannah trying to find out if I'm still alive: it shows she respects me enough to fear me, and she's trying to make contact with me to ascertain my whereabouts or if I'm still alive.

Five times she's tried to contact me and five times I've not replied.

So the radio doesn't give away my position, I've turned it down and her words are little more than a whisper.

I'm not sure if she knows I'm alive and she's aware I'm ignoring her on purpose. In her position, I'd keep talking in the hope my adversary is holed up somewhere, listening to my every word.

This may well be her plan, but it's not one I'm going to fall for. I've already returned to the beer cellar. The door is busted from where it was kicked in to rescue the guy I'd left in here, but the shelves at the back of the room are still in place.

The kitchens are across the hall, behind the reception desk, and they're where I should have gone before coming here.

I make my way to the kitchen and rummage around until I find what I need. A chef's sharpening steel works well as a short truncheon, so I slide one up my sleeve and grab a box of extra-long matches from the counter top.

As I move through the kitchen I keep myself low enough to not show through the windows of the serving doors.

I'm also careful not to knock any of the pots or pans. Everything in here is metal and in the middle of service there's more than a little noise. The last thing I want to do is knock something over and have a metallic clatter alert the terrorists of my whereabouts.

There's a pile of serving cloths dumped on a counter, so I grab a knife and cut two of them into quarters and stuff the pieces into the back of my rope belt. It tightens even further against me, but I'll be delighted if that's the worst discomfort I feel tonight.

Before I return to the beer cellar, I edge my way towards the dining room doors. I've no intention of going through them or trying to look through the windows. Instead, I'm checking on a simple device that will make my life easier.

Each of the four bolts that stop customers entering the kitchen in the middle of the night, via the exit and entrance doors, have been shot home. I'd expected as much – it makes sense to secure all possible exits from the area where the hostages are being held – but it's nice to have the confirmation.

I sidle across to the door that leads from the kitchen to the main corridor. This is used by servers delivering room service, and has a slatted blind across its window.

There's a fraction of a gap either side of the blind, and I position myself so I can peer through it.

I don't see anyone at the dining room end of the corridor, but there are a pair of terrorists at the main entrance end.

They're maybe five feet back from the door and they both have their guns trained that way.

I grab a bag of sugar as I leave the kitchen and make my way to the beer cellar again.

Now I know the location of two of the terrorists, I can start putting my next plan into action.

My first move is to climb up the shelving and pop the access hatch open. Like the kitchen, this functional part of the resort has a proper ceiling and there's a way to get above it.

I place all my supplies up there then pull out my radio and put it to my ear. Hannah has gone from trying to get a response from me, to telling me what she's about to do.

'Did you hear me, Boulder? I want to know where my explosives are, and if you don't tell me, I'll start killing hostages. Say, one every minute, until you tell me where you've stashed my explosives. How does that sound to you? How many deaths can your conscience take before you give in and tell me? One? Two? Maybe it's a dozen, so I'll start with the youngest, those who have the most life yet to be lived.'

As much as I want to reply to her, I keep my silence. I don't even move my grip of the walkie-talkie in case I press the send button and let her know that I still have it.

So far as I can work out, her threat is an empty one. If she starts killing people she'll have a revolt on her hands and, until she's ready to leave, she'll always have a use for some of the hostages. The youngest ones will be the most valuable to her and there's no way she's going to sacrifice them without certain knowledge that I'm aware of her attempts to communicate with me.

I almost miss the most significant part of what she's saying, or not saying as the case may be, but a part of my brain registers it.

If she knows about the explosives being missing, it means she's sent one of her men to check them. Which means either someone is outside and about to come in, or he's come back in without me noticing. If he's outside, he must have a radio, and if he's back in the building, he's come in via the balcony or one of the emergency exits.

In case he's outside and about to come back in, I push on with my latest plan and pull the cork from a cognac bottle, roll it across the floor, and clamber up the shelves. The sooner I get myself out of sight, the better my chances of seeing the sun rise.

Chapter 67

Sharon is aware things have changed in the dining room since the windows were shot out. The female terrorist has reassigned a large portion of her men.

The curtains have been opened and there's two terrorists standing guard by the broken glass. Another pair have been positioned by the doors leading to the main entrance.

Three of the remaining four are standing over the hostages, while the man with the clipboard has assembled the dozen customers who've yet to take a second visit to Fleming's office into a line outside the door.

Since the last one came out a minute ago, no one else has been ushered in.

Sharon doesn't know what the reason for this is, but it's not at the forefront of her thoughts. All she wants to do now is get her hands on a weapon and join the fight.

The pain in her face is beyond excruciating and it's adding to her fury at the terrorists' actions.

What they did to her was bad enough, but to threaten three innocent children, so she would give up Boulder, was cruel on another level.

The biggest surprise to Sharon is the effect Boulder is having on the terrorists' plan. Not only have their numbers dwindled by half, those left are now edgy and nervous. This means they're not at their best. Their decision-making skills will be compromised, leaving them vulnerable.

However, she doesn't believe that Boulder will be able to take down all of the terrorists himself. What she has to do is find a way of arming herself so she can join the fight.

She knows she's a long way from her best and she can only open one of her eyes, but neither of these facts is enough to deter her.

Sharon expects to die if the terrorists aren't stopped, and because she believes this, she has nothing to lose. The idea that she'll die before the night is out terrifies her, but the thought of dying without fighting back fills her with shame.

The biggest barrier she's got is that the guards are all spread out, and the odds of her being able to take down one, and grab their weapon, before being shot by another are slim to non-existent.

There is a glimmer of hope for her though. The nearest guard is a bald guy who has spent more time ogling the women than intimidating the men.

In Sharon's mind, he's nothing more than a lecherous pervert, but in the circumstances that's a good thing, as it shows a weakness she can bend to her advantage.

The server who's holding her down is young and pretty, and Sharon had already spotted the guard checking her out whenever he could.

That's why she's using the girl as a distraction.

Her idea has put the girl in danger, but as Sharon expects them all to be slaughtered anyway, all that will happen is the danger to the girl will move from imminent to immediate.

Sharon knew that to get the girl to cooperate she would have to remember her name. She'd trawled her way through her memories of conversations when the girl was around and remembered her getting into trouble for never fastening the top button of her blouse. RidgeTop isn't the kind of place where the waiting staff are expected to flirt with the customers or flash a little flesh to keep them coming back, yet the girl had done it anyway.

There is every chance the girl is a gold-digger, who's only taken the job in the hope of snaring a rich husband, but as far as Sharon's plan is concerned, the girl's brazenness will be a plus.

Sharon had placed a hand on Brooke's shoulder and pulled her forward so she could whisper in her ear. Every word she'd spoken sent pain shooting through her jaw, but she'd said everything she needed to, regardless of the agony.

The girl tried to refuse at first, to suggest another way, but after a minute's persuasion she agreed to do as Sharon asked.

Brooke removed her shirt, rolled it into a ball, and handed it to Sharon who'd used it to dab at the wounds on her face.

If Sharon's own shirt hadn't been covered in blood she would have used that and kept Brooke out of it. For Sharon, showing her bra was no different to wearing a bikini top, it's only the change in venue that makes the difference. At least that's the case with the comfortable sports bras that Sharon favours.

Brooke's personality, and possible agenda, has extended to her underwear: her bra is designed to be seen. There's little doubt in Sharon's mind that the girl's underwear will be a matching set, something she hasn't worn herself since the day she gave up on her marriage.

From the corner of her functioning eye, Sharon can see the guard is paying a little too much attention to Brooke.

The girl has an arm across her chest in an effort to cover herself, but Sharon can tell from the tension in the girl's arm that she's deliberately pressing her chest hard, to squeeze her breasts upwards, in an effort to make them appear bigger.

Sharon gives Brooke a mental pat on the back. Not only is she playing along with the ruse, she's doing all she can to make it work.

Brooke stands and walks towards the bald guard. He points his gun at her, but it's not her hands he's watching.

Sharon knows how the conversation will go. She's put the words into Brooke's mouth.

Whether or not the guard lets the girl get some water to bathe her wounds is immaterial. The whole purpose of the request is to distract the guard and establish a habit.

His head shakes, and he points towards the hostages. He's obviously sending her back, but Brooke has more nerve than Sharon has given her credit for. She unpeels her right arm from her chest and uses it to point at the bar as she repeats her request.

The bald guard locks his eyes onto her chest and leaves his arm out indicating that Brooke should return to where she came from.

Brooke holds her stance for a few seconds then turns away from him shaking her head.

Sharon is delighted with the exchange. Because the guard was focused on Brooke's chest he hadn't threatened her in any way, which means he sees her as a source of entertainment rather than a threat.

She pities Brooke for the fact that she's bound to be even colder than she is. Including the terrorists, everyone is doing whatever they can to keep warm.

The cold is the least of their worries, so Sharon settles down to wait for Brooke to carry out the next part of her plan.

A single shot ringing out from the office causes her head to snap up. The movement sends waves of pain shooting through her shattered jaw.

As much as the shot has startled Sharon, it confuses her more. The female terrorist is in the office by herself, and she doesn't believe that she's committed suicide or pulled the trigger by mistake.

With no one there to shoot, the reason for the shot is a mystery.

While a part of Sharon wants to question why the shot rang out, she knows she must forget about that, and the hostages' visits to the office, and concentrate on what's happening in the dining room.

If she survives the night, she'll find out what happened in there, and if she is to see the morning sun, she knows she has to focus on her plan and be ready to strike at the opportune moment.

Chapter 68

Instinct forces me to take on the rigidity of a statue when I hear the gunshot. I've gambled that Hannah is bluffing, but a part of me is terrified I've called it wrong. The gunshot is what I've been dreading.

Except it's not followed by the right noises. I know I'm a good thirty yards or so from the dining room, but I'm sure I'd hear screaming and shouted outrage had Hannah shot one of the kids.

I hear nothing except a whisper from my pocket.

'That's one, Boulder. How many more will there be before you tell me where my explosives are?'

I grab the control knob on the walkie-talkie and twist it to the off position before stuffing it back in my pocket. The less I hear from Hannah, the less she'll be able to get inside my head.

By not answering her, I'm screwing with her mind and that's the way I want to keep it.

Although my rationalisation makes sense I'm still filled with doubts. I wonder if she has really shot a hostage, or if she fired a shot into the floor in case I'm playing the game I am.

A part of me can't help but wonder who she chose – if she's been true to her word. While my earlier thinking was that the children are the most valuable hostages, there's an awful lot of wealthy and important people in the resort tonight, which means any one of the customers would suffice should she need someone's head to put a gun to.

I think of the people in the room that I have something of a feeling for: Sharon Bairden and I hit it off due to our shared memories of Glasgow; Hank, the sous chef, is a decent guy – he is the one who cooks the staff meals and he does so without any of the attitude you usually get from chefs. The only other person in the room that I care about more than others is the young lad, Daniel, and most of those feelings are projections.

I've never had kids, nor wanted any until I met Taylor if I'm honest. My mother has rattled on for years about me being the only person who could make her a grandmother, but I've never been in, or wanted to be in, a serious relationship.

When I found myself in one, I did start to wonder about settling down and raising a family. I had even been prepared to put someone else's needs above my own.

On a Monday morning, after Taylor had left my flat to go to work, I found myself thinking about kids; and despite everything I've said to Mother on the subject I found myself *wanting* kids.

I blame that lazy hour for the way I'm feeling right now. I'd let my imagination run free that morning and had conjured up pictures of the children I wanted.

A boy and a girl were the obvious starting points, but I'd gone past there and imagined the people I wanted them to be. The boy would be the eldest and his sister his junior by no more than two years.

He'd squabble with her the way I had with my sister but, like me, he'd always protect her from bullies and make sure she was safe.

Both of my children would be well-behaved, and my fictional versions had them smart enough to choose whatever career they wanted, but their intelligence would also see them possess sufficient street smarts to keep them out of trouble.

Their manners would be good, and as they grew into teenagers they'd be able to hold a decent conversation with an adult.

Most of all they were children any parent would be proud of.

That's why I've found myself caring about Daniel, he's a real-life version of the son I'd imagined having. Everything about him – from his nature to his respectful ways – is how I'd wanted my son to be. The way he talks impresses me; he doesn't speak like a normal teenager, all hashtag this, OMG that, he talks like an adult. The limited bits of conversation I've had with him have shown he's very smart and he relishes a puzzle. He's alert to what's going on around him and he gets subtext and unspoken words better than a lot of adults. I'm confident he'll go far in life, and I see elements of my better qualities in him.

The best thing about both Daniel and my imaginary son is that neither of them have my faults, which means they would grow up to be a better person than I am and, other than health and happiness, that's all a parent can hope for their child.

I push all of these thoughts from my brain and refocus on my latest plan.

Chapter 69

I work my way along the ducting, between the false ceiling and the floor above, until I've got myself in the area I want to be.

It's not easy to move around up here when carrying supplies but I manage it. Crawling along the duct is a lot better than trudging through snow and it's many degrees warmer, but my hands and feet are still numb.

I lean away from the ducting and reach down to lift one of the ceiling tiles to check I'm in the right place.

Once I've confirmed I am, I start finalising my preparations. First, I put one of the rags from my rope belt to one side and arrange the remaining seven pieces so they lay flat on top of one another. I then fold the pile of cloths over the barrel of one of the pistols that is tucked into the rope at my waist.

The length of rope in my pocket is used to tie them in place.

As silencers go, it's makeshift, but it's the best I can do in the circumstances. I'm not confident it will muffle all the noise from the pistol being fired, but as long as it muffles most of it, it'll serve its purpose.

With that part of my preparation complete, I remove the cork from the bottle of cognac I brought with me.

I splash the amber spirit on the rag that isn't wrapped around the pistol barrel until the whole thing is damp.

My fingers reek of cognac by the time I've rolled the scrap of cloth tight enough to press two inches of it into the neck of the bottle.

As tempting as it is to suck the cognac from my fingers, I settle for rubbing my hands on the pipe lagging.

I remove the ceiling tile I lifted earlier and use the light that floods upwards to get my bearings.

Now that I'm about to light one of the matches, I'm grateful for their length; the last thing I want to do is set fire to my hands.

When I touch the lit match to the cognac-soaked wick, it flares at once. I shake the match out and toss the bottle of cognac down towards the one I opened and rolled along the floor earlier, before clambering into the crawl space.

It doesn't matter that it misses the first bottle, it lands close enough to ignite the cognac that has spilled from the rolled bottle. Nor does it smash, but that's fine as well. When the flame gets past the wick it'll explode.

The sugar I poured into each of the bottles will cause the burning cognac to stick to whatever it comes into contact with.

As planned, the blaze sets off the fire alarm, which in turn activates the sprinkler system. The alarm is nothing less than a klaxon, and the jets of water from the sprinklers are spraying the whole corridor.

I don't waste time watching the fire. The assault rifle is in my hands, and before I've counted to ten, the terrorists who were at the other side of the doors burst into view.

They recoil at the suddenness of the flames, but it's the last reaction they ever have.

I'm no marksman, but I can hit two man-sized targets at a range of six feet. They crumple where they stand, and as they're falling to the ground the bottle of cognac explodes and showers their bodies with glass and burning alcohol.

The alcohol-fuelled fire won't burn for long under the spray of water coming from the sprinklers, but if luck is on my side, it'll burn long enough to hide their bullet wounds from any quick examinations their buddies give them.

I drop the ceiling tile back into place and set off for my next destination; setting a fire and drawing this pair of terrorists out is only the first part of my plan.

Chapter 70

The double impact of the fire alarm and the cold water from the sprinklers is enough to cause panic and confusion in the dining room. Some of the hostages stand, as if getting ready to evacuate, but the terrorists guarding them wave them back to a sitting position.

Sharon's first instinct is to leave the building as well, but as she's starting to rise she realises the fire alarm must be to do with Boulder.

Whether he is screwing with the terrorists, the way he had when he shot out the front windows, or has some other reason for triggering the alarm, it doesn't matter. The simple truth is, every one of the terrorists looks nervous.

No longer are they exuding quiet confidence. As their numbers dwindle, so does their surety.

She can imagine the doubts flooding their minds. The huge explosion was enough to sow the first seeds, but every action since has worsened things for them.

With their colleagues continually leaving the room and not returning, thoughts of abandoning their plan and escaping while they can are bound to be entering nervous minds. Next will come a decision of mutiny, followed by the terrorists speaking to each other and looking towards the office.

The female terrorist emerges from the office, points at one of her men and then to Fleming.

The other terrorist walks across to her but Fleming pushes himself backwards.

Sharon watches with distaste as the terrorist crooks a finger at Fleming and gets ignored. The manager's reaction showcases the dictionary definitions of both cowardice and denial.

It's obvious why the female terrorist wants Fleming: he's the manager of the hotel and, as such, he'll know how to switch off the alarm and the sprinklers. It's clear he hasn't considered this. With every passing minute he's showing himself to be nothing more than a corporate drone rather than a real leader.

Sharon is tempted to offer to switch off the alarms herself, but she knows the female terrorist won't let her leave the room with one of her men as she's already identified herself as trouble.

Fleming will just have to suck it up and do as he's told.

Despite the blaring of the klaxon and the cold from the water, Sharon can't help but admire Boulder's cunning in setting off the fire alarm.

Not only is the noise disorientating, but the cold water will chill the terrorists and slow their movements. Coupled with the psychological effects of the action, it's clear to Sharon that Boulder is not just tough, he's smart as well.

The noise from the klaxon is a nuisance and is sure to trigger headaches, but it's the water that's a greater concern for Sharon.

She's tough enough to withstand being cold for a while, but with a sub-zero wind blowing through the room it won't take long for people to become dangerously cold.

It may take a while for hypothermia to kick in and frostbite to develop, but being soaked through is likely to increase the risk of people succumbing to either condition.

Sharon doesn't believe Boulder would want to wantonly risk people's lives this way, so she reasons that he must have an end game in mind and it's going to be soon. She's pleased at the thought, although she can't help but worry that the female terrorist will arrive at the same conclusion.

In front of her, Brooke's bare skin has a bluish hue to it, and like so many of the others she's straightened a table and is hunching under it to shelter from the water sprinkling down from the ceiling.

Brooke is looking her way with expectancy in her eyes. Sharon wonders what she's asking, when she realises the girl is waiting for the nod from her to carry out the next part of their ruse.

Sharon shakes her head and gives Brooke the best smile her battered face will allow. This isn't the right time for them to act, but she knows it's coming soon.

Chapter 71

I lie in wait above the plant room door. I've moved a ceiling tile an inch out of place so I can see any movement below me. To shut off the sprinklers and the alarm they'll have to access the control panel, which is located in the plant room.

As there's a code that needs to be keyed in to deactivate the alarm, I suspect one of the terrorists will bring either Fleming or Ed the maintenance man to switch it off. There will be a gun at their backs, but I've already thought of a way to deal with that.

With the klaxon blaring I can't hear footsteps approaching, but I can see shadows crossing the floor.

I tighten my grip on the pistol and prepare myself.

It's Fleming's comb-over that comes into view first. He pulls a key from his pocket and I see him tilt his head to one side as he looks at the door. I'm guessing either the lock has been shot out or the door has been kicked in by one of the terrorists.

He won't like that: any small piece of damage to his fiefdom is taken as a personal insult. I'm sure when he learns it was me who soaked his precious hotel by setting off the sprinklers he will fire me.

That's fine. If I get out of this alive, and somehow manage to not end up in prison for all the homicides I've committed, I plan to drive south until I'm somewhere that's warm all year round. Being from Glasgow, I have a natural tolerance to cold weather, but tonight has given me enough cold to last me the rest of my life.

Fleming pushes open the door and takes a step forward. I can see the gun at his back, and the top of a terrorist's head.

The terrorist stands guard at the door, which is what I expected him to do. I use my left hand to slide the ceiling tile further over and extend my right hand downwards. The pistol in my hand has my substitute silencer attached and I'm aiming it right at the top of his head. It'd be easy to shoot him now, but his gun is still trained on Fleming so I have to wait until the alarm is silenced. Before I pull my trigger, I have to be certain that if the terrorist pulls his trigger in a death spasm, he won't shoot Fleming.

As soon as the noise stops I say two words loud enough to be heard past ears still ringing from the alarm's piercing note.

The terrorist does as he's instructed and looks up. It's not that he's obeying me, he's just giving an instinctive reaction to an unexpected command.

As his head tilts back, his gun comes up towards me. It's a great mix of human reaction and military training that makes the gun point where the eyes are looking.

Once I'm convinced his gun isn't pointing at Fleming, I pull my trigger.

The terrorist gets two bullets in the top of his head. At the range of a foot I wasn't going to miss; the second was my way of making sure.

He slumps down in a heap as Fleming's head appears in the doorway.

'Kirk. It's me… Boulder. Listen up and listen quick.'

Fleming cranes his neck further round the door and looks up at me. I'm sure he wants to say something, but his mouth is opening and closing without any sounds coming out.

I don't have time to deal with his shock so I start firing instructions at him.

The first thing I tell him to do is to drag the terrorist into the plant room. When he's in there he has to check the phone lines. If there's a new router in place of the one that serves the resort, he's to remove it and give it to me.

'Should I plug our one back in?'

'No. Absolutely not.' I don't waste time explaining it to him, but if all the cell phones in the dining room suddenly get a connection, they'll start pinging and beeping and that's sure to draw Hannah's attention. While it would be nice to screw with her some more, I don't want to push her too far and I don't want her to find out that I've cut her connection until she discovers it for herself. Plus, if some of the hostages start trying to call or send messages, they will be putting themselves at risk of reprisals.

'How can I go back in there? The second I turn up without my guard they'll think I've killed him.'

Fleming has a point, or he would do if he wasn't a nine-stone weakling with a dodgy comb-over. The only people who could believe he's killed an armed man with his bare hands wear straightjackets or aluminium foil hats.

'Run back in, shouting "don't shoot"; tell them the guard got into a gun fight with me and you ran for your life.'

'Why can't I just hide out somewhere?'

His cowardice makes me want to drop down and recalibrate his sensibilities, but I don't have time for that. Besides, if I don't want him to rat me out at the slightest pressure, I have to keep him onside. Also, sending him back without his escort, with a black eye or a bloody nose, is akin to putting a noose round his neck.

'Two reasons: one, sooner or later they'll coming looking for you and the guy I just shot, and the chances are they'll find you. Two, I need you to pick up that guy's pistol and put it under your shirt, in the back of your pants. When you get back in there, sit where you were for ten minutes then move so you're beside Sharon Bairden – make sure nobody sees what you're doing. Give her the gun then tell her that when I come in, she's to take out the guards nearest her.' I have one last use for him. 'The terrorists, how many of them are left in there and where are they?'

Fleming's eyes glaze over as he thinks before giving his answer. I learn there are four guards covering the hostages, two by the front window, and Hannah is still using his office.

'Tell Sharon, if she takes the two by the windows, I'll deal with the rest. Now go.'

He goes – not without swallowing a few times first, but he goes.

I know in my heart that, by telling him to take a gun in for Sharon, I'm putting his life at risk. It's not a decision I came to lightly, but if I'm to succeed in rescuing the hostages I'll need some help.

I just hope Fleming can be trusted not to ditch the pistol rather than deliver it to Sharon.

Chapter 72

The control room has become a whole lot busier since the cableway started moving. The police team are poised, ready for an attack, and Ogden has stationed a spotter on the roof and equipped him with a huge torch so he can see into the cars before they arrive in case they contain explosives.

Nathan has Attwood, Ogden, and an FBI special agent called Riley with him in the control room.

The air in the room is stale, yet Nathan can feel the sense of anticipation. He's already told the others in the room that the next car to appear will be the first one to have travelled all the way down from the resort.

As much as Riley might outrank Ogden, he is the only man the FBI had available to send, and therefore the only resources he has at his disposal are those he can commandeer from the police captain. The two men have had their pissing contest, and now they are working together in the kind of uneasy truce that usually requires the services of the United Nations.

Ogden's radio crackles into life.

'Got the car in view. I can see no occupants or any obvious explosives.'

Nathan eases back the controls so the car slows as it approaches the station. As soon as it appears from the snow, all four men give it their focus.

'What's that? Are those safety notices?'

Both Nathan and Attwood say no at the same time.

Nathan turns back to his control desk and stops the car at the point where passengers would board or disembark.

The four men all move towards the door as one. Despite it being his domain, Nathan has the good sense to let the others go first. He's as keen as them to know what the papers that have been stuck to the door are, but he figures he'll be lucky if he ever finds out.

As the others file into the station, Nathan looks past them and sees two members of the assault team approach the cable car with their guns aimed and ready for use.

By the time Nathan has joined the others in the station, the cable car has been declared clear by the two cops, and both Ogden and Riley are in front of the door.

Nathan steps forward when Ogden calls his name. 'Yes, Captain?'

'This door, can you see any strange wires or anything unusual about it?'

Nathan gives the door a quick but thorough examination. He gets what the captain is hinting at. The idea the terrorists may have booby trapped the door is a real and terrifying prospect, but he doesn't see anything untoward.

'It looks normal to me.'

'Good.' Ogden grasps the handle and slides the door of the car open.

Nathan doesn't realise he's holding his breath until he jumps at Ogden's hollered request for evidence bags.

From the glance Nathan had of the papers while he was examining the door, he'd seen they were a message to him from Boulder. While he doesn't think they'll hold evidence against the terrorists, he's seen enough cop shows to know that procedures have to be followed.

As soon as the three sheets of paper are placed in separate evidence bags, Nathan feels a strong grip on his arm; he looks round and sees it's Riley.

'Come with me, please. Ogden, the control room, if you will.'

Although the FBI man's words are polite, there is no doubt in Nathan's mind that he's just received an order, not a request.

Attwood tries to follow them but Ogden plants a hand in the middle of his chest and closes the door in his face.

The three evidence bags have been laid across the control desk, and Nathan is invited to read them.

The handwriting is terrible, but at least the author has used block capitals to make the notes more legible.

He reads each page twice so he can comprehend every word. When he's finished he looks at Riley, who rolls his hand indicating he should speak.

'He's genuine. Where he says about Deadwood Attwood, that only broke yesterday morning, there's no way the terrorists can know about that.' Nathan explains where the nickname came from, but neither man reacts to it.

'And the rest of it, what do you make of his claim that he's taken out a dozen of the terrorists, including their pilot *and* their helicopter?' Riley's tone is both incredulous and respectful.

'I hardly know the man. I've only seen him once or twice.'

'He's on the right side.' Ogden pushes his cell phone back into a pocket and looks at Riley. 'When I heard his name earlier, I had him checked out. He has a bad habit of getting mixed up in stuff he shouldn't be anywhere near, but until we can get a team up there, he's the best hope the hostages have.'

Riley draws back his shoulders and looks up at Ogden. 'Are you condoning a civilian taking vigilante action, Captain?'

'You're damn right I am. I've lost a dozen men to these terrorists. You've read the message the same as I have. They shot that piste basher with a goddamned rocket launcher. Maybe a civilian shouldn't be running around taking on terrorists, but if what he says about the place being rigged with explosives is true, we should be building a statue of the man for the lives he's saved, not arresting him for his methods.'

While Nathan is enjoying watching the two men go at it, they're both missing the most important detail. Rather than point it out to them, he turns his radio to channel three, as per the instruction on the second page of the message, and hands

Captain Ogden the evidence bag with the third part of the message in it.

As he waits for the radio to crackle into life, he stares out of the window that faces the mountain.

'Nathan, can you restart the cableway please?'

Nathan understands the sense in Riley's request; as long as he's got the cars stationary, Boulder can't send any more messages or start to evacuate hostages – if he's successful in his attempt to eliminate the terrorists.

As he throws the lever over, he can't help but wonder what kind of man Boulder is to keep risking his life for others. If he'd been up there, he wouldn't have sent messages down in the cable cars, he'd have been in one himself.

Boulder had refused that option and chosen to stay up there with the aim of saving the lives of strangers. To Nathan, that choice showed all kinds of bravery, and maybe a little insanity.

Ogden steps forward from the back of the control room, his cell in his hand. 'Right, that's that done. And there's been more praise for this Boulder guy.'

When he's finished speaking, Ogden knocks on the window that overlooks the station, and points at a cop who's almost as big as he is. When the cop looks his way, Ogden gestures for the guy to join them in the control room.

'What are you doing, Captain?'

'I'm going up in the next cable car.'

'No way are you doing that.'

As Riley glares at Ogden, the cop enters the room.

'You're damn right I am. And I'm doing it alone so I don't risk the lives of any more of my men.' Ogden turns to face the cop. 'I need your body armour, helmet and weapons.'

The cop looks at Ogden. 'Sir, I'd like to volunteer to come with you.'

'Your request is noted, appreciated, and denied. I'm going up alone. Give me your gear, please.'

As the cop strips off his equipment, Riley tries to order Ogden not to go up the mountain, but the burly captain just ignores him.

Nathan keeps his face neutral, but inside he's backing the captain. Boulder will need all the help he can get, and the way the captain has chosen to take action himself, rather than delegate the danger to his men, speaks volumes about him.

The worry for Nathan is that Ogden may be too late to save Boulder. At least twenty minutes have passed since the message was written, and there will be a minimum of another fifteen before Ogden arrives at the resort. Thirty-five minutes is a long time for anyone to be battling against terrorists.

Chapter 73

Sharon can't help but wince at the way Fleming returns to the dining room. To her way of thinking, it's a miracle he hadn't got himself shot when he burst through the door. Had he not had the good sense to raise his hands above his head, and shout to announce his arrival, she's sure he'd be dead by now.

She watches as the terrorist who'd had the clipboard marches up to Fleming, his gun aimed at the manager's nose. Somehow, Fleming manages to raise his hands another couple of inches.

Sharon can see the two men speaking but she has no idea of what's being said.

Fleming has the gun removed from his face and gets directed towards the hostages.

Once he's under the watch of one of the guards, the man who'd put the gun under his nose marches to the office where the female terrorist is holed up.

Sharon can only think of one reason as to why the terrorist who had escorted Fleming from the room hadn't returned with him: he's fighting with Boulder.

She now wants to get involved in any way she can, but she still doesn't have a weapon beyond her fists and feet.

Brooke's arm is close to hers, so she gives the girl a nudge with her elbow and keeps her eyes fixed on Fleming. 'Go and see if the bald guy will let you go to the restroom. If he does, go, and come back to me. If he refuses, don't sit near me when you return. Keep an eye on me, and when I nod your way, get up and make as much of a scene about it as you dare.'

Sharon puzzles at Fleming's return. In the normal run of events he's a stickler for professionalism, and carries his slight frame with a stiffness she's always thought was his way of trying to appear larger than he is.

Since the terrorists launched their attack, he's had the slumped posture of a defeated man. Now, he's walking that little bit taller, and regaining some of his usual stiffness. This tells her he has a purpose. The way he's appearing to scan the mixture of hostages and staff seems false to her. From the moment Debbie Boitoult screamed, he hasn't looked anyone in the eye.

Fleming catches her eye and holds her stare for a second.

There's something about the way he's arranged his face that tells Sharon he's trying to give her a message.

As Fleming sits down ten feet away, Sharon can hear Brooke trying to persuade the bald guard to allow her a trip to the restroom.

The guy just shakes his head and points to the corner of the room, his meaning implicit.

Brooke pouts and flounces away from him in what Sharon considers to be a masterful performance.

The desire to find out what Fleming wants with her is burning at Sharon, but the way he has kept away tells her that he's trying hard not to be obvious. She's on the point of revising her opinion of him when she realises how wrong she is.

Fleming isn't acting of his own accord, he's not subtle or brave enough to do what he's doing without an external force guiding him. The way he came back without his guard tells her that the hand pulling his strings belongs to Boulder.

If Boulder has taken the guard out and spoken to Fleming before sending him back, he must have a message for Sharon. The message will be a request for help, or an instruction for her to carry out at a certain point in time.

For a moment, she fantasises that Boulder has sent a weapon in with Fleming, but she doubts he would gamble with the man's life. If the terrorists had frisked Fleming on his return and found he was carrying a weapon, they'd have killed him, or at the very least crippled him in some way.

Sharon watches as the female terrorist gives Fleming a hard stare then goes to the doors past the restrooms.

The woman draws her pistol and takes a peek through the doors.

When her head comes back in, her face is twisted in fury.

Within seconds she's beside the clipboard guy and is issuing orders that are accompanied by frantic hand gestures.

Two of the guards covering the hostages are sent to guard the doors. That leaves just two terrorists, plus the clipboard guy and the woman to watch over them.

Sharon hopes the men will rebel against their leader, but from the way they're obeying her commands, it looks as if that's a forlorn hope. She guesses the woman is aware of the threat and is planning to make their escape before it happens.

If that's the case, it means the clock is ticking for everyone, but until she finds out what Boulder has told Fleming, and Boulder himself acts, Sharon knows there's nothing she can do except make sure she's ready to act when the time comes.

With an icy wind blowing errant flakes of snow into the dining room, and the soaking from the sprinklers, Sharon is shivering – along with everyone else in the room. She flexes her feet and tucks her legs beneath her backside to make use of her core heat. Her hands are buried into her armpits, but she knows she can't retain this position for long. The discomfort is bearable, but the way her legs are positioned won't enable her to spring into action.

Sharon doesn't know when her chance to act will come; all she knows is that she'll get a second or two's warning at the most.

Chapter 74

I lay the terrorists' router on top of a ceiling tile and make my way back to the beer cellar. Before I climb down, I pull the walkie-talkie from my pocket and turn the channel selector.

'Nathan. Are you there?' I know there's a proper way of speaking through a walkie-talkie, using words like 'copy' and 'over', but I'm not familiar enough with the protocol to use the right word at the right time so I don't try. Sometimes it's better to embrace ignorance than be too clever and get things wrong.

'Copy you. Is that Boulder?'

'Yeah.'

'We've got the FBI and the police here. One of the police is making like a pregnant salmon.'

That's good news, but the next voice I hear is a bit more demanding. In this situation I'd expect nothing less from the police or FBI guy who's been assigned to this mess.

'I need you to identify yourself, Boulder. Why is the resort's manager nicknamed Deadwood Attwood? Over.'

'Because the maid who cleans his room found a packet of boner pills on his nightstand yesterday morning. Who am I speaking to?'

'Special Agent Riley. I'm in charge of this incident. Over.'

As much as I want to tell Riley that he's not in charge of anything to do with 'the incident' as he calls it, I bite my tongue. When you've unlawfully killed as many people as I have tonight, pissing off the most senior cop around isn't the wisest of ideas.

'I hear you, Special Agent. As I'm up here and you're down there, do you have any suggestions about how I can save the hostages? The fact you're speaking to me tells me you got my message; therefore, you'll know about the explosives I found and their location.'

I let him have a few seconds to think. An FBI Special Agent cannot condone vigilante action; therefore, he can't tell me to storm the dining room. However, the decision about how to save the hostages is now in his hands. The way he tells me not to engage with the terrorists again will tell me what he's really saying to me.

'I copy what you say regarding the explosives and their former location. This information suggests a significant risk to the lives of many innocent civilians. I'd like to think that risk will be reduced at the earliest opportunity. However, I have to say I cannot condone any of the perpetrators of this heinous crime being murdered in cold blood before a response team can arrive on the scene.'

I'm tempted to reply with 'copy that', but I'm not going to be an asshole to him. He's just given me the green light to rescue the hostages, so long as I don't kill any of the terrorists without them having tried to kill me first.

The terrorists are all carrying guns and will shoot me on sight. As far as I'm concerned, that constitutes them trying to kill me. With them having superior numbers and firepower, no quarter can be given by either me or Sharon when I make my move.

Chapter 75

Ivy scowls at Alfonse, although she knows it's not his fault the police report doesn't say if Jake is alive or dead.

The furniture, walls and everything else in Alfonse's apartment has either been scowled at or is waiting in line for its turn. She's been worried about Jake before, mostly in the last year. Since he got mixed up in a murder case, his life has been under threat from one force or another on almost a weekly basis.

What she can't work out is why he keeps risking his life and putting her through so much torment. She's positive she has twice as many grey hairs as she had this time last year. To Ivy, it's almost as if Jake is trying to punish her for something.

A series of thumps on Alfonse's door interrupts her scowls.

When she opens the door, the grim face of Chief Watson is staring back at her.

Her knees buckle, this is the moment she's been dreading. A cop knocking on the door in the middle of the night is never good news. It's rarely even bad news. Invariably, it's the worst news imaginable.

Not one of Ivy's limbs possess the strength to move. She just slumps to the ground and looks at Chief Watson. Every fibre of her soul is willing him not to speak. Not to utter the words his mouth is opening to form.

'Mrs Boulder, Mr Devereaux.' Ivy notices he's being formal and using their surnames. This has to be the moment her worst fear is realised. 'I need you to come with me. Boulder, well, Jake, has gotten himself into a situation where there's a significant threat to life.'

'Is he alive?'

Ivy wants to kick and punch at Alfonse for asking the question whose answer may break her heart. It's cruel, insensitive, and a huge step across the line.

'He was the last I heard. Now, get a move on, I need to get you to the station where I can protect you.'

'Come on, Mrs B. Let's go.'

When Ivy takes the hand Alfonse is offering, she feels his grip tighten and a gentle pressure on her arm as he hauls her to her feet and wraps an arm around her waist.

With the strength returning to her limbs – now she knows Chief Watson wasn't there to deliver a death notice – Ivy realises she was wrong to loathe Alfonse, even if it was for a split second. He's a good man, who'd left a party without complaint just so he could assuage her fears. Her son is lucky to have such a good friend and the next time she speaks to Jake, she'll make sure he knows it.

Ivy notices, as they leave the apartment, Alfonse has his laptop in his hand.

She wants to demand answers from the chief, as to why they're being taken to the station for protection, but the man's gruff manner stills her tongue as she collects her thoughts.

Jake has told her about the chief's habit of kneading his temples when he's under stress, and even as he's driving the mile across town, Chief Watson keeps swapping the hand he's holding the wheel with so he can knead each temple in turn.

When they arrive at the station, the chief leads them to what Ivy assumes is his office. She takes a seat beside Alfonse in front of a cluttered desk. Chief Watson has plonked himself in a seat that squeaks every time he moves.

The chief stops kneading his temples long enough to lay both his hands on the desk, palms upwards in a helpless gesture.

When he speaks, Ivy can see the stress he's carrying in his eyes as he looks at her. 'I know you're going to have a lot of questions, but I have to tell you there's been a terrorist attack at the ski resort where your son has been working. Boulder, sorry, Jake; well, Jake being the man he is, started fighting back against the attackers. Somehow, they learned his name, and when he was able to get a message out, he asked that you and your husband and daughter, along with Alfonse, were protected in case they tried to use any of you as a means of leverage.'

'What do you mean "leverage"? Explain yourself, man.'

Ivy sees the flash of anger cross the chief's face, but she doesn't care about hurt feelings, not when her son's life is in danger.

Alfonse lays a warm hand on her arm. 'I think he means they want to make Jake stop fighting back, or hand over something they want.'

'Is that what you're trying to say?'

'Yes, ma'am. According to what I've heard, the terrorists had rigged the supports for the dining room and a balcony with explosives and positioned their hostages where they'd be killed in the collapse. Jake has dismantled the explosive charges and hidden them.'

Ivy can't help but notice the glance the chief sends Alfonse's way. It's like he's telling him to keep his trap shut and not ask any questions. She can tell she's not being given the full story, but she doesn't care, she's heard enough to allow her to work out the rest.

The way Jake has been since he left Casperton is all the evidence she needs to complete the picture. His grief at losing Taylor, coupled with his biological need to right wrongs, will have led him to strike back at the people who've attacked the ski resort.

The news he's now taken up disarming explosives shows her just how far her son will go in his efforts to shed his guilt. Other than his safe return, all she can hope is that whatever he does tonight proves to be enough to restore the balance his life needs, because if it doesn't, he'll keep searching for karmic resolution until he gets himself killed.

Chapter 76

I tease the door of the beer cellar open enough to allow me to peek along the corridor. There are no terrorists in view, so I open the door a little further and look the other way.

As there's still no sign of them, I pad my way along to the cableway station and check the mechanism is still running.

Nathan's comment about one of the police imitating a pregnant salmon was an ingenious way of letting me know that at least one cop is coming up in a cable car. As soon as he'd said it, I knew what he meant: pregnant salmon swim upstream to spawn, and for the cops at the bottom of the mountain, upstream means uphill.

The guy who'll be coming will in all likelihood be one of their finest warriors. A man trained in using a variety of weapons and hand to hand fighting. The possible arrival of such a man, or men, is the reason I gave a written description of myself and the clothes I'm wearing in my message. To find myself under attack, from cops with orders to kill everyone holding a gun, is the last thing I want after everything I've been through tonight.

With this area checked, I make my way along the corridor until I can once again slip inside the kitchen.

As I walk across the tiled floor I can hear my shoes squeaking. Either they've now got the right level of dampness to make a noise, or I didn't notice it the first time I was in here.

Either way, now I'm about to attack the terrorists in their metaphorical stronghold, I need every piece of stealth I can get, so I take off my shoes. My socks are sodden as well, so I remove them too and drop one in each shoe.

I'm sure the floor should feel cold to my feet, but I haven't felt anything below my knees for the best part of an hour.

I cross the kitchen at a half crouch and make my way to the service doors – as the doors that open into the dining room are known. By the time I get there, I have claimed one of the ornamental side plates the chef loves to use and the waiting staff hate.

While very decorative, the dinner plates, which are part of a set, are large and cumbersome, meaning the waiting staff can't carry as many as they'd like. Because of this, they have to make more journeys between the kitchen and dining room.

Another reason they don't like the plates is their fragility. Each plate has to be handled with care, even thunking one down from an inch above a table has been known to crack it.

For use as a distraction, their fragility makes them perfect.

Now I'm at the doors, I'm faced with a dilemma. The door on the left only opens inwards, for staff returning into the kitchen, whereas the one on the right opens into the dining room, for waiting staff carrying plates from the kitchen. It's a standard arrangement in restaurants to keep the staff from pushing at doors from each side.

If I go through the right door, it will act as a shield and, if I'm fired upon, thanks to the presence of a closing mechanism, the door will swing shut behind me should I need to duck back into the kitchen. The left-hand door will need a hand to open it, and as soon as I step into the doorway I'll be exposed on all sides.

This should be a no brainer, apart from one key detail. The bar is two paces to the left of the doors. My plan of using shock and awe tactics may well work fine, but if it doesn't, the bar is waist high and fronted with timber panels that are at least an inch thick. In other words, it's a great place to be when someone's shooting at you.

It wouldn't be a problem if the door on the right was hinged on the right, but it's hinged on the left, which means to get to the safety of the bar, I'll have to go far enough past the door that it closes behind me, and then turn left.

In the end, I decide to try the right door first, and if being sneaky doesn't work, I can always revert to using the one on the left. I've already locked the door I used to enter the kitchen, so if they work out I'm in here, they'll have to come in after me rather than sneak round behind me.

Before I start to go through the door, I cross to the griddle and grab the squeezy bottle of cooking oil that's always to hand. Next, I check the side door that has the blind, in case the terrorists I killed earlier have been replaced.

They haven't, so I check to make sure the door is bolted shut and return to the service doors.

I bend down and aim the squeezy bottle's nozzle at each bolt in turn and dribble a few drops onto their barrels. Once the oil has had a few seconds to run down the length of the barrels, I tease the bolts open.

Thanks to the oil, neither bolt makes so much as a whisper of sound.

Undoing the top bolts is a little trickier thanks to the circular windows in each door.

To make myself as inconspicuous as possible, I rise to my feet in a slow, deliberate movement. I have my side to the left of the 'in' door, which allows me to look through the window and survey the majority of the dining room.

I can see Hannah, Clipboard and one other terrorist. They all have their guns at waist level and are training them on the hostages.

My left hand raises the bottle of oil and I tear my eyes from the window long enough to glance and aim a healthy squirt of oil at the bolt. A second later I have the bolt undone and I'm bending down to cross beneath the windows so I can repeat the action at the right-hand side of the door.

With both bolts undone, I'm ready to go through the door and effect my rescue.

Except I'm not.

My hands are shaking, and my head is filled with doubts. When I go through the door, should I lie on the floor and use my shoulder to open it, so I can snipe at the three terrorists I can see?

Or should I burst through and charge at them, so the shock and awe will make them hesitate for the split second it will take me to gun them down? Maybe it would go better if I tossed the fragile side plate at the wall behind them, so they turn, and I can shoot them in the back?

In the end, I do nothing … yet. I know where three of the terrorists are, but that leaves four unaccounted for.

My best guess is that two are still stationed by the windows, and the other two have been sent part way along the corridor – perhaps to where the restrooms are.

I check my watch and see that Fleming's ten-minute wait after returning to the dining room has yet to pass.

There's no chance of me succeeding if I don't have Sharon armed and able to deal with the two men by the windows.

I rise to my feet with my left shoulder against the central column between the service doors.

My legs feel rubbery, but unless I see something that forces me to act, I can do nothing except wait for a few minutes until I'm sure Fleming has passed the pistol to Sharon.

Chapter 77

Sharon sees Fleming move a little. He's inching her way, but he's still got a few feet to make up.

To help him, she shuffles her backside in his direction.

With nine feet separating them, and four people filling that gap, there's no easy way they can get close enough for him to pass on his message without it being obvious to the terrorists that they're up to something.

She catches Brooke's eye and gives the girl a distinct nod.

Brooke rises to her feet and goes towards the bald guard.

The predictable way his eyes go to Brooke's chest sickens Sharon, yet she knows his lechery is the best distraction they have. The girl's skin is blue from the cold and Sharon can see goosebumps all over her upper body, but that doesn't seem to bother the lecherous guard.

'Come on, please let me go to the restroom?' Brooke's voice is loud enough to carry across to Sharon.

'No. You can piss in the corner or piss your pants. Your choice.'

'Don't be so gross. I mean, right, look at me, look at the size of me, I'm no threat to you. All I want is to go to the restroom.'

The bald guard has a smile on his face as he points at the corner again.

'You'd like that, wouldn't you? Bet you'd love to see me pull down my pants and squat in the corner.'

Brooke's voice has risen to a shout and her performance is giving Sharon the distraction she needs to close the gap between her and Fleming.

As Sharon is crawling one way, the manager is coming the other, and they end up side by side, wedged between two of the kitchen porters.

Sharon feels Fleming reach behind her back and press something metallic between her and the wall she's leaning against.

His lips brush her ear. 'When Jake Boulder comes in, he wants you to take out the two terrorists at the windows.'

'Got it.'

As soon as the words have left her mouth, Fleming is off again, shuffling away from her. She reaches behind her back and feels the reassuring shape of a pistol grip.

She leaves her hand behind her back and watches as the female terrorist approaches Brooke and the bald guy.

When Brooke sees the woman coming her way she goes to back off, but she's not quick enough. Her punishment for haranguing the guard is a slash from the female terrorist's knife that leaves a wide horizontal canyon through her nose.

It's a terrible price to pay and Sharon feels guilty for asking the girl to get mixed up in her scheming.

Sharon knows it's her imagination, but she feels as if the pistol in her hand is calling to her, asking for the chance to put a bullet in the female terrorist's brain.

As much as she wants to give the pistol its wish, she stays her hand. She can accept dying if she's able to kill the female terrorist first, but her issue is that the other terrorists will fire her way with their submachine guns.

Sharon is aware that, even in trained hands, submachine guns aren't famed for their accuracy. She knows that a large portion of the bullets fired her way will miss her and will instead strike the bodies of those around her.

It's one thing for her to sacrifice her own life, but to risk the lives of others is unthinkable. She was brought up in a staunch Catholic household and, while her faith has lapsed, she knows she'll never find absolution if she causes the deaths of others.

As she fights her anger, she takes solace in the fact that when Boulder makes his appearance, as Fleming has suggested he will, she'll be in a position to help him eliminate the terrorists.

Chapter 78

The scream I hear goes right through me but I hold my nerve. From what I've witnessed and overheard, a near topless woman has gotten into it with one of the guards over a requested restroom visit.

As much as I don't like to think Sharon or Fleming would endanger someone else, I suspect the girl's behaviour is a distraction that one of them has created so the gun could be passed between them.

The minute or two I've been looking through this window, not moving, has given me time to think about the terrorists' goal. Every possible scenario has run through my mind as the night has passed, and it's only now I think I may have the answer. To verify my thinking, I have a couple of questions for any one of the customers who've been taken into the office, but that can wait.

I shrink back a little as Hannah returns to where Clipboard is. When she's beside him, she gives a 'come here' wave. If she's summoning the other two terrorists she's playing right into my hands. Having all five in a tight group will make shooting them a whole lot easier.

When I have that thought, I'm attacked by a crisis of confidence. Not only will I be killing them in cold blood, which is something Riley has warned me not to do, but I'll also be killing a woman.

It's not that Hannah doesn't deserve to die; her actions tonight alone have proved many times over that her death would make the world a safer place. It's that I don't know if I can gun down a woman, regardless of how much she may deserve it.

I suspect it will be different if she attacks me and I have to defend myself, but other than a playful tap on a girl's ass in the window between goofing and fooling around, I've never hit a woman and I'm not sure I can bring myself to do it.

I see a pair of terrorists emerge from the corridor end of the dining room to join the group of three, and that's when Hannah waves the other two forward.

This is a sudden change I'm not at all comfortable with. If Hannah has got all her troops in the one place she must be leaving. Had she been leaving along the corridor, she'd have called the ones by the window forward to join her, and then left. The same goes if she was leaving via the balcony, she'd get the corridor guys first and then go towards the balcony.

The way she's called all her men into one place tells me she's got one last thing to do before she leaves. I suspect her plan is to kill all the hostages and use the time until dawn to look for me. If all seven of them are together and using proper cover, they'll be a lot safer.

As I burst through the door, with my automatic rifle chattering away, I'm aware of someone moving at the far end of the room. It's one of the hostages and I think they're trying to get outside, but I don't give them any more than a fleeting thought.

The knot of five people isn't as tightly tied as I'd like, and while I see my bullets transform Clipboard's head into a bursting watermelon and thud into the bodies of Bald Man and one of the other guards, I miss Swimmer altogether.

I'm unsure whether or not I've hit Hannah but, amid the clatter of my rifle, the shrieks of the hostages and the acrid smell of gunfire, enough of my senses are untainted for me to witness her dropping her weapon and clutching her right arm with her left.

Swimmer runs off at a tangent, which prevents me from trying to shoot him as he's running in front of the hostages.

It's fair to assume that he's about to start shooting back, so I plant my right foot into the carpet and turn to run for the bar.

How Sharon is getting on is unknown to me, but for the time being I'm more concerned with not letting Swimmer put any holes in me.

When I'm three paces from the bar I launch myself into a headlong dive. It's not a moment too soon as Swimmer opens fire.

All the bottles and glasses at the back of the bar, that I'd polished until they gleamed, explode in a shower of fragments.

I don't like how vulnerable I am. With all the glass that's raining down, I can't look up to see if Swimmer is standing over me as I'll be blinded.

Chapter 79

Sharon has the pistol in her hand, pointing at the nearest guard, before Boulder has the chance to squeeze his own trigger.

The guard is ten feet away and she's used a pistol often enough to put two rounds in his chest before he can react.

It's not so easy for her to get a shot at the other man she's been tasked with taking out.

This guy has a buzz cut and fast reactions.

Even as she is rising to her feet and swivelling her body to face him, he's bending over and grabbing one of the hostages.

The man he's got in a headlock is around sixty and has a pallor that comes from a lifetime spent under artificial lighting. Sharon has taken his lunch to his room on each of the days he's been here. The scene was always the same: he'd have his laptop on the writing bureau and he'd chat for a moment before pressing a generous tip into her hand. As much as she liked the guy, she'd never taken to his waspish wife.

The terrorist hauls the old guy to his feet and jams a pistol in his ear.

They're twenty feet away, and at that distance Sharon isn't confident that she won't hit the wrong man.

If she had a pistol she was familiar with, and two working eyes, she may have taken a chance and made the shot, but in the current circumstances, she wasn't going to add the extra ounce of pressure to the trigger unless the pistol was turned on her.

She flicks her eyes across for a fractional glance to see how Boulder is getting on.

Three of the five terrorists he ambushed are down, and the woman is clutching her left wrist. She's down, but not out. The fifth guy is firing at the bar, where she presumes Boulder is taking cover.

Sharon is tempted to put a shot past the guy with the buzz cut and into the guy shooting at the bar, but she knows, as soon as she pulls her trigger, the guy with the buzz cut will pull his in the mistaken belief she's shooting at him.

The fact that the other guy is an extra ten feet away makes the odds of hitting him low, so she'll have to fire a few shots to make sure she takes him down. That's not something she's prepared to do as it'll give the one with the hostage more than enough time to shoot her. Plus, she's no idea how many bullets are in the pistol's magazine.

She trusts that Boulder would have given her a full magazine if he could, but she can't ask him right now, and the only other way to find out is to keep shooting until the bullets run out.

The old man's lips are moving in a soundless motion.

Sharon sees he's looking down at his wife and telling her that he loves her.

When he lifts his head, he catches Sharon's eye and winks at her.

His lips move again. He's speaking without sound, but Sharon doesn't need to be a lip reader to recognise he's saying, 'on three'.

'One.'

'Two.'

Sharon adds a half ounce to the pressure on her finger and centres her aim on the old man's forehead. Once he makes his move, her aim will be at the centre of the terrorist's face.

'Three.'

Everything in Sharon's world crawls to a halt. There are no sounds, or external movements, all she sees is the old man starting to slide down the terrorist's body.

The terrorist is pulled forward by the old man lifting his knees, so his entire weight is being supported by the arm that the terrorist has around his throat. He reacts to the old man's movement by pulling his trigger a fraction of a second before Sharon pulls hers.

Chapter 80

I'm not sure where Swimmer is, but I need to find out before he kills me. Glass is still raining down on me, but I figure he can't have much ammo left in his clip.

I half wriggle, half roll myself onto my side with my back against the bar's rear wall. In front of me are bottle fridges full of various beers.

I slide a fridge door open and take out three bottles.

I then draw my feet up and manoeuvre myself until I'm in a squatting position. I lean right and toss a bottle of beer over the counter in the general direction of where I think Swimmer is.

The next bottle I toss is sent from where I'm squatting, and I lean left before tossing the third.

I grab my rifle and set off running to my right, straightening to my full height as I go. My bare feet are crunching on the broken glass that litters the bar floor and, for once tonight, I'm grateful for the cold that has numbed them. They'll hurt like hell when they thaw out, but until then their numbness is giving me a chance to fight back.

When I burst out from behind the bar, I see Swimmer is ten yards back and he's shooting left of where I was, which means he's fallen for my ruse.

There are hostages cowering behind him so, when I start firing, I make sure any of the bullets that miss him fly high enough to also miss the hostages.

It's a good job I'm aiming high, as not one of the three rounds I fire before the ammo runs out hits its target.

My luck changes for the better when, the moment he turns his weapon my way, Swimmer's submachine gun clicks on empty as well.

I don't waste time offering prayers of thanks to any deity. Instead I keep running and launch myself at him.

As I fly through the air I'm swinging the rifle in my hands at his head.

He sees me coming and, rather than trying to strike out at me or defend himself, he drops his weapon, grabs my arms and lets my momentum roll him backwards.

The sole of his boot gets planted into my stomach and when he straightens his leg I find myself flying backwards and upside down through the air until I land in a heap.

By the time I've squirmed my way upright he's standing in front of me. With great care and deliberation, he removes his pistol from its holster and his knife from its sheath.

My first thought is that I should rush him. He's ten feet away and, while at that range it's not likely he'll miss, it's not guaranteed that his first shot will kill me.

My second thought is that I'm about to die; that everyone else in this room will die because I'm a rotten shot and missed my chance to shoot him.

My third thought tells me to get over myself and do something.

Swimmer isn't doing anything. He's just standing there. Waiting for me to make the first move.

I do the same thing. As soon as he goes to move, I'm going to attack him with everything I have. I'd sooner go down fighting than cowering.

'You killed my brother and a lot of my buddies. You're going to pay for that. I'm going to peel your face off and shove it down your throat until you choke.'

When he's finished speaking he tosses his gun behind the bar.

It's clear he wants to punish me and make me pay for the deaths of his brother and his buddies.

I'm comfortable with how he feels. I've been there myself and know exactly how an internal rage can dominate all other thoughts.

By rights, he should have used the gun to make me an easier target. A shot in one of my legs, or my gut, would have left me at his mercy. That he didn't take it shows his confidence.

It's hard to argue with his belief that he'll win the fight.

He's got at least five inches and forty pounds on me.

And a knife.

He's also a lot fresher than I am. For the last few hours, he's been inside where it's warm and dry, while I've been running around a mountain in a snowstorm. Fair enough, he'll have gotten wet and a little chilled in the last hour, but he hasn't been cold for hours. Nor has he been punched and kicked the way I have.

Every advantage he could have over me is right there at his disposal.

I feel for my own weapons but find them missing. One or another of my headlong dives must have dislodged them. Maybe it was being thrown across the room by Swimmer that did it. The cause doesn't matter, I'm down a pistol and a knife. Even the sharpening steel I took from the kitchen would give me a chance against Swimmer and his knife, but that's no longer inside my sleeve.

The one advantage I've got over Swimmer is his over-confidence. I expect he's going to toy with me, cut me several times without doing any real damage other than hurting me. His desire to inflict pain will stop him going for a quick kill.

As we square up to each other, the odds are so heavy in his favour only a fool would bet on me.

I'm not a fool, but as it's my life on the line, I'm not of a mind to make things easy for him.

Chapter 81

Sharon doesn't have time to register her bullet smashing into the terrorist's face and blowing his brains out of the back of his buzz cut.

All she's aware of is the female terrorist's shoulder crashing into her ribs and driving her backwards.

As she staggers back, she trips over someone's leg and crashes onto her back hard enough to loosen her grip on the pistol.

The terrorist is on her before she can even start to rise.

The woman's legs are straddling her and the punches she's throwing are enough to take the pain Sharon had previously felt and multiply it into a blur of agony.

Sharon curls her arms over her head to protect her face, and writhes to free herself. She's not successful, but she feels a pause in the rate of punches so she moves an arm enough to let her see what's happening.

If the female terrorist is reaching for her knife, Sharon knows she'll need to be aware of it and ready to counter any strikes.

She sees a wicked smile on the woman's lips and a knife comes into view. It's just as she feared.

Sharon expects the worst.

The best happens.

Something slams into the female terrorist's back hard enough to jolt her forward. When Sharon looks to see what's happened, she sees one of the customers holding a chair.

It's not an adult. None of the men in the room have come to her aid.

It's a child who's had the guts to act. Specifically, it's a boy of around fifteen. The smart kid whose name Sharon doesn't know.

He swings the chair again, but this time the terrorist is aware of what he's doing and grabs at the chair, yanks it out of his hands, and throws it back at him.

One of the chair's legs smashes into the boy's face and opens up a cut above his eyebrow.

The boy's mother flies into the female terrorist and knocks her off Sharon, as she rains wild blows at the woman who's injured her son.

Sharon scrambles to her feet as a loud scream pierces the air.

The mother rolls off the female terrorist with a knife handle protruding from her stomach. Bright red blood seeps past the hands she's clasping around her wound.

The terrorist is on all fours, presenting too good a target for Sharon to pass up, so she takes a vicious kick at her head.

The thunk from her soft work shoe connecting with the terrorist's head isn't as satisfying as it would have been had Sharon been wearing her old combat boots, but it still sounds good.

She repeats the kick then pounces on the terrorist and rolls her over so she can rain blows onto her face.

Time after time she throws her fists into the face of the vicious killer until she feels the fight has been knocked out of the other woman.

With her opponent incapacitated, Sharon scrambles off the woman and goes to retrieve her pistol.

Once the gun is back in her hand, Sharon returns to the terrorist and stands over her.

She kicks the woman's shoulder three times until a bloodied eye opens and looks up at her.

Sharon wants the terrorist to know she's going to die, she wants to see the fear in her eyes and relish the terrorist's anguish as she realises that, not only has she lost, but losing is going to cost the woman her life.

'No.'

The single word is spoken in a calm tone with just enough authority to prevent Sharon from squeezing the trigger.

A hand touches her arm and exerts a gentle force to shift Sharon's aim away from the terrorist's head.

'Don't do it, ma'am. She deserves to die in prison. Let her spend the rest of her life there. Don't be like her, you're way better than she is.'

'You're right.'

Sharon doesn't just say the words to appease the speaker. She agrees with him and his logic. The way that her agony and rage have almost driven her to kill a defenceless person shames her.

When she looks round to address the man who's spoken to her, her mouth drops open in surprise.

It's not a man, but the boy who'd come to her aid. As shamed as she feels by her own actions, she hopes every adult in the room is feeling ten times as bad. A child has shown more guts and humanity than any of the adults who are present.

While his mother lies bleeding, he's found the time and reason to prevent her from executing the female terrorist.

People like this kid give her hope for the next generation.

Chapter 82

The knife flashes again and I feel its sting as it slices through the sleeve of my jacket. That's the fourth time he's slashed at me and the third time he's made contact.

So far, this fight is going the way Swimmer is dictating, and if it carries on in this vein, I'm not going to survive it.

As I back away from him I bump into something.

My hand goes behind me and I feel the soft upholstery of a chair. I know from our position in the room that it will be a solid tub chair that's too heavy and cumbersome to be used as a weapon.

I jink left and wait for him to follow.

I don't know where I'm leading him to, but if I'm not within his reach he can't use his knife on me.

He takes a half step to his right and turns his body to face me.

The way he's moving suggests he's trying to back me into a corner, or up against an obstacle – like the tub chairs.

I'm not at all keen on the idea of being cornered, so I take two steps to my right.

As a rule of thumb, when faced with an opponent with a knife I'd remove my jacket and wrap it around my left arm so I could reduce my risk of stab wounds and keep my right hand free to punch or counter-punch. That's what I would do, had I not tied a rope around my waist as a belt.

I can't even loosen the knot as I had made sure it was well enough tied to stay knotted, regardless of my actions.

Because of the knife, I can't get close enough to him to land any blows of my own.

I have no problem with catching the odd punch if it means I can land a fight-ending blow of my own, but when my opponent has a knife rather than fists, I know that any contact from him could deliver the kind of wound that would incapacitate me.

He dances forward like a fencer and aims a slash at my head.

I manage to lean far enough back so his knife misses my face, but when his arm returns with a backhand slash, it's dropped to waist level and I feel the knife slice into my stomach.

This has gone on way too long for my liking, and every time he adds a new cut to my body, the more he's weakening me.

The problem I have is working out how to attack him without exposing myself to a wound that'll debilitate me.

My bare feet are useless as weapons. If I had shoes or boots on I could dislocate his kneecap with a kick, but with bare feet, all I'll achieve is a set of broken toes.

He dances forward and feints before taking a step back. I have to concede more ground, and that's when I feel my shoulder bump against something solid. I can go left or right now, but I can no longer go backwards.

Again, he dances forward with his knife moving so fast it's little more than a blur.

If this swing had connected with me it would have opened me up from my left shoulder to my right hip.

Before he can reverse his thrust, I twist, so his chest is against my back, grab his wrist with my left hand, and loop my right arm over his elbow and lift up.

This kind of arm bar is a standard move in many forms of martial art, and I'm exerting all the pressure I can to either snap his elbow or force him to release his knife.

The problem with knowing such fighting moves is that there's every chance your opponent knows them too. And more importantly, they may know how to counter them.

Swimmer is no novice, and before I've put enough pressure on him to achieve either of my aims, he's yanked his arm backwards and out of my grasp. The knife in his hands cuts my side as his hand is drawn back.

Rather than allowing him time to regroup and come at me again, I whirl round and slash my left arm upwards to deflect his knife arm up and away from my body, while throwing a swinging roundhouse with my right.

I'm aiming at his body and I'm not fussy where my punch lands. A solid blow to the liver, kidneys or solar plexus will stun any man long enough to allow you to pick your spot for the next blow.

Swimmer has twisted enough for my punch to glance off his stomach.

I've put so much power into the blow that I rotate until I've got my back to him again.

He tenses his muscles and starts to draw his right arm in. The knife in his hand is moving towards my face and there's nothing I can do to stop it.

Both of my hands are wrapped around his knife arm, but he's got his left hand wrapped over his right and he's using both of his powerful arms to pull the knife towards my eye.

I've seen what happens when a knife is plunged into an eye and it's not something I want to experience myself.

The knife is now so close to my face its tip is blurring out of focus.

I do the only thing I can do in the circumstances and shift the emphasis of my exertions.

Rather than pushing his arms out, which isn't working, I push them upwards. By doing this I'm altering the balance of power. I'm pushing upwards with all my strength, whereas he's pressing down. Regardless of how strong he is, without something to push off, even the strongest person in the world can't push downwards with anything more than their own bodyweight.

I allow the action to force my head and shoulders towards the floor and away from his knife. I release the upwards push at the same time as I drop to my knees and haul down on his arms.

The combination of my weight and my sudden change in thrust, coupled with the fact I'm pulling with him rather than offering resistance, means the knife now arcs towards his chest.

In an ideal world the knife would slip between his ribs and pierce his heart.

It clumps against his sternum instead.

I roll away to one side and scramble to my feet.

At least when I face him, I now have my back to the room rather than the corner he was trying to pin me in.

He steps forward a half pace. He's learned I'm not the patsy he thought I was and he's now taking me as a serious threat.

I stand my ground and feint the same defensive up-swinging arm that I've just tried on him.

It's what he was expecting, and he ducks his arm back out of reach before lunging with a stab towards my stomach.

I wrap both my hands around his arm as I jump backwards.

He's now off balance and over-extended so I twist his arm until I hear cartilage tearing.

The knife drops from his hand, punctuating his screaming with a thud as it hits the floor.

Swimmer steps forward far enough to allow him to swing punches with his left hand, but I don't let go of his wrist until I hear the snap of bones splintering.

I straighten and jab his eyes with extended fingers.

He howls as he uses his good hand to reach up and protect his eyes.

Right about now I'd usually bury a boot into an opponent's groin but, as I'm barefoot, I use a knee instead, and put enough force behind it to lift him up onto his toes.

Whether or not his current blindness will be permanent remains to be seen, but for now it's making him vulnerable.

The punch I land on his jaw is hard enough to break two of my knuckles, but I don't care. I've knocked out a few people over the years, but never has it felt as sweet as this.

As he's crumpling into an untidy heap I remember there may be other threats in the room.

I cast my eyes around and see live hostages and dead terrorists.

Sharon is standing over Hannah with a gun in her hand, but from her body language, I can tell she's guarding the woman rather than threatening her.

I walk towards her and see the mess of bruises and cuts on her face. I also see Daniel crouched beside his mother. There's a cut on his head and a knife in her gut, but I can find out about them later.

Chapter 83

As I stand beside Sharon I realise how much is still to be done and how little leadership there is in the room.

I point to Fleming. 'Go to the cableway station and get a roll of duct tape from Steve's toolbox and bring it here. When you've done that, go back and reconnect the phones and the router.'

I retrieve the walkie-talkie and press my thumb against the call button. 'Nathan, you there?'

'Copy that, I'm here and at your service. What's the state of play?'

'So far as I'm aware, the terrorists are all defeated. If that salmon you mentioned is armed, tell it to stand down. Also, get more salmon up here, along with a team of paramedics. We've got a woman with a stab wound to her stomach, another three with severe facial injuries, and a lot of people who're chilled to the bone. A couple of the terrorists may need a band aid or two as well.'

I stand in front of the assembled crowd and raise my hands for silence. When I speak, I make sure I have a smile on my face and avoid using any words that may be similar to those used by Hannah.

'Hey, folks. I think the threat is over, but to be on the safe side, I want you all to stay here until the police arrive. Once they have secured the building properly, we'll be able to start shipping you out, or, at the very least, we'll let you get some warm, dry clothes from your rooms.' I look at the head chef, an obstinate man who views his kitchen as a personal kingdom. 'I'm sure some soup and coffee will also be made available for those waiting to be evacuated.' The approving nod I get from the chef makes me revise my opinion of him.

Somewhere at the back of the room someone starts clapping. By the time I've taken three steps towards Sharon, every hostage has risen to their feet and is applauding me.

As nice as the intent behind the sentiment is, it's wrong. I've killed men tonight and I've disabled others. I expect to face arrest for my actions, and quite possibly one hell of a lot of jail time.

While I appreciate the back-slapping and the handshakes that are coming my way, I don't feel like I've earned thanks, much less praise. None of the people rejoicing in my actions will be aware of what it's like to live with the fact you have taken a life.

There's a reason that I'm walking towards Sharon, and it has nothing to do with Glaswegian kinship, and everything to do with the man who's five paces behind her.

I pass by Sharon, grab the guy by his collar and pull him onto the most vicious headbutt I can deliver.

He drops in an untidy bundle and I let him lie there moaning in pain.

Fleming returns, so I instruct his brother to use the tape to bind Hannah, Swimmer and the man at my feet.

The faces that were cheering me a minute or two ago are now looking at me in puzzlement. Maybe a couple of them will work out why I dropped the guy in the yellow shirt, maybe they won't.

Before the security boss binds Hannah, I remove the backpack she's wearing. I spotted it during my charge from the kitchen, and if it holds what I think it does, it's the key to everything that has gone on here tonight.

Rather than reveal to everyone what I'm doing, I step into the manager's office before opening the backpack. When I do, I find a laptop and a lead with a USB connection at one end and a range of different connectors at the other. I've had enough kinds of phones and tablets to recognise that this lead will connect anything to the computer or laptop it's plugged into.

I pull my phone out of my pocket and look to see if it has battery and a signal. It has a lot of the latter and only a little of the former.

There's only one person in the world I trust to look at this laptop, so I call Alfonse on the off chance he's still awake.

He's said nothing more than my name when I hear a shriek that forewarns me of a maternal lecture.

Mother comes on the line. The only reason I tolerate the tongue lashing she gives me for risking my life, yet again, is that I can hear the relief in her voice and the catch in her throat.

I tell her to put Alfonse back on the phone.

She does so after only a minute's more lecturing.

Alfonse listens as I tell him about the laptop and my suspicions. He tells me to open the laptop, plug my cell into it and then call him back from another phone in ten minutes.

While he's doing that, I grab a pistol from one of the fallen terrorists and head towards the cableway station to meet the salmon.

I have the gun held in front of me as I go, but if any of the terrorists have escaped, they're in hiding now. The police team can find them.

As I stand waiting for the cable car, I'm fighting yawns as my body comes down from the exertions of the night.

To protect myself in the event of the salmon mistaking me for a terrorist, I have positioned myself under a light and I have the pistol hidden by my side.

When a cable car appears out of the snowstorm, I can see it houses a burly figure dressed all in black.

Chapter 84

Daniel releases his mother's hand and follows the bartender to a space where they can talk. Once the terrorists had been defeated, one of the customers stepped forward and said he was a doctor; so, after the doctor had told him the knife had missed all his mom's vital organs, Daniel left the man to tend to his mother.

He was glad of the doctor's presence as it reassured his mother and meant she was getting the best help available.

What he doesn't understand is why the bartender attacked the guy in the yellow shirt. It's a question that he needs answered.

'I heard what you did, you're a brave one and your mum should be proud of you.'

Daniel doesn't answer. He's not sure how to. As far as he's concerned, he just saw a good person fighting an evil one and had helped. To him it was as simple as that. Good should always triumph over evil.

'The customer you hit – I figure you've got a good reason for hitting him, but I can't work out what it is.'

A lazy smile touches the bartender's bruised lips. 'Maybe you'd like to take a guess before I tell you?'

Daniel returns the smile. 'I don't know. Nothing I can think of makes any sense.'

'When I came in, the terrorists were gathering in group. I think they were going to shoot all the hostages. Out of the corner of my eye I saw the guy sneaking out.'

'There's nothing wrong with that, I'd have done that if I could.' Daniel thinks the bartender has it wrong about the guy. 'And how are you sure he's the guy who sneaked out?'

'Three reasons. One, he's the only person wearing a bright yellow shirt. Two, I remember him from yesterday. He and his wife were arguing and the looks they were giving each other spoke of hate, not love.'

'And the third?' Daniel is following the logic, but he's intrigued as to where it's going.

'That's the big point.' The bartender's smile fades. 'He resisted the terrorists so much that he got his wife killed.'

'I remember her body being carried out, but that doesn't explain why you hit him.'

'Because I think he was the one who killed her.'

'Huh? Why do you think that?'

The bartender explains his reasoning, and to Daniel it all makes perfect sense. He doesn't know how, but the bartender has worked out what was really happening in the office, and what he says about the guy in the yellow shirt makes perfect sense.

Daniel extends his right hand. 'Thank you, sir. Without you, me, my mum and everyone else in here would be dead by now.'

The man winces as Daniel grips his hand and shakes it, but he doesn't let go. To Daniel, he looks sad, wistful almost. It's like he's somewhere else in his thoughts and that place is both comforting and distressing.

He doesn't know what's troubling the bartender, but he knows he'll come through it in his own way.

Chapter 85

I'm in the office talking to Alfonse via the desk phone when Captain Ogden bursts in. He's a bull of a man and I can imagine him as a former linebacker, who always managed to blitz his way past the guards so he could sack the opposition quarterback.

I gave him a rapid update on the events of the evening when I met him off the cable car. He listened to my report and asked the right questions at the right times. In my opinion, he's the ideal man to deal with the fallout from this evening's events.

As soon as he entered the dining room, and slapped cuffs on Hannah, Swimmer and the guy in the yellow shirt, he got on his radio and started issuing orders at a rate similar to machine gun fire.

Once Ogden had taken control of the dining room, I found a chair and borrowed a pair of tweezers from a female customer and pulled seventeen pieces of broken glass from the soles of my feet while they were still numb.

Give Ogden his due, he waits until I've finished speaking to Alfonse before he talks to me. I'm not sure how someone can pace back and forth while tapping their foot with impatience, but he manages it.

'Right, Boulder. A tactical team is sweeping the building and the area outside for any terrorists you didn't kill or disable. Do you want to tell me what in Sam Hill this is all about?'

I tell him everything that has happened in the last few hours, including my own actions. There's not one part that I leave out. Confessing to multiple homicides isn't the wisest thing to do, but with every admission, a weight falls from my shoulders.

They say unburdening is good for the soul and I'm finding that to be true.

Ogden doesn't take any notes as I speak, but I can see by the way he's focusing on me he's taking it all in.

'So, this was all about money?'

'That's right.'

The sums of money involved have boggled my mind, but after getting confirmation from Daniel that my theory was right, I couldn't help but marvel at the ingenuity behind the crime.

In a modern twist on kidnapping, Hannah and her gang had forced every one of the customers to pay their own ransom using digital banking. Not only had they moved the maximum amount of money per day, they'd had a second bite at the cherry by repeating the action after midnight. Once the ball had dropped, there was a whole new day, week, month and year, which let them double their earnings.

Alfonse is on the case and in the short time he's been looking at Hannah's laptop, he's found more than enough evidence to guarantee she will never walk down a street again.

For Ogden's benefit, I repeat what I've surmised about the guy in the yellow shirt.

'When his wife was killed, he was brought out of the office within ten seconds of the shots being fired. If it was the terrorists who'd killed her, they didn't have time to force him to transfer the money. That means they gained nothing from killing her other than the effect it had on the other hostages. Also, the man's a braggart, and I heard him talking about how his company is one of America's largest arms manufacturers. You don't know it yet, but the terrorists had a rocket launcher, explosives and a military helicopter. That's not the kind of stuff you can buy at a corner store; plus, through his company, he'd have contact with private security contractors, many of whom are best described as mercenaries. As I was about to burst into the dining room, the terrorists were getting ready to execute everyone and he was trying to sneak out. One of the terrorists was looking at him but was letting him go. For me, that confirmed his collusion.'

'Why would he be robbing people here though? Surely he's got plenty of money?'

'To instil fear in people. With the outcry for tighter gun regulations every time there's a school shooting, he wanted to scare people into buying guns to protect themselves. A terrorist attack is also a good way of getting rid of his wife without a costly divorce.'

'Jeez, that's twisted on all kinds of levels.'

'It's the modern way of it, Captain. He was just the first person to realise that in today's world, provided they have their cell phone or tablet on them, a kidnap victim can pay their own ransom. The way he used this knowledge to also make money for his company, and get rid of his wife at the same time, was just him getting all his ducks in a row.'

'Yeah well, you figured it out and you stopped them.' Ogden steps forward and shakes my hand. 'Damnit, Boulder, you're a goddamn hero.'

The grip he has on my hand is making my broken knuckles squeal in protest, but I manage not to yelp, even if I can't hide the wince from my face.

'I sense a "but", Captain.'

His face morphs in a flash from happy to annoyed. 'You know?'

'That you're going to arrest me for homicide?' I shrug. 'Yeah, I knew that when I killed the first terrorist.'

'Then why did you confess?'

'Because, as we say in Glasgow, the truth will always out. A room full of people saw me gun down three men. There's also a trail of bodies around here and I'm the only one who wasn't a hostage all night. Therefore, it must be me. Plus, there are six terrorists still alive to testify against me.'

'Dammit, Boulder, you know I don't want to arrest you, don't you?'

'I know, Captain. I also know there's no way that you can let me off with what I've done.' I hold my hands out. 'Do your duty, Captain.'

Chapter 86

My Mustang normally eats up the miles of road like a hungry shark, but today I'm playing it cool. The last two weeks have been interesting to say the least.

After our conversation, rather than slapping a pair of cuffs on me, Captain Ogden had allowed me to get my things from my room and sent me down in a cable car with Sharon and two of his men.

The FBI arrested Sharon and me when we exited the cable car, although it was the gentlest and most courteous arrest I've ever known. At every point in the proceedings we were cared for, and while Sharon was shipped off to hospital for the injuries to her face, I was put in the back of an FBI SUV and taken to their field office in Montpelier.

Special Agent Riley had led the questioning, after he'd made sure a doctor attended to my wounds.

As I'd done with Captain Ogden, I held nothing back. Unburdening myself a second time wasn't as fulfilling as the first, but it still made a difference.

Riley did what he was paid to do and kept questioning me about each part of my actions in a dozen different ways. He was trying to trip me up and find inconsistencies in my story, but he couldn't because I was telling the truth.

Because of the seriousness of my crimes, I found myself in court on the seventh of January. I'd expected my trial would have taken months to arrange, but, as I'd confessed, there was very little to delay the proceedings.

The judge was a stern looking woman who, as my trial went on, appeared to be irritated by the prosecution counsel as she fixed him with one withering stare after another.

I stuck to my policy of telling the truth.

The lawyer representing me worked for one of New York's top law firms, and he had a team of a dozen paralegals behind him. I would never have been able to afford such a lawyer, but one of the firm's partners was a hostage at RidgeTop Resort and she had arranged pro bono representation for me.

After two days of wondering if I'd ever taste freedom again, the judge ruled that all the homicides I had committed were either in self-defence, or at the defence of others, and had it not been for me, not only would the terrorists have been able to steal just over two billion dollars, but they would have killed one hundred and eighty-seven people.

The vast sums were incomprehensible to me, but I learned from Alfonse that one of the customers, a Leslie Trouseau, was a big shot in finance, and from the accounts he managed, the terrorists had got more than half of their loot.

Trouseau was shot in the shoulder during the evening but, from what I'd heard, he'd been a hero and had risked his life to give Sharon a clear shot at one of the terrorists.

Thanks to Alfonse's digital skills the money had been traced to its final destination: an offshore account owned by the man in the yellow shirt.

Special Agent Riley had found digital tampering on the resort's reservation system, which explains how Hannah and co had known how much to extort each customer for. With a full customer list, she would have been able to do research into their lives and wealth.

I exit the turnpike on the freeway signposted for Miami and prepare to take a vacation.

Before Captain Ogden had put me on the cable car, one of RidgeTop's customers had come forward and handed me a beer glass stuffed with money. He'd gone round every customer and collected over twenty thousand dollars.

I sent a third of the money to Alfonse and told him to treat my mother to a nice meal and the biggest bunch of flowers he could buy, and for him to keep the rest. Another third was given to Sharon. Without her help I'd never have succeeded in storming the dining room. Nathan had been the grateful recipient of two kegs of beer and a case of bourbon. As for the final third: me having enough money to take a break is good, having so much I'll become idle and bored isn't.

I have one last thing to do before I consider myself to be on vacation, so I scroll through the names on my phone until I find Doctor Edwards. I don't want to speak to him, but I know I need to. One way or another I need to deal with my guilt and get my head straightened out.

As nice as bourbon is to drink, it's nothing more than a short-term solution, and, while I have several thousand bucks in my pocket, I couldn't afford all the bourbon it would take to eradicate my guilt.

The End